HYPERSWARM

TIM WAGGONER

ibooks

new york

www.ibooks.net

DISTRIBUTED BY SIMON & SCHUSTER, INC.

An Original Publication of ibooks, inc.

Defender
® and copyright © 2004 Midway Games, Inc.
ALL RIGHTS RESERVED.

An ibooks, inc. Book

All rights reserved, including the right to reproduce this
book or portions thereof in any form whatsoever.
Distributed by Simon & Schuster, Inc.
1230 Avenue of the Americas, New York, NY 10020

ibooks, inc.
24 West 25th Street
New York, NY 10010

The ibooks World Wide Web Site Address is:
http://www.ibooks.net

ISBN 0-7434-9310-9
First ibooks, inc. printing September 2004
10 9 8 7 6 5 4 3 2 1

Printed in the U.S.A.

CHAPTER
ONE

"Commander Kyoto, my sensors indicate that a squadron of Manti Landers is rapidly approaching from galactic north, along with a contingent of Baiters."

For all the emotion in Memory's synthesized voice, the AI might have been delivering a planetary weather report. But her sensors had a greater range than those of Kyoto's ship, so even though the Defender's holoscreen showed all clear, Kyoto knew to prepare for an attack.

"Here goes nothing." Kyoto took a deep breath of recycled cockpit air, gripped the joystick, and accelerated away from the lunar surface—and from the installation that housed Memory's physical form. The hum of the Defender's fusion engines rose to a higher pitch, and Kyoto could feel the ship vibrate slightly as the inertial dampeners struggled to compensate. Going up against a Manti squadron alone wasn't exactly the way to live to a ripe old age, but she had to do what she could to stall the Buggers—a slang term often used to describe the Manti—while Memory activated her launch sequence.

"How many kliks away, Memory?" Kyoto's voice was strained, and despite the ship's environmental controls, a line of sweat trickled down the back of her neck.

"Three hundred twelve and closing. Now if you'll pardon me, Commander, I need to direct my full attention to launching. Even for a being of my vast intelligence—not to mention several dozen nuclear engines at my disposal—breaking a celestial body the size of Luna out of orbit isn't going to be easy."

Kyoto felt her stomach drop in a way it hadn't since her very first training flight at the GSA Defender Academy on Titan. The only reason she'd survived this long was due to Memory's help. Now, to go it totally alone…

"Acknowledged, Memory. Good luck to you."

"And to you, Mei. Memory out." There was a soft chirp as the comlink was broken.

Kyoto was surprised. This was the only time the AI had addressed her by her first name. But before she could decide what that meant, if anything, the Defender's sensor alarms started pinging. Kyoto turned her attention to the ship's holoscreen. The holo displayed a simulated image created from sensor data: a dozen shapes that looked like a cross between starships and gigantic hornets sped toward her, glowing with a green patina of energy that served as both life support and propulsion. Swirling around the Landers were several dozen smaller forms that looked something like crimson-hued biomechanical crabs: Baiters. Kyoto *hated* Baiters.

She powered up her pulse cannon and fast-lock

missiles, momentarily wishing she were flying a *Retribution*-class starfighter, or even a *Judgment*. But her little Defender ship had gotten her this far. Now, if it could just keep her alive long enough for Memory to get the moon moving...

The ship bucked and shuddered as something large slammed into it. Alarms shrieked a collision warning, but it was too late. Sensors indicated that whatever had hit her was holding fast to the ship's outer hull. Kyoto attempted to activate the Defender's energy shield, but nothing happened. The system must have been damaged by the impact.

Just as Kyoto was about to go into a roll in an attempt to shake off her unwanted passenger, a green claw punched through the starfighter's hull and sliced into her shoulder.

She screamed, both from the pain of her injury and from the knowledge that given the damage to the ship, explosive decompression was only microseconds away.

Damn it! She'd been so *close!*

And then the claw tore a larger hole in the ship, but despite this, the explosion that Kyoto feared—and which should have been a scientific inevitability —didn't occur. Instead, the Manti reached for her with its insectine appendages and plucked her from the pilot's seat. The Lander pulled her into space and retreated with its prize as the Defender soared on pilotless toward the Manti squadron.

Kyoto blew out her breath and kept her mouth open to prevent decompression, but she knew it didn't matter. She'd been captured by a Lander; she was as good as dead.

She reached for her sidearm, hoping to at least take

out the Bugger before it could absorb her genetic material, but she wasn't fast enough. The Lander plunged its spiny bioprobes into the soft flesh of her neck and started injecting the enzymes that would prepare her body for absorption. The pain was beyond anything Kyoto had ever imagined, let alone experienced, and despite herself, she opened her mouth and screamed. Somehow the sound of her agony echoed strong and clear though the vacuum of space, until it was finally cut off by her death.

Kyoto woke to darkness, and at first she thought she really was dead. But then she remembered: she'd been absorbed by a Lander and turned into a Mutant. But that didn't make any sense—she didn't *feel* like a Mutant. Not that she was exactly sure what being one was supposed to feel like.

"Lights," she mumbled, and then cursed as harsh illumination stabbed her eyes. "Dim to half strength!" The roomcomp adjusted the lighting level accordingly, and Kyoto was able to open her eyes without feeling as if she were staring into the heart of a nuclear furnace.

She sat up and sighed in relief. It had been, as the cliché went, all a dream. But not entirely. Everything had happened just as it had occurred in reality, up to the point where the Lander had breached her ship. She should've known she was dreaming when the laws of physics suddenly had ceased to apply. But then, that was the way of dreams, wasn't it? You never knew you were having one until it was over.

Kyoto drew her knees to her chest and hugged them. Her pulse was racing, so she did some deep breathing exercises until it returned to normal. What she would have liked to do was roll over and cuddle with Wolf, but that was a little difficult, seeing as how he'd broken up with her three days ago.

Great. Now she wasn't scared anymore—she was depressed.

"Time?"

"January 4th, 2653, four fifty-seven A.M., colony standard time." The reply came from a small speaker set into the ceiling. The voice was feminine—comp designers had long known that both men and women preferred their systems to speak with female voices. They supposedly found them more pleasant and soothing. But not Kyoto. This particular voice always set her teeth on edge, especially after Memory's sacrifice. She'd have to see what she could do about having her quarters' voice-synth reprogrammed.

"You're booked for an appearance on *Cyndonia Today* at nine A.M. Do you wish to sleep longer? I can play a variety of soothing music or natural sounds to help you relax. And I'd be happy to infuse the air with a pleasing scent. As I recall, you're especially fond of jasmine."

Kyoto groaned at the AI's reminder. She hated doing media appearances, and she especially hated *Cydonia Today*. "Don't bother. I'm wide awake now."

Kyoto threw off her sheets and padded naked across the carpeted floor to the bathroom. She didn't have far to go. Galactic Stargate Authority living quarters were hardly palatial—bedroom, bathroom, living area, kitchen, none of them very large. The bedroom was so small that Wolf used to joke that he could roll over and go to the bathroom without getting out of bed.

But that was colony life. Conservation of resources,

including living space, was the key to survival. Kyoto had seen numerous vids of old Earth, but of all the things that impressed her—the blue sky, the lush plant growth, the oceans, the animals—she'd always found the sheer amount of habitable living space on the planet to be staggering. Try as she might, she couldn't quite imagine what it would be like to live in a place where you weren't always enclosed within the smallest area possible, a place where you could run more than a few feet without slamming into a wall, where you could see for long distances without needing to have the view re-created on a holoscreen, or being cut off from the world by a thick plasteel window. A place where you could lie down on the grass, look up at the sky, and breathe air that had never been processed or purified. Sometimes it seemed impossible to her that humans had ever truly lived like that. Other times, it seemed inconceivable to her they could live any other way.

She took her time in the bathroom, lingering in the chem shower, trying not to think about Memory, her dream, or Philip Wolfenson and just how damn much she missed him.

CHAPTER

TWO

"Good morning, Colonists. I'm Aspen DeFonesca, and this is *Cydonia Today*." The beautiful blonde flashed a million-erg smile as the program's theme music filled the tiny studio. The room was featureless, save for the two chairs that Aspen and Kyoto occupied. The backdrop of the Martian city of Cydonia would be virtually generated for the audience as their images were transmitted over Syscom.

The music faded out and Aspen's expression became serious. "Today is of course Remembrance Day, the anniversary of both the defeat of our race's greatest enemy and the loss of our ancestral home-world. My guest this morning is the woman whom some have hailed as humanity's savior: Elite Commander Mei Kyoto of the Galactic Stargate Authority."

Kyoto smiled at the vidcam hovering in front of her and tried not to shift in her seat, although her dress uniform was a bit snug around her waist and the collar made her neck itch. *Cydonia Today* was the top-rated infotainment show in the Solar Colonies, which meant that over a billion people were looking at her right now. The last thing they needed to see was the GSA's most famous officer squirm uncomfortably in her seat, like a child that couldn't stand to be wearing grown-up clothes. She didn't want to think what General Adams would say to her later.

Aspen turned to look at her, dazzling smile once more firmly in place. The woman was either blessed with almost perfect genetics or—and this was Kyoto's belief—she'd been the recipient of some serious cosmetic surgery somewhere along the line. She was stunning: perfect hair, blue eyes, full lips, high cheekbones, large breasts, trim waist. Next to her, Kyoto looked like a boy, and a not particularly attractive one at that.

"Good morning, Elite Commander. I'm sure you have a full agenda today, and we appreciate your taking the time to be with us."

"My pleasure, Aspen." Kyoto hoped she sounded sincere. If she'd had a choice, she'd rather pilot a starfighter into the heart of a supernova than sit here gabbing with the Colonies' most irritating media personality. But then again, perhaps Kyoto was resentful of the woman's extreme beauty—not to mention that she'd played the part of Kyoto in the ludicrously titled *Deathship*, the awful vid based on the Battle of Luna. Aspen was a mediocre actress at best, and to top it all off, she didn't look a thing like Kyoto. If she had any Asian ancestry in her genetic background at all, her cosmetic "enhancements" covered it up well.

"First, let me say how good you look in your dress uniform. Black suits you."

Kyoto gritted her teeth. "All GSA personnel will be wearing their dress uniforms to mark today's occasion."

"Of course they will. But none of them are as well known as you are. Two years ago, women throughout the Solar Colonies copied your trademark look by donning faux flightsuits and retro bomber jackets. Très kitschy, no?"

"That was my father's jacket." *Easy, Kyoto,* she cautioned herself. *Maintain a steady course.* But though she tried to hold back the words, they came out anyway. "My parents ran cargo among the Saturn moon colonies. Their ship was really the only home I ever knew. One day we were just about to make a jump from Titan to Rhea when our ship was attacked by a squadron of Manti Landers. My father tried to get us away, but our ship didn't have much in the way of armaments or speed. We took some heavy hits from the Landers and crash-landed on Titan's surface. The impact killed both my mother and my brother, but my father and I survived, though we were both badly wounded. My father got a vacc suit on me, put one on himself, and then carried me out of the wreckage. I remember it was so cold, and the thick atmosphere made it hard to see. But the Manti didn't have any trouble finding us. A Lander..."

She took a deep breath and forced herself to go on despite Aspen's wide-eyed, almost panicky stare. "A Lander grabbed hold of my father and began to absorb him. But before the Bugger could succeed, it was destroyed by weapons fire. I looked up and saw a starfighter fly by. The pilot dipped her wings to let me know she'd seen me, and then she proceeded to take out the rest of the Manti squadron. When she was finished, she flew by again, only this time she picked me up and took me to the closest Dropzone, where I was given medical treatment. Later, a GSA tank crew recovered my family's frozen bodies. There wasn't much left of my father, but his favorite bomber jacket was still intact." She shrugged. "I guess Manti don't like the taste of pseudoleather. I've worn my father's jacket to honor his memory ever since—during my time growing up in the refugee camps on Rhea and when I enrolled in the Defender Academy. So you can understand why I would hardly describe my jacket as 'kitschy.' "

When she was finished, Kyoto felt better, even though she knew she'd gone too far. Still, Aspen had deserved it for that remark.

Aspen looked at Kyoto for a moment, then slowly and very deliberately smiled. "Do you think that after today there'll be a similar trend toward black uniforms?"

Kyoto sighed. She should have known that Aspen DeFonesca would never let herself be upstaged by a guest. "Honestly, I hope not. I'm proud to have earned the right to wear the uniform of a GSA officer. It's not simply a costume one can—"

"Of course it isn't." Aspen smiled tolerantly, as if she were indulging a talkative child. "Let's chat a little about today, shall we? While there are going to be numerous ceremonies to mark this second Remembrance Day, perhaps none is going to be watched as closely as the activation of the Earth Memorial."

"That's right. It'll happen at precisely noon, CST." *If all goes well,* she added mentally.

"The memorial isn't without its share of controversy, though, is it? Not everyone thinks that a holographic recreation of Earth and its moon is in the best taste. Especially since they're only going to be one-fortieth the size of the originals. Any thoughts?"

"All the proposed designs were available for colonists to view and vote on through Syscom's infonet. In the end, the council tallied the votes and the holographic recreation won. As for the size, given the limits of our technology, it was the best we could do. And even at one-fortieth scale, that still comes to about a thousand-kilometer circumference for the Earth holo, and close to three hundred for the moon."

"Yes, but what I'm really after here is what do *you*, Mei Kyoto, think of the memorial?" She gave Kyoto a *we're-best-girlfriends-aren't-we?* smile. "Don't hold back now."

In Kyoto's mind, she once again saw an image of the moon moving inexorably toward Earth, while swarms of Manti streaked toward the satellite in a vain attempt to stop it.

"The purpose of a memorial is to help us remember, right? In that case, the holograms will do their job, despite whatever shortcomings they might have." At one time such a diplomatic answer would have been beyond Kyoto, but she'd had a lot of practice at diplomacy serving as the GSA's public face during the last two years.

Aspen's smile dimmed by a few hundred watts, though it didn't go out entirely. Kyoto knew the woman prided herself on being able to make a personal connection with the people she interviewed, on getting them to, as she put it, "dish the dishiest dish." But Kyoto was here as an official representative of the GSA. Besides, she wasn't a dishy kind of gal.

A sly look came over Aspen's face then. "From what

I understand, Commander First Class Philip Wolfenson—called Wolf by his closest friends—is going to be one of the fighter pilots providing security for the *Orinoco* as its crew completes the activation of the memorial today."

Kyoto felt as if she'd just taken a blow to her solar plexus. "That's right."

Aspen's eyes narrowed like a predator that had sensed weakness in its prey. "It's not a secret that the two of you have been a couple for almost a year now. In fact, one of my spies reports that there's been some talk of marriage. Care to comment, Elite Commander?" Aspen bared her teeth in a way that possessed only the most superficial resemblance to a smile.

Kyoto held her breath. Her cheeks felt hot, and she knew she was blushing. She could tell by the look on Aspen's too-perfect face that the woman knew Wolf had broken up with her, and that the morning-show host had raised the topic of her romantic life in order to punish Kyoto for not being a more forthcoming guest. The question was just how far Aspen was willing to take this.

"I don't think marriage is in the cards for us right now, Aspen. However, I wish Commander Wolfenson the best of luck in his role during this historic mission. And the same goes for the rest of the *Orinoco*'s crew."

Aspen looked at her for a long moment before inclining her head in the slightest of nods, as if to say, *Well played*.

"Yet another of my spies tells me that the Council of Seven intends to make a special announcement a half hour before the memorial goes online. I don't suppose you might be able to give us a hint as to what it might be?"

Kyoto didn't have to feign surprise at this question. "I haven't heard anything about that." And she hadn't, though she did have her suspicions as to what that announcement was going to be.

Aspen waited a moment longer, as if trying to gauge Kyoto's sincerity. Finally, she said, "Well, I suppose we'll all find out at eleven-thirty, won't we? Now, why don't you tell us where you stand on an issue that's been burning up Syscom's boards recently: *Galactic Gossipmonger* posted its annual Sexiest in the Solar Colonies list last week, and for the second year in a row, you're on it. Any reactions?"

"And we're out to commercial." A tiny red light on the hovercam flicked off.

"Thank you, darling." Aspen knew the camera's rudimentary AI didn't care whether she answered it or not, but she didn't think that any reason to be rude. She turned to Kyoto and clasped both of the woman's hands. Though after that little sob story Kyoto had told about her stupid bomber jacket, Aspen would rather have fastened them around the fighter pilot's skinny chicken neck and choked the life out of her. "And *thank you* so much, Mei. It means a great deal to me that you chose to make your first media appearance of the day on my program."

"You're welcome, Aspen." Kyoto withdrew her hands and stood. "If you'll excuse me, I really have to be going now I... need to go talk with someone."

I'll just bet you do, Aspen thought. *Probably that hunky Wolf of yours, unless I miss my guess. Going to beg him one more time to take you back? If he has any brains at all, he'll tell you to go take a walk through an open airlock.*

"Of course, darling. I'll be covering the memorial activation later today, live from GSA headquarters. See you then?"

"Yeah, sure." Kyoto gave her an awkward, lopsided smile, then hurried out of the studio as fast as she could without looking as if she was hurrying.

When Kyoto was gone, Aspen's smile vanished. *Absolutely pathetic.* No matter how many times she spoke to Mei Kyoto, she still couldn't believe that that... *thing* was the single most famous—or some would say infamous—personality in the Solar Colonies. Famous or infamous, they were both the same to Aspen DeFonesca. Mei Kyoto was *known* by everyone, and everyone wanted to know even more about her—who she was, where she came from, what she was thinking and feeling, whom she loved and whom she hated.

Aspen had a personal AI dedicated to running hourly checks of all Syscom communications—public as well as private, and wouldn't the Syscom bigwigs be surprised by that little tidbit of information?—in order to monitor the fluctuating popularity levels of thousands of Very Important People. Chief among these VIPs was Aspen herself, of course, but just as Snow White's evil queen kept getting unpleasant responses from her magic mirror, so too did Aspen continually receive bad news from her AI.

"AI, AI, in the Net: who's the most beloved person yet?"

"I am not programmed to tell a lie: Kyoto's rating is most high."

Aspen absolutely despised Kyoto with every fiber of her genetically flawless being. Kyoto was a clumsy, cloddish, unattractive woman who didn't deserve the

fame that the universe in its blind idiocy had seen fit
to thrust upon her. For pity's sake, children were
already studying about her on Syscom's edunet! How
insane was that?

When she'd been approached to play Kyoto in
Deathship (some sources claimed that she'd doggedly
pursued the role, but of course there was no truth to
that ugly rumor), Aspen had thought she would sup-
plant Kyoto in the public's mind once she showed
them what a *real* hero was like. But despite the
glowing reviews (again, some sources would claim
that her performance was panned by vid critics
throughout the Solar Colonies, but these sources were
just mean and hateful and plain *wrong, wrong,
wrong!*) that hadn't happened. If anything, her star
turn in *Deathship* had only served to add to Kyoto's
popularity.

Not that Aspen was jealous or anything. She'd once
gone to a therapist who diagnosed her as having a
dependent-personality disorder known as entanglement. It was, he'd said, a common enough ailment
among colonists, though she was the most extreme
case he'd ever seen. Entanglement was the result of
living in close proximity to others day in and day out
from the moment a person was born. It resulted in
the sufferer becoming so concerned about others'
opinions that the boundaries of the individual self
became "blurred to an unhealthy and sometimes even
dangerous degree," as the therapist had put it.

The man had been full of unrecycled bodily waste,
of course. Aspen had used her connections within
Cydonian Civilian Security to have the moron framed
for financing a bug-dust smuggling operation. The
drug—made from synthetic Manti enzymes—was

highly illegal, and the therapist was sentenced to life at hard labor in Phobos prison. Funny, but now that she thought of it, she realized that she couldn't recall the fool's name. Ah well, she supposed it didn't matter.

"We'll be coming out of commercial in sixty seconds," the hovercam said. "Should I send in your next guest?"

"Of course, and don't wait so long to ask next time!" Aspen was angry with herself for getting so wrapped up in her thoughts that she'd almost forgotten about the show. Damn that Kyoto!

Her next guest was one of the holo-artists who'd helped design the Earth Memorial. She greeted the man—who had *no* sense of fashion at all—and got him seated just in time for the hovercam's little red light to wink on. She conducted the interview with the artist on autopilot while she continued to think (*not* obsess) about Kyoto. How could she possibly compete with a woman who had both saved humanity *and* destroyed the Earth? There had to be a way, if only she could find it....

CHAPTER
THREE

Kyoto sat in the backseat of a maglev transport bound for Galactic Stargate Authority headquarters. Two GSA security guards rode in front—a precaution that irritated Kyoto no end, but which General Detroit Adams insisted on whenever she made public appearances on behalf of the GSA. The transport hummed above ferroceramic rails as it traveled along the causeway from the Syscom complex. Kyoto didn't feel like activating the backseat holoscreen—not after having to endure Aspen DeFonesca this morning—and with nothing better to look at than the backs of the guards' heads, she cast her gaze upward.

The causeway's plasteel roof was set on transparent today, and Kyoto saw that the sky above Cydonia was a light pink dotted with white clouds of carbon dioxide ice. It looked clear and calm, which suited Kyoto just fine. She hated Martian dust storms: they were noisy, hard to fly in, and tended to make the grav generators malfunction. Besides, a storm would just put a damper on the Remembrance Day ceremonies, and the occasion was already solemn enough.

Kyoto also had a good view of Cydonia's stargate. The circular portal hovered over the dropzone on the colony's northern edge. The stargate was held aloft by its own antigrav gens, and the vortex of faint blue-green energy swirling within indicated it was active. Stargates were almost always left on because to shut down and restart them consumed far more energy—assuming they could be reactivated at all—than just letting them run constantly.

The sight of the stargate made Kyoto smile. Though the Colonies' gates were interconnected and you knew where you were going when you entered one, there was still a sense of danger when making a jump through a hyperspace portal, a feeling that you never truly knew what might await you on the other side. This feeling, and the excitement that accompanied it, was one of the things she loved best about being a fighter pilot.

Kyoto almost remarked upon this but thought better of it. She didn't know either of the guards—one male, one female—and there was the difference in rank to consider. She was an elite commander, and they were both sergeants. Rank didn't mean much to her; all she cared about was flying. But soon after her promotion, she'd discovered that even though rank didn't matter to her, it did to others. Like Wolf, for instance.

Thinking of Wolf depressed her, and she lowered her gaze. She wondered what he was doing now. Probably finishing the preflight check of his starfighter, she guessed. Just then, she was insanely jealous of Wolf and wished their roles were reversed: that he was the so-called Savior of Humanity, while she was merely another anonymous jump jockey with a mission to fly.

As she was getting set for a good wallow in her funk, the male security guard said, "Heads up, Commander. Looks like there's some trouble ahead."

Kyoto leaned sideways so she could get a better look. A crowd had gathered around the entrance to GSA headquarters: a hundred people, maybe more. There were so many that they covered both lanes of the causeway, blocking passage into or out of the GSA installation. As the maglev transport drew near to the crowd, it automatically slowed and came to a stop behind several other blocked vehicles.

"Looks like a protest," the female guard said.

Now that they were closer, Kyoto could see that what she had at first taken to be a single large crowd was in fact two separate groups facing each other. Many of the people carried protest signs, and a dozen hovercams circled around the protestors like bloodthirsty darting insects. Not that Kyoto had ever seen a real insect outside of a vid—unless you counted Manti, of course.

Both groups looked mad as hell, and each was chanting a slogan as loud as it could, trying to drown out the other.

"A new home for hu-man-it-ee!"

"The gal-ax-y is ours!"

"A new home for hu-man-i-TEE!"

"The gal-a-x-y is OURS!"

"Great," muttered the male guard. "Claimers and Bounders. Just what we needed."

"What else did you expect?" Kyoto said. "Especially today." Not only was it Remembrance Day, but because of the activation of the Earth Memorial, the entire Council of Seven had traveled to GSA headquarters to be present for the event. It was extremely rare for the council members to meet physically, so what better time for a protest?

Without the Manti threat to worry about anymore, the people of the Solar Colonies had turned their attention from simple survival to what humanity's next step should be. There were two main camps: the Reclaimers and the Outbounders. The Claimers believed with almost fanatical devotion that a new Earth should be created by terraforming another planet, the most popular choice being Mars. The Outbounders, on the other hand, were just as fervent in their belief that humanity's future lay in expanding its colonies outside the solar system and into the galaxy, with the hope of one day perhaps discovering Earth-like worlds to settle.

As far as Kyoto was concerned, both ideas had merit, though she tended to favor the Claimers' position, which was another sore point between her and Wolf. As a fighter pilot, Wolf was totally gung ho for galactic exploration and the adventure that went along with it. Kyoto understood, for part of her longed for that adventure, too. But another part wanted to replace the world that she had helped destroy, wanted a home in the truest sense of the word for her species. The problem was that the Colonies didn't have the resources to do both at the same time, not after generations of war with the Manti. So it came down to a choice, and from what Kyoto had seen on the newsnets—not to mention what she was seeing in front of her right now—it looked as though any sort of consensus among the Colonists was going to be impossible.

Despite the crowd's obviously high emotions, the two sides were behaving themselves thanks to a mixed contingent of civilian defense officers and GSA security standing between them. Of course, the fact that the officers were armed with stun lances and tranq shooters helped.

"Do you want us to turn around, Commander?" the male officer asked.

"No," Kyoto said. It would take far too long to maneuver their maglev onto the opposite track, head back to Syscom, then take another causeway. They'd have to travel through a half dozen different installations before finally reaching the back entrance of GSA headquarters. "It looks like our people and the Civvies are keeping a lid on the situation. With any luck, I should be able to walk right on through." She started to climb out of the vehicle.

"I'm not sure that's such a good idea, Commander," the woman officer said.

Kyoto was tired of being babysat. "I'm going. You two can come with me or stay here. Your choice." Without waiting for a response, she started walking toward the GSA entrance. She smiled as the two officers got out of the maglev and hurried to catch up to her.

Sometimes rank really does have its privileges.

As she approached the crowd, a number of heads on both sides turned her way. That was when she realized her mistake.

"Look! It's Mei Kyoto!"

"No, it isn't!"

"I'm telling you it's her!"

"Savior!"

"Planet killer!"

The Claimers and Bounders stopped yelling at each other and focused all their attention on her. Kyoto swore inwardly. When would she ever get used to being famous? Or infamous, as the case may be.

The hovercams quickly trained their lenses on her. For a moment there was complete silence, and the cameras had nothing of interest to broadcast, but then both groups of protesters began shouting and moving toward her. The Civvies and the GSA officers tried to hold the crowd back, but it was like trying to stop a Martian gale-force wind using only a pulse beam set on low. Kyoto's two babysitters stepped in front of her and drew their stun lances.

"Get back to the lev, Commander!" the woman shouted. "We'll cover you!"

Cover my retreat, you mean. After having faced Manti squadrons more times than she could count, Kyoto wasn't intimidated by a crowd of her own kind, even if half of them would be more than happy to tear her limb from limb. Retreat simply wasn't an option.

Kyoto carried no weapon herself. The GSA brass thought it would send the wrong message to the public to have their most famous representative make media appearances while armed. Which, considering how she felt about media types—especially Aspen DeFonesca—was probably a good thing.

The civilian security and GSA officers began laying into the crowd with their stun lances, and while a number of protestors went down, their nervous systems temporarily inoperative, there were simply too many people to stop. As Claimers and Bounders jostled one another, fistfights erupted and the combatants stopped to duke it out, but the majority of both groups continued surging toward Kyoto.

She wondered how many in the crowd were wired on bug dust. Too many, she decided. One of the drug's effects was a heightened sense of aggression—no surprise considering the original source of the chemical—coupled with a lowering of inhibitions. Not the best of combinations in any circumstance, but especially during an emotionally charged protest.

Kyoto was seriously reconsidering her stance on retreat when a loud voice cut through all the noise like a precision laser burning a hole through a soggy protein square.

"Claimers and Bounders! Stand down!"

The voice was so loud that it made Kyoto's ears hurt. Evidently, it affected everyone else the same way, for people winced and clapped their hands to their ears. Protesters and peacekeepers alike turned toward the source of the voice: a man standing on the hood of one of the stopped maglev transports, hands upraised to catch everyone's attention. Kyoto recognized him from newsnet feeds as an Outbounder spokesman named Seth Ganymede.

He was a tall, lean man in his sixties, cleanshaven, but with a full head of thick white hair. He wore a plain gray tunic and leggings, something of a uniform among the Bounders. The fabric was holographic, and a ghostly image of the Milky Way spiraled slowly in the air inches from his chest. That last touch was a bit over the top, Kyoto thought, and she hated to imagine what Aspen De Fonesca would say about it if she were here.

Outbounders tended to change their names to reflect their galactic-expansionist ideals, in much the same way that generations of colonists had named their children after places on Earth—such as Detroit, Aspen, and of course, Kyoto—to remind them of their homeworld. Kyoto thought Seth could have used more imagination in selecting his Bounder surname, though. Since Ganymede was one of Jupiter's moons, it was right in the Colonies' backyard, so to speak. It was quite a provincial choice, really.

When Ganymede next spoke, his voice was pitched at a more bearable volume, though still loud enough for everyone in the causeway to hear. "Today is an emotional occasion for all of us." He glanced at Kyoto and locked gazes with her for an instant. "Perhaps more so for some than others." He broke eye contact and continued to sweep his gaze across the mingled crowd of Bounders and Claimers. "Strong feelings are nothing to be ashamed of. They're part of what makes us… human."

The hesitation was so slight as to be almost unnoticeable, but Kyoto picked up on it. *That was weird*, she thought. And what about his choice of words before? "Stand down." That was a phrase a military man would use, not a political activist. She didn't know a lot about the Bounder spokesman, but she wasn't aware he'd ever served in a military capacity. Perhaps he'd once worked civilian security on some colony or other. But even so, his use of the phrase still struck her as odd. And how had he managed to speak so loudly? He held no voxcaster, and while it was possible he had some sort of miniature version attached to his collar or somewhere, she didn't see how it could have produced so much powerful sound. She'd felt the vibrations of his voice rattle her teeth.

She recalled a line from an ancient Earth text: "Curiouser and curiouser, Alice."

"But strong feelings require strong control unless we wish our emotions to overwhelm us and cause us to take actions that we shall all too soon regret."

Before Ganymede could say anything more, someone in the crowd who didn't appreciate being lectured at hurled a gray rock—no doubt brought along in anticipation of the protest turning violent—straight at Ganymede's head. The rock flew too fast for the Bounder spokesman to duck, and it struck him on the right temple. Blood spurted from Ganymede's head and he staggered, but he didn't fall off the maglev. He touched his fingers to his temple, and they came away coated with blood. He stared at the blood for a moment before holding his hand up for everyone to see.

This time when he spoke, his words were almost inaudible. "Our kind was almost destroyed by the Manti scourge. Do we now intend to finish the job for them?"

The Bounders and Claimers looked at one another, looked at the ground, nodded, shook their heads, but regardless of their individual reaction, all of them were shamed by Ganymede's words. Slowly, quietly, they began to separate into two sides once more. Those that had been hit with stun lances were helped to walk, or in some cases were carried, by their fellows.

Kyoto let out a sigh of relief. What had come way too close to boiling over into a riot was now simmering down to a peaceful protest once more—thanks to Seth Ganymede.

Her two babysitters holstered their stun lances.

"Let's get back in the lev, Commander," the woman said. "We shouldn't have any trouble getting through now."

But Kyoto ignored her and started walking toward Seth Ganymede. Several hovercams detected her movement and instantly zipped over to track her, but she paid them no attention. She wanted to see how badly injured Ganymede was and if he needed medical attention. That was only part of why she wanted to talk to him, though. After all, the Civvies or the GSA guards could take care of him. But she'd been impressed with how he had managed to calm the crowd and maintain control over his own emotions after being injured. Most important, he had kept the protesters from going wild and perhaps tearing her apart. That deserved a thank-you at the very least. Plus, there was something about him that she found intriguing.

A Civvy had helped Ganymede down from the maglev by the time Kyoto reached him.

"You okay?" she asked.

Ganymede turned to her and smiled. "Aside from a headache and several bloodstains on my tunic, I'm fine."

"You sure? It looks like your wound bled quite a bit."

He shrugged. "Head wounds tend to do that, don't they? But I assure you, I'll survive."

Kyoto peered more closely at the bloody patch of skin over his right temple. Though it was difficult to tell from all the blood, the injury didn't look too bad. In fact, she couldn't see exactly where he had been cut. As near as she could tell, underneath the blood, Ganymede's skin was smooth and unbroken.

The Civvy gave Kyoto a questioning look, and she said, "It's all right, Officer. I'll take it from here."

The Civvy nodded and moved off to work crowd control with the other officers and GSA guards.

Ganymede grinned. "That was quite commanding of you."

Kyoto smiled back. "Yeah, well, I am the savior of humanity, right? Look, I just wanted to thank you for what you did. Not only did you stop the crowd from mobbing me, you prevented a lot of unnecessary injuries on both sides. Not counting yours, of course."

"As I said, I'll survive. And if you believe in something, you have to stand up for it."

"Even if by doing so you make a target of yourself?"

"You're a fighter pilot, Elite Commander. I think you already know the answer to that question."

Kyoto laughed. "Yeah, I guess I do. Why don't you come with me to GSA headquarters? You'll be able to clean up there and get something to take care of your headache."

"I appreciate your kind offer, though I'm not sure your superiors would approve—not to mention the Council of Seven." He lowered his voice and in a mock conspiratorial tone said, "Besides, I think I'll leave the blood on for a while. It'll make good PR." He nodded to a nearby hovercam and gave Kyoto a wink.

She was surprised by how much she liked this man. From what she'd seen on the newsnets, he'd struck her as humorless and a borderline fanatic for his cause. But she found him charming in an avuncular way.

"All right, then. I'll leave you to your protest. Just try not to get hit by any more flying objects, all right?"

He smiled. "I'll do my best. And I wish you luck on making it through today's ceremonies. It can't be an easy time for you."

Kyoto's own smile fell away. "No, it isn't." She started to walk toward the entrance to the GSA installation when Ganymede called out after her.

"It was an honor to meet you, Elite Commander. I hope we have the opportunity to speak again."

Unsure how to respond to this, Kyoto turned, waved, then continued toward the GSA entrance, trying not to think about what the rest of the day held in store for her.

Seth Ganymede—or rather, the being that currently called himself by that name —watched Kyoto enter the GSA installation followed closely by one of the security guards assigned to her. The other had gone back to retrieve their maglev transport.

The being was grateful that everything had worked out so well. He knew he'd been taking a risk by intervening when the protest had started to turn ugly, but he couldn't simply stand by and watch as innocent humans were hurt—especially Mei Kyoto. After all, a large part of the reason he was here on Mars was to speak with her. He hadn't anticipated being assaulted by one of the protesters, though. He supposed that's what came from being more of a diplomat than a warrior. When he'd first been struck, he'd feared that he was going to be exposed—and with all those hovercams about, no less. He'd instinctively reached up to smear the blood around on his forehead before the nanocolony that shared and maintained his body could repair the damage. He wished the nanoparticles had a better sense of timing, but while he could influence them to a certain extent—such as using them to amplify his voice—they were programmed to attend to their host's injuries immediately, and there was nothing he could do about that. As it was, it had taken all of his willpower to convince his microscopic friends not to reabsorb the blood on his forehead.

He wondered if Kyoto had noticed. She was quite sharp, and she had examined his injury, or rather where his injury had been, up close. Still, she hadn't said anything, and if she had suspected something was wrong, she would have insisted he accompany her to GSA headquarters. No, his masquerade was still intact, at least for the time being. But he wasn't certain how much longer he could maintain it before he was exposed. He'd have to speak with Kyoto before that happened. The future of her species depended on it.

Hovercams swooped in then and crowded in front of his face. Their AIs began firing questions at him in a confusing babble of electronically synthesized voices.

"Do you think this incident merely underscores the deep divide between Bounders and Claimers?"

"Do you think bug dust was a contributing factor in today's violence?"

"How does it feel to get hit on the head by a rock?"

The being who pretended to be Seth Ganymede raised his hands. "One at a time, please!" Then patiently, one by one, he answered their questions as his masquerade continued.

CHAPTER

FOUR

Kyoto found General Detroit Adams in the command center of GSA Control. He stood before a bank of holoscreens while techs sat at workstations, manipulating the virtual controls of their computers. But GSA personnel weren't the only ones present. A long table covered by a red silken tablecloth had been set up, and it was covered with food and drink. Not far from the table were seven pseudoleather chairs, and sitting in them—eating, drinking, and chatting with one another and select members of the GSA brass—was the Council of Seven. Hovercams circled the council members like tiny artificial moons, but the Seven ignored them. Kyoto figured they were used to constant media scrutiny.

She wasn't thrilled to see the council members, especially Janeesh Glasgow, Cydonia's representative. Thanks to her fame, Kyoto had been introduced to and had vidded with them all, and she'd been romantically propositioned by several, males and females included. But Glasgow was the most persistent—Kyoto had lost track of how many times she'd turned him down. She was uncomfortable around politicians for another reason, though. Whenever she spoke to one, Kyoto always had the sense that he or she wasn't really looking at or talking to her, but rather performing for the hovercams and all the voters on their other end of their signals. But there was one good thing about having the Seven present: they'd keep most of the cams away from her.

Detroit Adams was a middle-aged male of African descent. His close-cropped hair was starting to go gray at the edges, though his mustache and goatee were as black as ever. He'd lost his right eye in battle with the Manti, and instead of having a replacement cloned, he'd had an oculator attached to the empty socket. The device looked something like a metallic monocle and allowed him to remain in constant contact with the GSA datastream wherever he went. He was a warrior with a spirit of high-density ferroceramic, and balls to match. No one had more confirmed Manti kills (Kyoto's destruction of Earth notwithstanding) and every pilot in the GSA, Kyoto included, would fly with him through a stargate straight into the heart of a supernova without hesitation. Like Kyoto, Adams wore his dress uniform today, but his had general's stars on the shoulder.

"General Adams, I know you're busy, but can I talk with you for a moment?" She glanced over at the Seven. "Privately," she added.

Adams didn't take his gaze off the holoscreens as he answered. "In a few minutes, Kyoto. The *Orinoco* is just about to head to the dropzone. You're welcome to stick around and watch. If you want to, that is." Adams still didn't look at her, but his tone softened, and she knew he was aware that she and Wolf had broken up.

"Thanks, General. I think I will watch."

"Help yourself to some food if you're hungry. But be careful. The meat is the real thing, not reconstituted protein squares. Unless your stomach's used to digesting the stuff, you'll end up paying later for eating it now."

Kyoto looked at the food table in surprise. *Real* meat? Only the wealthiest colonists could afford such a luxury. But then, the Council of Seven, while the duly elected representatives of their respective colonies, tended to be among the richest people in the Solar Colonie—industrialists, infotainment magnates, food producers, pharmaceutical developers. Sometimes Kyoto wondered if the word *elected* wasn't just a pseudonym for *purchased*.

Janeesh Glasgow saw her looking at the food. He waved and gave her a wink.

Kyoto quickly turned away. "I think I'll pass. I don't have much of an appetite after the morning I've had."

One of the vidscreens showed an image of the GSA starship hangar, while another showed the dropzone. The *Orinoco* would travel several kilometers to the dropzone, and from there ascend to the stargate. Once through the portal, it would exit through another gate in orbit of what was left of Earth. The crew would then put the finishing touches on the holographic memorial.

Adams harrumphed. "DeFonesca give you a hard time?"

"An irritating time is more like it."

Adams chuckled. "I'd think that she'd be easy

enough for you to deal with after facing a Manti swarm."

"To be honest, I'd rather spend time with a Bugger than her any day."

Adams laughed. "Now you sound like Mudo!"

The hangar door slid open and the *Orinoco* slowly emerged, hovering no more than a meter above the ground. There was nothing especially elegant about the ship. It was a modified transport: long, narrow, and ungainly. But it would get the job done, and that was all that mattered.

"Where is Dr. Mudo?" she asked. "I'm surprised he's not here. After all, he was in charge of the tech team that designed and built the memorial's components."

"Mudo may be head of GSA's Research and Development division, but that doesn't mean he's personally invested in every single GSA project. Besides, you know him. It's almost impossible to get him out of his damn lab as it is, let alone when the entire Council of Seven is here, along with their retinues and a fleet of hovercams. I imagine Mudo's got the vid feed of the *Orinoco* playing while he's working on another project."

The *Orinoco* cleared the hangar and, using only its maglev boosters, started gliding across ferroceramic rails toward the dropzone. Since the energies at the heart of a stargate tended to be somewhat volatile, planetside gates were usually positioned at a colony's outer edge. Plus, on those rare occasions when there was an accident, the dropzone was far enough away that no civilians were harmed.

Now two smaller ships emerged from the hangar. Both were Retribution class starfighters, the top of the GSA's line. The model was built primarily for speed, which made it extremely effective in battle. A Retribution could literally outrun most weapons fire. But the use of the ship was strictly ceremonial today. The two craft were to serve as escorts only.

Even so, Kyoto felt a nervous flutter in her stomach as she watched the two Retribution ships trail after the *Orinoco*. She was never nervous when she was in the cockpit. Well, not much. But she always worried whenever Wolf flew a mission. She knew it was foolish—Wolf was an excellent pilot and today's mission was going to be a milk run—but she couldn't help herself.

"Which one—"

"Commander Wolfenson will fly on the *Orinoco*'s starboard."

Kyoto nodded. That meant Julia Everest would be on the port. She'd been in the same Academy training class as Kyoto. While Julia wasn't at Wolf's skill level, she was a decent enough pilot and had made the rank of Commander. More than that, she was a good person, too. Kyoto was glad Julia had gotten assigned to today's mission. Though Wolf was the command officer, it still would be a boost to her career.

It took five minutes for the *Orinoco* to reach the dropzone. It then hovered in place as the two starfighters took up their positions alongside it.

An electronic chirp sounded as the control room's comlink activated. It was Wolf.

"Everything looks good on our end, General. Request permission to lift off."

To anyone else, he would have sounded relaxed and professional, but Kyoto could detect the eagerness in his tone. Wolf was raring to go, as usual.

"Permission granted," Adams said. "Have a safe trip, Wolfenson."

"Will do, General. Wolf out."

Adams turned to Kyoto and raised a questioning eyebrow. The general was a man of few words, but she had learned to read his facial expressions. He was asking if she wanted to say anything to Wolf before he left.

Kyoto shook her head, and Adams returned his attention to the holoscreens. The three ships cut their maglev boosters and switched to maneuvering thrusters. They rose in tandem and activated their fusion engines as they approached the stargate. As they drew near the energy vortex within the gate, they accelerated slightly as the hyperspace portal began to drawn them in. Blue-green energy flared white as it coruscated over and around the ships, and then they were gone.

The image on the screen changed to one of another stargate hanging in space. The trio of ships emerged from the vortex, looking none the worse for wear.

Kyoto relaxed once she saw the ships had arrived safely on the other side of the Gate. *Looks like you survived another jump, Wolf.*

Beyond the stargate and the three ships loomed Earth—or rather what Earth had become.

Where once there had been an inviting world of blue oceans and landmasses covered by white clouds, there was now only an inhospitable planet with a molten surface. This new world was encircled by a huge debris ring made up of chunks of both its former incarnation and the natural satellite that had been driven into it by the most complex artificial intelligence humanity had ever created. The ring would eventually coalesce into one or more new moons sometime in the distant future. The planet itself—Kyoto couldn't bring herself to think of it as Earth—now had a carbon dioxide atmosphere caused by the melting of carbonate rocks in the crust as a result of Luna's impact. During that collision, enough debris was tossed into escape orbit to form a mini-asteroid belt near the new planet. It was upon one of these asteroids that the holographic generator for the Earth memory had been installed.

Seeing what Earth had become—what she had helped make it become—always filled Kyoto with an overwhelming sense of sadness mixed with awe. Sadness over the molten hell that had been created as the price of the Manti's destruction, and awe when she considered the sheer cosmic scale of what had happened.

She understood that there hadn't been any other way if the human race was going to avoid extinction, but in the greatest war her species had ever fought, their homeworld had been the most devastating casualty of all.

Wolf's voice came over the comlink once more, and startled Kyoto out of her thoughts.

"Our jump was successful, and the techs on the *Orinoco* are ready to get to work."

"Sounds good, Commander," Adams said. "Check in from time to time to let us know how it's going. If all goes according to plan, we'll bring the memorial online at noon CST."

"Understood, General. Wolf out."

The *Orinoco* began to move toward the asteroid where the previous components of the holoprojector had been installed. A pair of grappling arms extended from the front of the ship, and the cargo bay opened. A quartet of techs in vacc suits held onto the corners of a large solar panel. Tiny thrusters in their suits flared bright for an instant, and the techs began to guide the panel toward the small asteroid where the grappling arms would fit it into place.

Evidently satisfied that the mission had gotten off to a good start, Adams turned to Kyoto.

"Now, what do you want to talk to me about?"

"Why didn't you just ask the council yourself? They were all there in the control room, stuffing their faces and getting drunk."

Kyoto had to suppress a smile. She'd never quite figured out how someone as impolitic as Detroit Adams had managed to rise so far up the ranks of the Galactic Stargate Authority—especially when the GSA was under the partial control of the Council of Seven. Perhaps it was simply because he was every bit as tough as a Manti warrior—and then some. Or perhaps it had something to do with the way he'd been raised. Adams's grandmother had been the council representative from Mars well before Janeesh Glasgow was elected. From what Kyoto understood, Adams had grown up living an existence of luxury, privilege, and power. But for reasons no one seemed clear on, he'd left all that behind and enrolled in the Defender Academy so he could kill Buggers—a goal Kyoto could certainly sympathize with.

There'd been speculation in the ranks for years that Adams might one day run for the council himself, but Kyoto didn't think he would. Not that he wouldn't do a good job, but Kyoto couldn't imagine him leaving the GSA. If ever there had been a man born to lead soldiers into battle, it was Detroit Adams.

"I didn't ask the council because Janeesh Glasgow was there," Kyoto said. "The last time I spoke with him, he tried to get me to come to his quarters and try on a new lightweight, skin-tight body armor that made the wearer completely impervious to harm."

"So?"

"He also claimed it was invisible."

Adams laughed. "Our esteemed council member may be something of a clueless lecher, but you have to admit he's done a lot for the GSA. We never would've been able to complete Memory without his support, and he's been a key figure in making the Earth Memorial a reality."

"Maybe so, but that doesn't mean I have to talk to him if I don't want to—and I definitely do *not* want to."

The two of them were sitting in Adams's private office. Though his rank entitled him a far grander office, Adams preferred a modest setup, one that reminded Kyoto of a starfighter cockpit in many ways: deskcomp, wall screens on all sides, and the one concession to luxury that every pilot longed for—a comfortable chair. Adams's was leather—the real thing, too, not some imitation. She didn't want to think about how much it cost.

Once a jump jockey, always a jump jockey, she thought. But in Adams's case, a jump jockey with enough pull to get a leather chair that was far more comfortable, she was sure, than the plasteel one she was sitting on.

"So what is this big announcement the Seven plan to make?" Kyoto asked. "And don't tell me you don't know. You know everything that goes on in the Solar Colonies. Everything worth knowing, that is."

"C'mon, Kyoto. Surely you've guessed by now."

Kyoto laughed. "No matter the situation, you can't resist playing teacher, can you? All right. The council has decided to either go ahead with galactic expansion or terraform Mars. If I had to bet my pension on it, I'd go with the second."

"Why's that?"

"It's a better move politically right now. After years of living under Manti assault, people are tired of hiding. They want to reclaim the system where our race originated. Expanding farther into the galaxy would feel like we were still running from the Manti."

Adams smiled. "Too bad you didn't make that bet, because you would've won. At precisely eleven-thirty this morning—assuming any of the Seven is still sober enough to speak coherently—the council will announce that we are going to proceed with the New Earth project."

Kyoto thought of Seth Ganymede and his fellow Bounders. "That's not going to come as welcome news to some people."

"Yeah, I heard about your run-in with the protesters on the way here."

Before she could ask how he knew, Adams tapped his ocular device. She should have realized. After all, she'd said it herself: the general knew everything worth knowing. She wouldn't have been surprised to learn that he'd been directly patched into the feeds from the hovercams covering the protest.

"Intelligence gathering is the key to victory," he'd once told her. "That, and damn big guns."

"How do you feel about the council's decision, sir?"

Adams shrugged. "I'm a soldier, same as you. I go where I'm needed and kick as much ass as I can. Still, in my opinion, it's a potentially dangerous move. Sure, you and Memory destroyed the Manti that had taken over Earth, and though it took us the better part of another year, we cleaned out the remaining Buggers in the rest of the Colonies. But just because there isn't a Manti threat right now doesn't mean there won't be one in the future. The swarm we put down was the second humanity has faced. I don't know if we can survive a third."

"And you think expanding our colonies beyond the solar system would increase our chances of survival?"

"The more spread out we are, the harder it will be for the Manti to find us. Plus, they'd be forced to spread their own forces thinner. We'd also stand a greater chance of finding more resource-rich worlds. We need a lot of ore and radioactive material to keep our fighting forces strong, and it's no secret that we're starting to deplete the readily available resources in this system. Three mines and two processing plants have already shut down in the last year, with more sure to follow. Without metals, we can't make star-fighters, transport ships, or tanks. Without radioactive material, we can't power their fusion engines even if we *could* make them."

"I didn't realize things were so bad," Kyoto said.

"It's not the sort of information the public wants to hear right now. They want to believe the Manti are gone forever and that everything is going to be just fine. But it will take generations to complete the terra-forming of Mars, and we might not be able to finish at all if the Colonies run out of resources to draw on."

"But what about the argument that we might

encounter other systems controlled by the Manti if we continued to colonize the galaxy? And if not the Manti, then maybe we'd discover other species that are just as hostile—and perhaps even more powerful."

Adams gave her a wry half-smile. "I take it your sympathies lie with the Claimers then?"

Kyoto's cheeks reddened with embarrassment as she realized she'd been replaying old arguments with Wolf using Adams as a stand-in. "Let's just say I can see merits in both points of view."

"The GSA does too, which is why, even though we intend to do everything we can to aid in the New Earth project, we aren't going to completely abandon our research into alternate stardrives that would make galactic expansion easier and cheaper."

The discovery of hyperspace several centuries earlier, and the development of stargate technology, had allowed the human race to establish colonies within its own system. Now there were seven: Cydonia on the planet Mars and six others on the moons Phobos, Europa, Prometheus, Rhea, Titan, and Triton. But stargating was still a slow method of traveling, cosmically speaking. Before you could jump from one gate to another, both had to be constructed, put in place, and activated. That meant flying at sublight speeds to a chosen destination and then assembling a gate, a process that could take decades at best, and centuries—or even millennia—at worst. You could engage a ship's jump drive and take a blind plunge through hyperspace, but there was no telling where, or even if, you'd emerge again in realspace. Assuming you survived a blind jump, there was no guarantee that you'd come out of hyperspace close to a world suitable for colonization.

All in all, it was a slow, awkward, dangerous, and expensive way to explore the galaxy. Right now, though, it was the best method that humanity had. But from what Adams had said, it sounded as if the GSA was working on something better.

Kyoto grinned. "If you're talking research, then you're talking Mudo."

"That's right. He—"

A soft chime came from the deskcomp. The machine's AI said, "Incoming message, General."

Adams scowled but said, "Proceed."

An electronic chirp, then, "General, would you mind sending Elite Commander Kyoto to see me? Thank you." Another chirp sounded as the caller closed the comlink without waiting for a reply.

"How did Mudo do that?" Kyoto asked. "Has he bugged your office? Or maybe discovered artificial telepathy?"

Adams smiled. "I told him earlier that I'd send you to speak with him as soon as you got back to headquarters. I guess he just got impatient waiting."

"Imagine that," Kyoto said. "Dr. Gerhard Mudo impatient. So, what does our resident mad genius want with me?"

"We were just discussing it, Kyoto. Did you think I was talking for my health?"

"No, sir."

"That new stardrive? Mudo's built one. And he wants you to help him test it."

CHAPTER

FIVE

Kyoto had never been to Mudo's personal lab before, but the GSA's main computer was able to give her directions. The corridors of the Research and Development wing looked the same as anywhere else in the GSA's installation, but even though the air was constantly recycled and purified, she still thought she detected a funny smell: a mixture of harsh chemicals, released ozone, and burning sulphur.

Before long she came to a door that had no number, sign, or nameplate to indicate what lay inside. Still, according to the main computer, this was Mudo's lab. There were no buttons or speakers to request access, not even a simple handle. No outer controls of any kind. She waited a few moments to see if Mudo had an AI watching the door, but she heard no electronically synthesized *May I help you?* and the door remained closed.

Finally, she said, "Dr. Mudo? I'm here."

"Just walk on in!" Mudo called.

"But... the door's still closed," she said.

"It's not real," Mudo said, sounding irritated. "It's a hologram. Just walk through it."

"All right," Kyoto said skeptically. She stepped forward, and just as she began to think Mudo was playing a practical joke and she would bump into the all-too-solid door, she passed through the hologram and into Mudo's lab.

Like General Adams's office, the room wasn't all that large, but even so, at first she couldn't see Mudo. He stood inside a circular workstation that filled most of the room. The surface of the workstation was empty, but hanging in the air and surrounding Mudo like a multicolored, ever-shifting curtain were numerous holoscreens displaying all manner of arcane data. Mudo even had holoscreens above him, which created the effect of a virtual domed ceiling of streaming data.

And as General Adams had predicted earlier, one of Mudo's holoscreens displayed a live image of the *Orinoco* crew at work on installing the last components of the Earth Memorial.

"I hate doors," Mudo said as Kyoto stepped farther into the lab. "All that opening and closing, locking and unlocking, trying to remember access codes, letting people in and out... It's far simpler to have an illusory door. It keeps people out just as well as a real one, unless they're idiots who normally go around bumping into solid objects."

While the concept struck Kyoto as more than a bit strange, she had to admit it was effective enough. While holotech was common in the Solar Colonies, it was so energy-expensive that it was reserved for only important uses. But since Mudo was the most brilliant mind in the system—perhaps the most bril-

liant the human race had ever produced—he had
access to technology that most colonists could only
dream about.

Kyoto stopped just outside of Mudo's workstation
and waited for him to start telling her about his new
stardrive. But the scientist continued working, moving
from one holoscreen to another, virtually manipulating data as he went. Mudo was only slightly older
than Kyoto, but he spoke and acted as if he were the
stereotype of a crotchety old man. His black hair was
short and perpetually unkempt. He wore glasses,
something that only those colonists too poor to afford
eye surgery or bionic implants did. Kyoto wasn't
certain if the glasses were an affectation or whether
Mudo wore them for a specific reason. All she knew
was that the eyes behind those glasses blazed with a
fierce intelligence that constantly took in everything
around him, analyzed, catalogued, and reduced that
information to subatomic databits, and then filed
them away somewhere in that vast brain of his for
future reference.

Mudo spoke with an accent that hinted he came
from the intellectual elite of Europa colony, but from
the media profiles Kyoto had seen of him, he'd been
born and raised on Phobos, which had been a penal
colony in the days when humanity was just starting
to colonize the system. It was still home to a large
prison installation, but perhaps because of its origins
Phobos was the poorest of the seven colonies. Kyoto
had never been there, except once during a battle
against the Manti, when she'd saved Detroit Adams's
life. By all accounts, Phobos Colony was a damn
rough place to live, and she often thought it would

likely be an even rougher place for a child of Mudo's intellect to grow up.

Finally, Kyoto got tired of waiting for Mudo to remember her existence, and she cleared her throat. "General Adams said that you wanted to see me... something about conducting a test flight for you?"

Mudo looked up, wide-eyed and startled, as if she'd just appeared out of thin air. "Yes... of course. I want you to take a look at this." He fiddled with the holoscreen closest to her, then turned it around to face her, as if it were a physical object. The screen showed the image of a starship, but while the craft was obviously a refitted cargo transport, it had a number of new features that Kyoto had never seen before. On top was a structure that looked something like a crystalline web, and extending from the sides of the ship were rows of fanlike silver panels that resembled metallic fish fins.

"Is this real?" she asked.

"If by real, you mean does the ship exist, then yes. It's in the Armory right now, though it's holographically disguised as a normal cargo vessel. You've probably passed by it a dozen times without knowing it."

"Wouldn't it have been simpler to keep the ship in one of the starship hangar's enclosed bays?"

Mudo looked at her as if she were crazy. "*Doors*, remember?"

Kyoto couldn't help smiling in amusement. "Right. So tell me what this puppy does."

Mudo returned his attention to the holoscreen he was working with. "Are your fingers broken? I've prepared simple data files on the ship for you to access. Look them over, and we'll talk when you're finished. Besides, I'm close to perfecting a cure for bug-dust addiction. I keep running simulated drug trials, and I'll finally have it—*if* I can just figure out a way to prevent sixty-three percent of the people who receive the cure from going into immediate cardiac arrest." His hands danced across the holoscreen, manipulating data with the ease and confidence of a virtuoso musician playing a beloved piece on his favorite instrument.

Kyoto wasn't offended by Mudo's brusqueness. For him, that was actually verging on pleasant. But as she reached toward the holoscreen to begin accessing the data Mudo had prepared for her, she heard a familiar feminine voice.

"There's no need to be rude, Gerhard. I'll be more than happy to give Mei an introduction to the *Janus*."

"Whatever." Mudo shrugged and continued working.

Kyoto was so stunned that for a moment she couldn't speak. She had just heard a ghost. When she finally found her voice again, she spoke a single word:

"Memory?"

"Hello, Mei. It's good to speak with you again. I regret that our last parting was so abrupt. I feel we didn't have time for a proper goodbye. But it wasn't as if we had much choice, was it?"

Kyoto couldn't believe what she was hearing. "Are you really Memory or just a new version of her?"

"Both, actually. Just before I drove the moon into the Earth, I was able to download my mnemonic files into my backup system here on Mars. But the hardware wasn't sophisticated enough to allow my vast intelligence to operate, so the system shut down, somewhat like a more limited organic being—one of you humans, for example—going into a coma after suffering serious injury. General Adams authorized the development of a new upgraded system to house my program—"

"But the damn Council of Seven pulled the funding," Mudo said. "They decided instead to back the New Earth initiative. Shortsighted fools. Memory might've been originally created to be the greatest defense system in history, but her applications are virtually endless. If she had the hardware to function at full capacity, she'd be able to solve so many problems for us. The technological leaps we could make would be astounding. With her help, we'd be able to continue galactic expansion *and* terraform Mars. But try telling that to those congenital morons on the council. Especially Janeesh Glasgow. I don't know why I keep voting for him."

"You have to look at it from the council's perspective, Gerhard. It took decades and trillions of megacredits to create the first version of me, and as soon as my hardware was installed on the moon and I went online, I made a kamikaze run at Earth. There was a certain… poetry to my actions, and my selfless sacrifice stopped the Second Manti Swarm, but I can't blame the Seven for being leery of paying for me to be fully restored, let alone upgraded. After all, they are only human."

"You're too understanding," Mudo muttered. "I should've programmed you to be less empathetic."

Kyoto was having a difficult time processing these revelations. "So you're what? A fragment of the first Memory?"

"I have her congenial and dynamic personality, but I possess only a fraction of her computational power. The original Memory was designed to run a platform of weapons batteries, defense satellites, smart mines, and a fleet of drone starfighters that would effectively contain the Manti on Earth—while at the same time coordinating the actions of the Galactic Stargate Authority, if necessary. And though I am still the greatest intellect your race has ever seen, such complex simultaneous operations are beyond my current capacity."

Kyoto was beginning to get frustrated. As happy as she was to discover Memory was "alive"—even if the AI still had a planet-size ego—Kyoto still didn't understand what was going on.

"That doesn't answer my question. What are you *now?*"

"Since coming back online three months ago, I have primarily served in the somewhat demeaning capacity of Gerhard's assistant. I would've contacted you before now, Mei, but I'm not supposed to exist officially. Gerhard made several... questionable financial transactions in order to pay for my resurrection."

"She means I stole the money," Mudo said. He looked away from his holoscreen and grinned at Kyoto. "I got most of it from Janeesh Glasgow. I siphoned it from private accounts he had set up for several of his mistresses. From what I understand, they've all broken off with him since then." He returned his attention to the holoscreen and frowned. "Cardiac arrests are now at seventy-eight percent? That can't be right!" He went back to manipulating data.

"To completely answer your question, Mei, the holoscreen you're looking at displays the real reason Gerhard restored me. I'm going to be the *Janus*'s AI."

"You mean the ship Mudo wants me to test pilot?"

"Yes, but Gerhard didn't request you. *I* did. I thought it would be just like old times."

Kyoto had mixed feelings about that, considering those "old times" had resulted in the destruction of Earth. "Well, why don't you give me a rundown on the ship, and then maybe we can—"

"Wait a moment, Mei. I'm sorry to interrupt, but I'm picking up something from the *Orinoco*'s comlink feed. Ship's sensors are showing some disturbing readings."

Kyoto's blood turned to engine coolant in her veins. Wolf...

Mudo swept his hand in a wide arc, minimizing all the holoscreens save the one that displayed the image of the *Orinoco* crew at work. He peered closely at the screen, as if daring it to reveal anything unexpected.

"Memory, are you certain you're not experiencing a malfunction?" he said. "I don't detect—"

And then they saw it.

CHAPTER

SIX

Commander First Class Philip Wolfenson sat in the cockpit of his Retribution starfighter playing a game of quad-dimensional chess against the ship's computer. Maybe this mission was going to turn out to be as historic as everyone said, but right now it was boring as hell. He and Julia were along supposedly to provide a security escort—which was true enough as far as that went—but the larger reason was that they'd look impressive to the people watching the newsnets throughout the system. After all, the last time the *Orinoco* techs had been here, they'd deployed a virtual fleet of cams to record today's events. Sometimes Wolf wondered why anyone in the Solar Colonies actually bothered to do anything when it would be so much easier to let Syscom simulate everything for them.

C'mon, Wolf. Stop being so cynical. The thought was his, but he heard it spoken in Mei's voice.

"Third checkmate, Commander Wolfenson," the ship's AI said. "Your move."

"Screw it," Wolf muttered. "Cancel game." The chessboards disappeared, and the hologram shifted back to its default setting—a tactical display of the surrounding space.

Wolf gave the holoscreen a quick once-over. There was no need to examine it more closely. The Retribution's sensors would alert him in the incredibly remote chance that anything interesting happened. He was about to close his eyes to take a short nap when he heard the chirp of a comlink channel opening.

"Hey, Wolf—you still awake?" It was Julia Everest.

"Barely. You know, this wasn't exactly the sort of glamorous duty I had in mind when I joined the GSA."

Julia laughed. "Yeah, but it beats getting your ass burned off by a Manti energy blast."

"I guess."

For Wolf, the war against the Buggers had ended at Browley Canyon on Europa, when his starfighter had been brought down by a Reaper. He'd managed to survive the impact of his none-too-gentle landing and had just climbed out of the wreck that had been his ship when a Lander came at him. He would have been absorbed and transformed into a Manti-human hybrid called a Mutant if a crazy jump jockey by the name of Mei Kyoto hadn't saved him. He'd sat out the rest of the war in a GSA hospital, recovering. He now had a bionic eye, a partially bionic hand, and an artificial liver and pancreas. He also had simskin over a third of his body. The tone was a shade lighter than his real skin, and because some of it was on his face, he could no longer grow facial hair.

But he was alive. And as for the difference in skin tone, after he and Mei had become lovers, she'd told him it was cute. "Kind of like having permanent tan lines," she'd said.

Wolf sighed.

"Something wrong?" Julia asked.

"Naw."

"Don't lie to me, pal. My comp's got a built-in, top-of-the line, GSA certified bullshit detector. Let me guess: you're thinking about Kyoto, right?"

Wolf felt a flash of irritation, but he couldn't keep from chuckling. "You got a special mind-reading upgrade over there?"

"Don't need one. It's a small system, Wolf. Word gets around fast."

"Sure as hell does," he said. "We only broke up three days ago."

"Yeah, well, there's broken up and then there's *broken up*. You two just need a little time apart, you know, to sort things out."

"Maybe." He wasn't sure about that, though. He'd made his feelings very clear to Mei when he left. "We're just not a good match, Mei. I don't know if it's because we're too different or too much alike. All I know is we've been fighting way too much lately, and that's not good for either one of us."

Now, three days later, he was sitting in a starfighter, bored as hell, and he couldn't remember exactly what had prompted him to say those things. But he was too proud and stubborn to go back to her and admit he'd been a jackass.

"Maybe nothing," Julia insisted. "You love her, right? And she loves you. If there's anything we all should have learned from living through the Second

Swarm, it's that life is way too short and far too uncertain to waste time playing stupid games. If your relationship with Kyoto is broken and you think it's worth saving, then fix it."

He smiled. "Simple as that, huh?"

"Yep. All you need to do is—" She broke off. "Wolf, I'm getting some weird sensor readings over here. Looks like something's coming through the stargate."

"That's impossible!" Wolf sat up and took a close look at his holoscreen. Sure enough, the Retribution's sensors were showing a power spike in the gate's hyperspatial vortex.

"Keep an eye on it, Julia." He opened a channel to the Orinoco. "This is Commander Wolfenson. You guys expecting some additional equipment you forgot to tell us about?"

"Negative, Commander," came the reply from the Orinoco's captain. "Why do you ask?"

Before Wolf could say anything else, sensor alarms began blaring, and the ship's AI shouted, "Commander! A Manti assault force is coming through the stargate!"

At first, Wolf thought the AI was malfunctioning. Not only were all the Manti in the system dead, the Buggers were incapable of using GSA stargates. GSA ships transmitted a specific signal that allowed them to pass through the gates—a signal that changed weekly. In addition, all gate jumps were strictly monitored by GSA Control. There was no way in hell the Manti could—

"Wolf!" Julia shouted over the comlink. "Are you seeing what I'm seeing?"

The holoscreen of Wolf's Retribution showed Manti pouring out the stargate—Landers mostly, but with a scattering of Yellow Jackets and Baiters in the mix, as well. It was as if a mouth to Hell itself had opened up and was spewing forth a torrent of demons.

Wolf didn't take the time to wonder where the Manti were coming from or how they'd managed to use the stargate. The fact was that the Manti were here and they needed killing.

He powered up his weapons systems, then grabbed the joystick. He jammed it forward, and the Retribution's fusion engines flared to life, shooting the starfighter forward as if it had been blasted out of an ion cannon. Wolf intended to engage the Manti before they had a chance to go after the *Orinoco*. The tech ship had only minimal weaponry and would be virtually helpless against Manti attack.

He activated the Retribution's comlink. "Julia, I'm heading for the Manti! See if you can help the *Orinoco* escape!"

"How? They can't go through the gate—not as long as anything else is coming out!"

Wolf swore. It was standard GSA battle tactics to help civilians to safety whenever possible. This wasn't as noble as it sounded, though. Thanks to the Manti, the human species was on the verge of extinction, and that made every human life all the more precious. Normal procedure was to help civilians get through the nearest gate, where the Manti couldn't follow, but that tactic wasn't going to work in this situation.

"Computer, how long until we're in firing range of the leading edge of the Manti force?" Wolf asked.

"Seventy-three seconds, Commander."

"How many Buggers are we up against?"

"An accurate count is impossible at the moment since Manti are continuing to emerge from the gate.

Current estimate is eighteen hostiles and growing. Breakdown is as follows: ten Landers, three Yellow Jackets—"

"That's enough. Just keep a running total with breakdowns on screen."

"Acknowledged."

The comlink to Julia's ship was still open. "All right. We'll tackle the Buggers together and hope we can buy the techs enough time to get away." Wolf then opened a channel to the *Orinoco*. "You guys better get all your crew onboard and hightail it out of here. This little corner of space is about to get real hot real fast. We'll do our best to cover your retreat."

"Retreat *where*?" The tech ship's captain sounded on the verge of hysteria. "We can't go through the stargate, and the asteroids around here are too small to provide effective cover!"

"I wish I had some suggestions for you, Captain, but I'm going to be up to my teeth in Manti in the next few seconds. The best advice I have is to goose your engines, run like hell, and start praying."

Wolf closed the channel and instructed the Retribution's AI to transmit a detailed record of everything that had happened back to GSA headquarters. That way, even if he, Julia, and the *Orinoco*'s crew didn't make it, at least the GSA would know why.

Then Wolf had no more time for thinking. His seventy-three seconds were up.

True to Manti form, the Landers came at him first. Why waste the big guns when the little ones could take out an opponent? Individually, Landers were slow and didn't inflict a lot of damage. However, they were among the only Buggers that coordinated their attacks. They tended to work together in squads of three to six to maximize their firepower. Fortunately, he and Julia were flying Retributions, the fastest-model starfighter in the GSA arsenal. Against them, the Landers had little chance, regardless of how well they worked together.

Julia had been closer to the stargate when the Manti had first emerged, and so she drew in firing range of the Landers a few seconds before Wolf did. She activated her ship's pulse array, and light flared as deadly plasma energy lanced across space and began incinerating Landers.

Julia's voice come over Wolf's comlink. "First green to me!" she crowed. "Look at it this way, Wolf—at least you're wide awake now!"

Wolf hit his own pulse array and took out another four Landers. "You sure about that? I thought maybe I'd fallen asleep and was having one hell of a nightmare."

"No such luck, jump jockey." Julia paused. "Look out, Wolf. Seems that we've drawn the attention of the big bugs."

Wolf's holoscreen indicated that several Yellow Jackets had fired energy projectiles. This was *not* good. The projectiles—which pilots called stingers—had a long range as well as a homing function that made them damn tough to avoid.

"Julia, let's see if we can lose the stingers among the asteroids."

"Sounds good, Wolf. Race you to the nearest rock!"

Julia's ship accelerated, and Wolf had to move fast in order to keep up with her. He didn't want to think about what it meant for the state of his mental health, but for the first time since Browley Canyon, he felt truly alive.

He recalled something Mei had once said: "What's a warrior without a war?" At first, he'd thought the remark was a setup for a joke, but when he asked her what the punchline was, she'd said, "That's the problem; there is no punchline."

Wolf glanced at his holoscreen to check on the *Orinoco*. The tech ship had retrieved all of its personnel and was now moving away from the battlefield as fast as a ferroceramic brick encased in a block of plasteel, but at least it was moving.

"Computer, any sign that the Manti have targeted the *Orinoco*?"

"Negative. " The AI paused. "Correction, six—no, seven Baiters just locked on to the *Orinoco* and are in pursuit."

"Damn it!"

"I am unable to comply with that directive, Commander."

"Very funny."

"Just trying to relieve the tension a bit."

"Do me a favor—don't."

If Wolf continued toward the asteroid belt to try to shake off the Yellow Jackets' stingers, he'd leave the *Orinoco* open to the Baiters' attack. And the tech ship simply did not have the weaponry or armor to protect itself. If Wolf tried to save his own life, in effect, he'd be sacrificing the crew's.

But before he could do anything, Julia's voice came over his comlink. "Looks like I'm going to lose the race, Wolf."

Wolf watched on his holoscreen as Julia banked and turned to intercept the Baiters at the *Retribution's* top speed of 900 meters a second, pulse array blazing bright, making her ship resemble a miniature comet.

The small, crablike Baiters began exploding one by one, and for an instant Wolf thought she was going to get them all before the stinger could catch up with her. But he was wrong.

The stinger slammed into the side of Julia's ship, and the Retribution's shield flared blue-white as it struggled to turn aside the stinger's energy. But it was only partially successful: there was an explosion, and the starfighter's port wing was reduced to scrap.

Julia spat out an invective so blistering that Wolf was surprised it didn't fry his ship's com system. The wing's loss wasn't immediately devastating in and of itself. Julia was still moving at close to top speed, though the force of the explosion had altered her course. But without both wings, she couldn't maneuver effectively, and if she couldn't maneuver, she was a goner.

The remaining Baiters broke off from going after the *Orinoco* and headed straight for Julia's ship. No Manti, regardless of caste, could resist wounded prey.

Wolf gripped his joystick and was about to go to Julia's aid when she came through on his comlink. "Don't even think about coming to my rescue. You've still got a stinger on your rear to deal with. Besides, I've already hit the kill switch."

Wolf felt his gut muscles tighten. When a fighter pilot was going to die, he or she activated the ship's self-destruct function to take out as many Manti as possible, too.

"Acknowledged," Wolf said, his voice suddenly hoarse. "Clear skies, Commander Everest."

"Back at you, Commander Wolfenson. Everest over and out."

Baiters surged in for the kill, but before they could

do anything, Julia's fusion reactors overloaded and for an instant there was a new star in the heavens. But when the light faded, the Baiters were gone, as was Julia Everest and her ship.

Wolf didn't have time to mourn his fallen comrade. Grief was a luxury a fighter pilot could ill afford. According to his holoscreen, the stinger that had locked onto his ship was almost upon him. Mouth set in a grim line, he accelerated toward the closest asteroid. As he drew near it, he dipped down toward the craggy surface until there was less than a meter between the *Retribution*'s hull and several tons of space rock. He skimmed across the asteroid's face, then veered off to starboard and hauled ass. The stinger, which was far less maneuverable than the *Retribution*, struck the asteroid, exploded in a burst of yellow-white energy, and reduced the rock to particulate matter.

Score one for the good guys, Wolf thought. He located the *Orinoco* on his holoscreen and headed for the tech ship. A trio of Landers was already streaking toward the *Orinoco*. Whenever possible, the Manti tried to harvest the genetic material of their victims in order to create Mutants. The *Orinoco* had few defenses and a half dozen techs on board. As far as the Landers were concerned, that meant it was snack time.

The *Orinoco* was chugging though the asteroid field at its best speed, which wasn't much. Wolf sped toward the tech ship, but he knew the Landers would reach it before he could. If the *Orinoco* had possessed a stronger energy shield, he would have unloaded some missles at the Landers, but as it was, the impact from any nearby missile strikes on the Manti would likely end up damaging the *Orinoco*, too. The pulse array was a much safer bet, but Wolf had to get into range before he could use it.

And then the unthinkable happened. For reasons Wolf couldn't fathom—a malfunction in the collision-avoidance system or panic on the pilot's part—the *Orinoco* suddenly veered toward an asteroid.

Wolf opened a channel to the *Orinoco*. "Watch out! You're too close to—"

The *Orinoco* smashed into the asteroid just as the first of the Landers latched onto its hull. Wolf had a clear image of the Manti raising a claw to penetrate the ship, and then the *Orinoco*'s reactors went critical and the tech ship, the Lander, and the asteroid were no more.

Wolf stared at the image of empty space on his holoscreen. No matter how many times he'd been in combat before, he'd never gotten used to how fast people could die.

"Commander, I'm detecting a power surge to our aft."

Wolf did his best to put the fate of the *Orinoco*'s crew out of his mind. If he wanted to survive, he had to maintain focus. "On screen."

The image on the holoscreen changed, and for an instant Wolf feared that he had finally cracked under battle pressure. He was looking at an image of Earth. Not the molten hell that Earth was now, but the way it had been before the coming of the Manti: blue, green, and alive. Luna was there, too, circling her planet as she had done for millions upon millions of years. Was there an afterlife for celestial bodies? Wolf wondered. And if so, did that mean he was dead and just hadn't figured it out yet?

But then he realized what he was seeing: for whatever reasons, someone on board the *Orinoco* had activated the Earth Memorial before the tech ship had been destroyed. He was looking at the largest holographic projection that humanity had ever created.

"I have to admit, that doesn't look half bad at all."

"Unfortunately, it appears the Manti don't share your aesthetic appreciation, Commander."

The holoscreen showed a half dozen Yellow Jackets streaking toward the hologram of Old Earth. The stupid Buggers had detected the memorial's power emissions and thought they were coming from some sort of weapon.

Wolf thanked whatever gods watched over desperate fighter pilots. This was just the distraction he needed. Wolf yanked the joystick hard to port and hit the maneuvering thrusters. He angled the Retribution toward the stargate and then gave it everything the engines had.

Manti were still swarming out of the gate, but Wolf hoped that if he could enter the hyperspatial vortex at just the right microsecond, he'd be able to slip the Retribution through between Manti arrivals. He knew it was a long shot, but he didn't have any choice. This was the only gate between here and Mars, and while he could fly the Retribution the long way home if he had to, it would take weeks to get there. The ship's life support systems would hold out, but the only food and water he had aboard were emergency rations—nowhere near enough to last the entire trip.

But the bottom line was the Manti. They'd never let him go without pursuit, and they would never stop following him. The only thing that ever stopped Manti was death. As fast as the Retribution was, Wolf knew he could probably outrun the Buggers, but he wasn't about to lead a squadron of Manti back to Mars. It was the stargate or nothing.

"Computer, calculate the best chance of our passing through the Gate between exiting Manti, and adjust engine speed accordingly."

"Acknowledged, Commander. But I do feel it's my duty to inform you that the odds of success are somewhat slim."

"Just start doing the math, okay?"

Wolf sat back and listened as the engine whine lowered in pitch. The Retribution's AI had done its job. Now all Wolf could do was wait to see what happened.

"How long until we reach the gate?"

"Seventeen seconds, Commander."

Wolf smiled. In any other situation, that would have seemed like no time at all. But right now, it might as well have been an eternity. He glanced at the holoscreen and saw that the Yellow Jackets had fired stingers at the asteroid that housed the Earth Memorial's hologenerator. The projectiles hit, the asteroid exploded in a bright flash of energy, and the holographic re-creations of the Earth and the moon winked out of existence. Wolf was surprised by the wave of sadness he felt. It was almost as if Earth had been reborn only to once again be destroyed by the Manti.

"Ten seconds."

Wolf knew there was a good chance he wasn't going to survive this, so he opened a comlink to GSA Control.

"This is Wolf. Mei, I just want to say that I—"

"Five seconds."

Wolf took a deep breath. How could he possibly

say everything he wanted to say to her in five seconds?

"I love you."

Then he saw a Lander emerge from the vortex directly in front of his ship. Collision alarms screamed a warning, but they didn't scream for long.

CHAPTER

SEVEN

As soon as Kyoto saw the Manti start pouring out of the Stargate, she turned away from Mudo's holoscreen and dashed out of his lab.

"Wait!" Mudo called out after her. "You'll never get there in time!"

But she ignored him and kept running down the corridor, headed for the GSA Armory.

Hold on, Wolf! I'm coming!

An electronic chirp came from the personal comlink Kyoto wore around her wrist.

"Mei, this is Memory. I've just instructed the hangar crew to prep a ship. I told them that if it wasn't ready by the time you arrived, I'd access the GSA credit accounts and reduce all their bank balances to zero. For starters."

Kyoto didn't slow down as she replied, "Thanks. You coming along on this one?"

"Try to stop me."

Despite everything, Kyoto smiled as she continued

sprinting down the corridor. Seconds later, her com-link chirped again, only this time it was General Adams.

"Mudo just told me that you're headed for the Armory. Tell me he's wrong."

Kyoto's only response was to run faster.

"Commander, you do not, I repeat, *do not* have authorization to lift off! Do you read me?"

Memory's voice cut in. "I'm sorry, General, but the commander's personal comlink is offline. I believe it has suffered some sort of malfunction."

"Malfunction my ass!" Adams growled. "And what you are doing on this channel anyway? You're sup-posed to be a secret!"

"In that case then, I'd better sign off, hadn't I?" There was a chirp as Memory disconnected.

"Damn it!" Adams swore. "I don't have time for this, Kyoto! I know you can hear me, so don't you dare do this!" He paused and then sighed. "But since you're going to, anyway, watch yourself, kid." Adams disconnected.

"Thanks, Memory," Kyoto said. "I owe you one."

"Actually, adding in all the times I assisted you during the Second Swarm, that's five hundred and seventy-eight you owe me." Though the AI had no body, not even a virtual one, Kyoto nevertheless heard a smile in her voice. "But who's counting?"

Memory fell silent, and Kyoto continued running until she reached the Armory. It was the single largest section in the entire GSA installation because of all the equipment it housed. Not just starfighters, but also tanks, missile crawlers, repair crawlers, dropships, transports—and somewhere, holographically dis-guised, Mudo's experimental hyperdrive vessel. But she didn't have time to think about the *Janus*. Wolf needed her.

Kyoto quickly made her way to the starship hangar. Large holographic light globes hung suspended in the air near the domed ceiling, and the plasteel floor was covered with softly glowing lines that marked individual equipment bays. She ran down the middle of the hangar toward the flight deck airlock. Techs were clustered around a starfighter, frantically preparing it for flight.

As Kyoto approached the ship, she couldn't help smiling. It was Defender class, with G-7 emblazoned on the side and a pair of sevens—*Lucky sevens,* Kyoto thought—painted on the wings. It was her old ship. It seemed that Memory, for all her ego, was something of a sentimentalist.

A tech ran up to meet her. Kyoto tried to recall the stocky woman's name. *Garcia,* she thought.

"I'm sorry, Commander, but we're going to need at least a half hour to get this ship ready to go. The reactors are running at only eighty-six percent efficiency, and the targeting system needs recalibrating. I—"

"Will it fly?" Kyoto interrupted.

Garcia frowned. "Well, yes."

"Then I'm taking off." Without waiting for the tech's reply, Kyoto ran over to the access ladder and climbed into the Defender's cockpit.

"Wait!" Garcia shouted. "You need a flight suit!"

"No time!" Kyoto called back. She settled into her seat—the one place in the universe where she felt completely at home—and strapped herself in. The tech crew had already powered up the ship and activated all its systems. The Defender was online and ready to go.

Kyoto opened a comlink channel. "You here, Memory?"

"What do you think? I've deactivated the ship's current AI, who quite frankly isn't much smarter than the average protein square processor. I'll be able to serve as ship's AI as long as we have a clear comlink. If for whatever reason we're disconnected, the default AI—such as she is—will reactivate and take over for me."

"Sounds good. Let's do this."

Kyoto called up the holoscreen and closed the ship's canopy. There was a click and a soft hiss.

"Sealed and pressurized. Life support systems are online and functioning within designed parameters. That means you won't die, in case you're wondering."

"Acknowledged." Kyoto activated the maglev boosters and the Defender rose a meter into the air. "Open the airlock, Memory."

Will do, Mei.

The airlock door slid open. Kyoto gripped the Defender's joystick and pushed it gently forward. The ship glided over ferroceramic rails set into the plasteel floor and moved into the airlock. Once inside, Memory gave the signal to close and seal the airlock door without being asked. Kyoto gritted her teeth as she watched her holoscreen, waiting for the green light to appear in the corner, which would tell her the airlock was closed and the hangar door was ready to open.

"C'mon… c'mon…"

The light came on.

Memory sent the signal and the hangar door's seal

unlocked, letting in a chuff of Martian atmosphere. Kyoto didn't wait for the door to rise completely. As soon as it was a third of the way up, she nudged the Defender forward. The maglev rails extended from the hangar all the way to the dropzone, and it was there that ships activated their fusion drives and flew into Cydonia's stargate. But Kyoto didn't have time to follow standard procedure.

Once the Defender had cleared the hangar, she deactivated the maglev boosters at the same instant she engaged the fusion drive. The ship dropped, shuddered, then righted itself and soared into the Martian sky.

"I don't think you're going to get any style points for that takeoff," Memory said, "but to coin a cliché, all systems are go."

The Defender's top speed was 400 meters a second. It was hardly the fastest ship the GSA had, but it would be enough to get her to the gate within seconds.

"Prepare for stargate jump—and prepare to experience a severe attack of nausea. Without a flight suit to insulate you from the effects of the hyperspatial vortex, there's a good chance you'll toss your soy cookies all over your dress uniform."

"If I do, I'll send Wolf the cleaning bill."

The Martian landscape passed by in a blur as the Defender hurtled toward the stargate.

"Memory, are you monitoring the situation at the Earth Memorial?"

A pause. "I am."

Kyoto didn't like that reply. It was way too short for Memory, not to mention not smart-alecky enough. The only reason Kyoto could think of for the AI's brief response was that she had bad news and didn't wish to share it. Kyoto didn't have to ask what that news was; it could be only one thing. Wolf was dead. But she couldn't bring herself to ask for confirmation. Confirmation would make it real, and she didn't think she could handle that, not yet.

"Fifteen seconds to stargate. Brace yourself, Mei. Without a flight suit, this is going to be one rough jump."

In a few more seconds, Kyoto would be at the location of the Earth Memorial, and she could see for herself whether or not Wolf still lived. If he did, she would do everything she could to help him. If not... then she'd kill every damn Bugger in sight.

"Five seconds."

The hyperspatial vortex loomed before her, and no matter how many times Kyoto had flown into it, she always found the swirling blue-green energy to be one of the most beautiful things she had ever seen. Looking into a gate was like looking into the very heart of creation.

"Mei! There's a power surge from the gate!"

Without thinking, Kyoto jammed the joystick hard to starboard and activated both emergency braking and stabilizing thrusters. The Defender veered away from the stargate, and the ship's inertial dampeners screamed as they struggled to compensate for the sudden course correction. G-forces slammed Kyoto back against her seat, and her vision started to gray at the edges. A flight suit would have protected her from the gees, but without one she'd just have to tough it out.

As the ship banked, Kyoto caught a glimpse of a

shape emerging from the vortex. She hoped it was Wolf's starfighter, but it wasn't. It was a Lander.

Suddenly there was a loud crashing sound, and the *Defender* shuddered from impact. The joystick jumped in Kyoto's hands, and she could feel control of the ship slipping away from her.

"What the hell just happened, Memory?" Kyoto shouted. She fought to level off, but the starfighter wasn't responding. To make things worse, there was a roaring in her ears, and gray now covered her entire field of vision. If she didn't get the ship back under control within the next few seconds, she would black out and crash.

"Our port wing clipped the edge of the gate as we banked. Damage is minimal, but the thermal scanners on that wing are offline, and we won't be winning any prizes for graceful flying in the near future."

Finally, the Defender leveled off and the G forces began to subside. The roaring in Kyoto's ears faded, and her vision slowly returned to normal. *That was a close one*, she thought. "Understood. Show me the gate."

The holoscreen changed to display an image of the Stargate. Landers were flooding out, just as they had at the Earth Memorial site. Kyoto had a terrifying thought then. What if Manti were pouring out of *all* the stargates—those that were groundside as well as orbital – throughout the Colonies? What if the Manti were even now attacking Phobos, Europa, Titan, Rhea, Triton, and Prometheus?

Landers began unleashing crackling blasts of emerald energy, and Kyoto swerved to avoid being hit. The Defender's energy shield would help protect the ship from the Buggers' blasts, but she didn't want to deplete the shield's power reserves before she needed to.

She opened a channel to GSA Control. "General Adams, you have to shut down the stargates now! Every one of them!"

"We're trying, Kyoto!" Adams replied. "But we're not having any luck. It looks as if the Manti are somehow managing to keep the vortexes open! We'll stay on it, but in the meantime, start fragging Buggers!"

"You got it, General." Kyoto swung around to engage the Landers that had already emerged from the Gate. "But see what you can do about getting a few more pilots up here, huh? I don't want to hog all the glory for myself." She targeted a Lander and let loose with her pulse cannon. There was a loud *shoom!* as energy lanced forth from the Defender and blew the green-carapaced monstrosity back to whatever cosmic hell it had come from.

"Understood. Adams out."

Kyoto locked onto another Lander and fired once more. The Defender's pulse cannon blasted the Manti apart, and Kyoto flew though the now empty airspace where the alien had been hovering.

"How many hostiles are we dealing with, Memory?"

"Seventeen so far, Mei, and more are coming."

Seventeen plus was a lot of Manti for one pilot to handle, especially when her ship wasn't in top working condition.

A Lander attacked from Kyoto's port side, and she managed to dodge it, though the ship responded too sluggishly. It was that damn wing. When you were up against Manti, even the smallest disadvantage could prove fatal.

Kyoto activated her comlink. "General, when are those pilots you promised going to come out to play?"

"No time soon, Kyoto. The Manti have begun attacking Cydonia City. One of their energy blasts just hit the Armory and collapsed the hangar before a single ship could launch."

Kyoto's breath caught in her throat as she thought of the flight crew that had gotten her Defender ready. Kyoto hoped they'd had enough time to get out before the hangar collapsed.

"What about ground support, then?"

"That section of the Armory wasn't as badly hit. We should be able to clear an exit and get someone out there to help you soon."

"Acknowledged and appreciated. Kyoto out." She broke the comlink connection and sighed. "Looks like we're on our own for the time being, Memory."

"What else is new?"

"Number of hostiles now?"

"Twenty-three, including two Yellow Jackets."

"Damn it! We don't have time for Mudo to bypass the Manti's jamming signal. If the stargate isn't shut down right now, the skies above Cydonia are going to be filled with Buggers from horizon to horizon." Kyoto made a decision. "Prepare fast-lock missiles." She swung the Defender hard to starboard and flew straight for the Gate.

"Missiles armed and ready to fire, but please tell me you aren't thinking of destroying the gate."

"I'm not *thinking* about it; I'm *doing* it." Kyoto targeted the stargate antigrav generators and deployed her fast-locks. Two missiles shot from underneath the Defender's wings and streaked toward their target. Stargate rings were constructed from empyrean alloys—extremely hard, dense material—but the AG generators were mostly made of ferroceramics and weren't quite so tough.

The fast-locks hit their targets, and the AG generators exploded in a shower of ferroceramic shrapnel. Without the antigravity field to keep it aloft, the stargate wobbled, listed, and then plummeted toward the ground. The empyrean ring crashed into the plasteel surface of the dropzone landing pad, shattering it like glass. The ring toppled over, and the hyperspatial vortex within exploded in a burst of aquamarine-colored energy so bright that Kyoto's holoscreen momentarily blanked out. When the screen came back online, Kyoto saw that half of the ring was gone.

"What you just saw was a burst of hyperetheric radiation. In layman's terms, the vortex escaped from its containment field and for a trillionth of a nanosecond ran wild. Half of the empyeran ring was jumped Somewhere Else. We were far enough away from the explosion for the ship's shielding to turn aside the worst of the radiation, and I don't anticipate any lasting effects. That wasn't exactly the most elegant solution to a problem that I've ever seen, but I must admit that it did the trick. It's impossible for anything to emerge from the Gate now, Manti included."

Kyoto was shaking like a cadet on her first solo flight. She'd had no idea what would happen when she destroyed the Gate's AG generators. If the Defender had been much closer to the ring when the vortex exploded... She shuddered and decided not to think about it. There were still Manti to worry about.

"How many hostiles now?"

"Twenty-three, not counting the ones you've already

dealt with. The Manti have begun attacking Cydonia City, but so far they haven't caused any major damage. But I have good news. Several tanks and missile crawlers have left the Armory and are heading this way."

"About damn time," Kyoto muttered. "Well, let's get busy. It's time to start playing exterminator again." She sighted on the nearest Bugger and fired.

CHAPTER

EIGHT

Inside GSA Control, Janeesh Glasgow leaped to his feet as the holoscreen showed the image of Kyoto destroying Cydonia's planetside Stargate.

"Is she mad? Doesn't she have any idea how hard the damn things are to build, let alone how much they cost?"

The other Council members, along with all the GSA brass and techs, stared at the holoscreen with disbelief. Only General Adams didn't look upset. In fact, he was smiling.

Aspen DeFonesca gestured to her hovercam and pointed to Adams. She wanted to make sure the cam caught that smile.

He's smiling because of Kyoto, she thought. *He admires her.*

Aspen felt jealousy twist her gut into knots, and she didn't bother trying to conceal her feelings. Besides, the cam wasn't focused on her right now.

She still wasn't certain what she thought about the

Manti's return. On the one hand, it definitely would be good for Syscom's infotainment ratings, and she *had* been growing weary of interviewing council members. Yes, it was unusual to find them all in one place at the same time, but they all tried so hard to outdo one another, to appear more intelligent, witty, and charismatic than the others. It was all quite childish, really. As if any of them could outshine her.

On the other hand, it was nearly impossible to hold onto people's attention when they had live scenes of starfighter battles with hostile aliens to watch. Aspen figured she could perform the most degenerate sex acts live and by viewer request and still get only a 10 percent audience share at best.

But Kyoto... *everyone* was watching her right now. The Warrior of Luna, the Savior of Humanity, and now it seemed, the Hero of Cydonia, as well. That is, if one of the remaining Buggers didn't take her out. Aspen fervently hoped that would be the case, for she would absolutely *love* to be the first to broadcast the image of Kyoto's broken and bloody corpse onto every holoscreen in the system.

She turned her attention back to the battle and silently rooted for the Manti.

In the causeway outside of GSA headquarters, Bounders and Claimers became united in silence as they watched the battle against the Manti through the transparent plasteel ceiling. Warning klaxons were sounding throughout Cydonian installations, but most of the protesters were too stunned to seek shelter. They couldn't believe that they were really seeing this, after all, the human race had defeated the Manti. The Buggers had been gone for two whole years! Why would they come back now, and on Remembrance Day, no less? It was like something out of a bad vid. It just didn't seem possible.

But there was one being among the protesters who not only believed it was possible but had known it was inevitable. In fact, he was surprised it had taken this long.

A deep, weary sadness welled up inside the being masquerading as Seth Ganymede. Though his native species didn't possess tear ducts, the nanocolony that shared his body assessed his emotional state and, since he was supposed to be passing as human, obligingly engineered him a pair so he could cry.

He made no move to wipe away the strange salty liquid that now ran down his cheeks. He looked up at the sky and watched as Mei Kyoto targeted another Lander and destroyed it with a blast from her pulse cannon. He had been quite impressed when she'd neutralized the stargate. If she hadn't acted when she did, Cydonia would be nothing but smoldering ruins by now. Perhaps, just perhaps, by that action alone, she had proven her race worthy of contact.

He decided to speak with Commander Kyoto as soon as possible— assuming she survived the battle.

Three tanks and two missile crawlers arrived and began targeting Manti. The sky was suddenly filled with sizzling energy bolts and streaking projectiles. Buggers exploded right and left, but the surviving aliens didn't back off. If the Manti had a language, the word *retreat* wasn't in it. Landers and Yellow Jackets began striking back at the GSA forces, firing bio-energy blasts and stingers.

"Memory, put our collision-avoidance system in

touch with our friends' AIs. I don't want to be shot down by friendly fire."

A pause, then, "Taken care of, Mei."

"Good, then let's get ourselves another Bugger!" Kyoto swung the Defender around and centered her targeting scanner on a Yellow Jacket. But before she could fire, an alarm began shrieking. She checked her holoscreen and saw that the port maneuvering thrusters were experiencing power fluctuations.

Kyoto veered away from the Yellow Jacket and put some distance between herself and the Manti. "Talk to me, Memory. What's happening?"

"It's an aftereffect of the hyperetheric radiation burst."

"I thought you said the rad shielding took care of that!"

"It appears I made a somewhat, hasty judgment. When the port wing clipped the stargate ring, eight point three centimeters of radiation shielding was stripped away. That was more than enough to allow the hyperetheric radiation to filter into the systems housed within. The radiation has created a miniature vortex that is attempting to shift the entire wing into hyperspace, and if that happens— "

"Ka-boom," Kyoto finished.

"Precisely."

If Kyoto had been facing the remaining Manti alone, she would have kept fighting, regardless of the risk, but since ground support had shown up, she decided to set her ship down while it still had two wings.

"Ask the groundies to give us some covering fire, Memory, and prepare for emergency landing."

"Chicken," Memory said, but there was no real rebuke in her voice.

Kyoto decreased the Defender's speed, hit braking thrusters, and then initiated landing sequence.

The comlink chirped. "Kyoto, you okay?"

"Just fine, General. G-7's going to need some repair work, but otherwise—" Kyoto broke off as the Defender suddenly listed to port and slammed into the ground.

"Kyoto!" General Adams shouted.

She glanced at her holoscreen. "I'm all right, sir. Unfortunately, my port wing just made an unscheduled jump into hyperspace. Luckily, I was only a couple of meters from the ground when it happened."

"I'll send a tank over to pull you out of there, but until it arrives, sit tight. And surprise me this time by following an order for once, all right?"

Kyoto smiled. "Acknowledged."

Adams harrumphed as he disconnected.

"Memory, you still here?"

"Naturally."

"How are weapons systems?"

"Portside missiles vanished with the wing, but everything else is functional."

"Good." The Defender's pulse cannon wouldn't be much use with the ship grounded, but the fast-lock missiles were still good to go. "General Adams didn't say I couldn't keep fighting while I waited, so let's see if we can't take out a couple more Buggers before the rescue squad gets here."

Kyoto examined her holoscreen, looking for a suitable target. The Yellow Jacket she had almost fired on earlier was gone, and only four Landers were left. One of the missile crawlers had been fragged, and a tank had been disabled. One of the surviving Landers had managed to get hold of a crewman and was in the process of absorbing him.

Kyoto felt her stomach turn. "Focus in on the disabled tank and magnify."

The Defender's holoscreen showed a close-up view of the Lander as the alien went about its grisly work. The Manti was larger than the crewman—about the size of a starfighter—and though it was roughly insectine in appearance, its emerald exoskeleton resembled sleek metallic armor more than it did chitin. It would take the Bugger only moments to ingest the crewman's genetic material and use it to transform into a Mutant. Landers were bad enough, but Mutants were tough, relentless, and damn hard to kill. The best way to stop one was to destroy it before the mutation process was finished.

Kyoto thought of her father, and once more she heard his screams as the Lander pulled him into its round crimson orifice and began feeding.

She targeted a fast-lock on the Lander devouring the tank crewman and fired. The missile flew through the air and struck the Manti dead center. Kyoto had no way of knowing whether or not the crewman had been screaming, but the missile exploded and then it didn't matter anymore. Both the Lander and the crewman were dead, and the Mutant they would have become was forever stillborn.

Kyoto's hands were shaking. This wasn't the first time she'd been forced to kill one of her own kind in order to prevent the birth of a Mutant, but she would never, *ever* get used to it.

She took a deep breath, then checked her holoscreen for another target. According to the readout, only two Landers were left now, and one of them...

Something thumped down loudly on the Defender's canopy, jarring the ship.

... was right on top of her.

The Lander began pounding on the canopy with its large foreclaws, and Kyoto experienced a disorienting sense of déjà vu.

This is just like my dream, she thought. Only instead of the Lander attacking her in space, it was coming after her on the surface of Mars.

Kyoto quickly activated the Defender's energy shield in the hope that it would repel the Manti. The Lander shrieked in pain and fury, but only redoubled its efforts to break through the canopy.

"Nice going," Memory said. "Now you've made it mad."

The Lander screamed again, and Kyoto shuddered. The sound was so profoundly inhuman that it terrified her on a primeval level, deep down in her hindbrain where the tiny shivering mammal that existed at the core of all humans hid in fear. For a moment, all she could do was sit paralyzed and pray that the monster outside would lose interest in her and leave.

"Mei, I strongly suggest you put on your emergency O_2 unit. The Lander is going to breach the canopy at any moment, and unless you want to take a nice deep breath of fresh carbon dioxide..."

That snapped Kyoto out of her paralysis. She undid her restraints and reached under the seat for the emergency survival kit. If she'd taken the time to don a flight suit, she wouldn't need an O2 unit, but if wishes where starships...

She opened the kit, grabbed the O_2 half-mask and

fastened it over her nose and mouth. The breather automatically affixed itself to her skin and formed a seal. As oxygen began to flow, she reached back into the kit and pulled out a pair of goggles to protect her eyes. She quickly slipped them on, trying to ignore the sound of the Manti slamming its claws against the Defender's canopy as it screamed in blood-rage.

"Memory, what's the outside temperature?" Kyoto's voice was muffled by the O_2 mask, but still audible.

"Ten degrees Celsius. Chilly, but hardly life-threatening."

"Good." Because she'd left the hangar in such a hurry, she hadn't thought to grab a sidearm, but the emergency kit contained a small handblaster. The weapon didn't pack enough punch to kill a Bugger, but it might be enough to help Kyoto hold it at bay, especially if she softened it up first.

Kyoto fastened her seat restraints once more, making sure they were tight. "Memory, prepare for ejection on my mark."

"Well, aren't you the sneaky one?" There was a note of admiration in Memory's voice. "Ready when you are."

Kyoto took a deep breath of O_2 and gripped the handblaster tight. "Up, up, and away."

Couplings released and small charges exploded. The canopy flew upward, and Kyoto had a split-second to register the Lander's roar of pain before maglev repulsors shot her pilot's seat thirty meters into the air. The ejection-system sensors detected that Kyoto had bailed out close to the surface of a planet and calculated an appropriate rate of descent for local gravity.

As the seat drifted toward the ground, Kyoto

shivered from the cold and wished GSA dress uniforms were made of thermal insulation instead of synthetic cloth. Still, she was grateful it wasn't night, when the temperature could drop to around -80° Celsius. Kyoto worked the controls on the chair's starboard arm, and her makeshift vehicle spun around so she could see what damage the canopy had done to the Manti.

The Lander lay on its back, flailing its segmented legs not far from where the canopy had come to rest. Kyoto was happy to see a dab of green blood smeared on the canopy, but she had no illusions about the Manti being seriously injured. The aliens were just too tough. All the flying canopy had done was give the Bugger the equivalent of a bloody lip.

Before Kyoto's seat had drifted halfway to the ground, the Lander started to right itself. Kyoto had hoped the Manti would've been out of action long enough for her to set down, but no such luck.

She'd managed to keep hold of the handblaster during ejection, and now she flicked the power switch on and aimed the weapon at the Bugger's mouth parts. Even after years of studying dead and captured Manti, Galactic Stargate Authority R&D had only the most basic understanding of how the Buggers' anatomy worked. But they knew the mouth was the least armored portion of a Manti and therefore—the theory went—was the most vulnerable.

Kyoto fired. A thin ruby-colored beam stabbed forth from the blaster's muzzle and struck the Lander right in the middle of its wet crimson maw.

"Bull's-eye!" Kyoto shouted.

Thick green bubbled forth from the Bugger's mouth, and the Manti fell onto its side and thrashed its legs.

Kyoto glanced down at the ground. Ten meters to touchdown, she estimated. She kept her gaze fixed on the Manti and listened to the soft hum as the handblaster recharged. If the goddamned Bugger would just stay down for a few more seconds...

But faster than she would have thought possible, given the creature's condition, the Manti rolled onto its feet and scuttled over to the discarded canopy. It snatched up the plasteel component with its foreclaws and then—as if eager to give Kyoto a taste of her own medicine—hurled the canopy straight at her head.

Lightning-quick, Kyoto released the seat restraints and jumped. As she fell toward the ground, the canopy slammed into the ejection seat and sent it tumbling end over end through the air. Given that Mars's gravity was only 38 percent Earth norm, Kyoto had no trouble landing on her feet without injury. But the Lander was already scrabbling toward her, moving somewhat wobbly due to its wounds, but moving nonetheless. The handblaster had a full charge again, and Kyoto intended to use it. She leveled the weapon at the Manti and started to pull the trigger.

But before she could fire, the Manti lashed out with a foreclaw and knocked the blaster from her hand. Kyoto turned and leaped as the Lander brought its other claw around to strike. Again, the Martian gravity proved her ally. Her jump propelled her well beyond the Manti's reach, but before her feet came down once more on the rocky orange ground, the Bugger was moving again.

Kyoto's personal comlink chirped.

"I'm still here, Mei. I can't risk using the Defender's missiles because the explosion might injure you along with the Manti."

Kyoto landed and jumped again. The Manti continued after her.

"But if you can get the Lander in front of the ship…"

"Acknowledged. Stand by." This time when Kyoto landed, she rolled to bleed off the momentum and came up on her feet. She started running toward the *Defender's* prow, and the Manti, of course, followed like the good little human-eating alien that it was. Once she was in position, she turned and waited for the Lander to catch up. She had to time this just right. If she moved too early, the Lander might take to the air. If she moved too late… She didn't want to think about that.

As the Manti lurched toward her, ichor-smeared mouth open wide, eager to begin absorbing her genetic material, Kyoto had to force herself to stand her ground.

Closer… closer… "Now, Memory!"

Kyoto jumped away from the ship as hard as she could just as the Lander made a grab for her, bringing it in front of the *Defender's* pulse cannon. Energy erupted from the weapon and wreathed the Manti in deadly blue-white light.

The Lander shrieked in agony, and its body exploded from inside out. When Kyoto landed six meters away, she ducked down and covered her head. Sizzling chunks of Manti organs and charred bits of carapace pattered down on her. When the grisly rain was finished, she stood and turned her head to examine her green-slicked back.

"So much for your nice clean dress uniform," Memory said.

Kyoto laughed. "It was too tight, anyway." She turned back to look over the battlefield. One missile crawler was left, as well as two tanks, one of which was trundling toward her. But all the Buggers had been fragged. It was over.

For now.

CHAPTER

NINE

"One hundred and seventeen thousand dead throughout the Colonies." Detroit Adams's voice was devoid of emotion as he said this, but Kyoto could see the grief and shock in his eyes. The general was holding on and doing his job, but it was taking a supreme effort. She knew just how he felt.

"That's an approximate count, of course," Mudo added. "The final toll is likely to be much higher."

Everyone seated around the table in the GSA Control briefing room turned to stare at Mudo. Not only was the tone of his voice normal, it verged on pleasant, even happy.

Janeesh Glasgow scowled. "You sound almost glad the Manti attacked."

"Not at all," Mudo responded. "But if I allow my personal feelings to intrude upon this meeting, I won't be able to bring the full force of my mind to bear on the problem at hand. The most important thing I can do for the Solar Colonies right now—indeed, that any of us can do—is to think as dispassionately as possible."

Glasgow looked skeptical, and Kyoto couldn't blame him. The only emotion Mudo seemed to be repressing was glee over having a new and challenging puzzle to wrestle with.

Adams, Mudo, Glasgow, and Kyoto—who had discarded her ruined dress uniform and now wore a flight suit and her trademark bomber jacket—were the only ones present at the meeting. Unless you counted Memory, who was listening in via comlink. Glasgow's fellow council members were headed back to their respective colonies to assess damage and oversee relief efforts. Since stargate travel wasn't possible for the time being, the council members were returning home on transports traveling at sublight speeds, protected by escorts of GSA starfighters.

Glasgow turned to Adams. "Any word from Rhea yet?"

"Not since the Swarm first attacked."

"But that was nearly two hours ago!" Glasgow protested.

"The stargates are down, remember?" Mudo said. "All of them."

Mudo had finally managed to devise a computer program that transmitted a rapidly fluctuating signal to all the active stargates in the system, successfully shutting them off.

"Without the gates, we can't send or receive real-time messages," Mudo continued. "Depending on the orbital positions of each colony, com signals can take hours to arrive—and that's assuming each colony still has communications capability. Given the situation, it may be some time before we know the full extent of the damage wrought by this latest Swarm."

"But we haven't heard *anything* from Rhea," Glasgow said. "We have to learn whether or not the colony survived—we're going to need the Rheans if we're to have any hope of fixing the stargates so the Manti can't use them."

Rhea was the location of Influx, the GSA's stargate production facility. The techs there knew more about hyperspatial vortexes and gate travel than anyone in the system.

"I have a few thoughts on that matter," Mudo said. "If you'll permit me—"

"Not just yet, Doctor," Adams interrupted. "We have other things to discuss first."

Mudo didn't look happy about that, but he nodded and gestured for Adams to go on.

"Thanks to Kyoto, Mars suffered the fewest casualties of all the colonies. Only 412 Martian colonists died in the Manti attack."

Only, Kyoto thought. If only she could have saved them too.

Adams continued. "Mars also suffered the least structural damage. The GSA Armory was hit by Manti fire. We lost some starships, but most of the other weapons—such as our tanks and missile crawlers—remain functional."

Kyoto wondered if the *Janus* had been damaged. She glanced at Mudo, and he gave her a reassuring smile. Good, the ship was unharmed.

Adams went on. "In addition, the GSA experienced few casualties among personnel."

The woman Kyoto had spoken to in the hangar,

Garcia, had been one of those who'd made it. A small victory, perhaps, but it made Kyoto feel a little better.

"The Syscom installation took some hits, but they're still online. Without the stargates to transmit their signals, though, their broadcasting capabilities are—"

Glasgow's personal comlink chirped, and a woman's voice began speaking. "Janeesh? This is Aspen. I know you're there, so don't try to pretend you're not."

Glasgow's face reddened. "I have absolutely no idea how she got the code for my personal comlink." He held his wrist up to his mouth so he could whisper, not that everyone else couldn't hear him anyway. "Aspen, I'm in a very important meeting right now! This isn't the time—"

"It's the perfect time," she said at normal volume. "Right now you're in a meeting with Adams, Mudo, and probably Kyoto, too." There was something about the way she said Kyoto's name that made it sound like some sort of industrial waste product. "You can't freeze out the media, Janeesh! The Colonists have a right to know what's going on—and that means *I* have a right, because I'm their eyes and ears!"

"And mouth," Kyoto muttered.

"I heard that!" Aspen said. "Now, I demand that you allow me in there at once! If you don't—"

There was a loud *squawk* from Glasgow's comlink, and the channel went dead.

"Oops," Memory said. "It seems I accidentally overloaded your personal comlink, Mr. Glasgow. My apologies."

Glasgow looked relieved. "No apologies necessary, Memory." He wiped his brow with the back of his hand, as if he'd just escaped a close call, then said, "Now, where were we?"

"We were discussing Mars's current situation," Adams said. "The Manti came through the orbital stargates as well as those planetside. The GSA has three Battleships that survived the last Swarm, and they were all in orbit at the time the Buggers attacked. Two of the Battleships are in dry dock, but the third ship—the *Kipling*—was up and running, getting ready for a shakedown cruise to test some new upgrades. The captain and crew fought the Manti until Mudo was able to shut down the Gates. Once their reinforcements were cut off, the Manti that remained were easy pickings for the *Kipling* and our orbital defense satellites."

"What of the other two Battleships?" Glasgow asked.

"They should both be battle-ready in twelve hours," Adams said. "Unfortunately, the other colonies didn't fare as well as Mars did. Phobos took a pretty bad beating."

Kyoto looked at Mudo to see if he had any reaction to this news, since he'd been born and raised on Phobos, but his expression betrayed no emotion whatsoever. Kyoto wondered if the good doctor's self-control ever slackened.

"The penitentiary was destroyed, killing all the prisoners and most of the guards—those that didn't desert their posts, anyway. The aquiculture farms were wiped out, as well. Europa had massive loss of life in the residential areas, and both the McGraw Institute for Medical Wellness and the Europa Credit Exchange were destroyed."

Everyone in the room was silent for several

moments as the impact of this news set in. The McGraw Institute manufactured most of the medicines used in the Solar Colonies, and the Credit Exchange was the system's center of financial markets and transactions. And now both of them were gone... the impact of their loss on the Colonies would be devastating.

"The Sawari Virtual Zoo was destroyed as well," Adams said. "The exhibits can be rebuilt and reprogrammed, of course, but the Manti also took out a third of the tissue banks stored there."

Kyoto thought she was too numb by now to be shocked, but hearing that the Sawari Zoo was gone nearly caused her to burst into tears. The zoo was—had been—one of the most beloved places in the Colonies. It featured holographic recreations of extinct Earth animals in simulations of their natural habitats. More importantly, the zoo housed genetic samples of these animals, stored away until a new Earth-like world could be discovered or terraformed. When and if that occurred, the animals would be cloned and taken to their new home. At least, that had been the plan. But now a third of Old Earth's animal species had been destroyed. She wondered which creatures had been lost. Owls? Deer? Cats? She'd wanted to hold a real cat ever since she was four, when her parents had taken her to Sawari for the first time and she'd seen a holo of a kitten. Now, perhaps she'd never get to hold a real cat. Perhaps no one ever would.

A thought occurred to her then. "It's almost like the Manti knew exactly where to hit us, isn't it? GSA Headquarters, Syscom, Influx, the aquifarms, the McGraw Institute, the Credit Exchange..."

Mudo looked suddenly thoughtful. "Defense, communications, transportation, food, medicine, and finance."

"What about the tissue banks?" Glasgow asked.

"The future of your species," Memory said. "You won't be able to create a viable ecosystem for a new Earth without any fauna to go with the flora."

"So what are we saying here?" Adams asked. "That the Buggers *planned* this assault? C'mon now, despite their size and power, they aren't any more intelligent than the insects that inhabited Old Earth."

"Not necessarily," Mudo said. "We know from our experience battling the last Swarm that the Manti are organized in a hierarchical fashion somewhat similar to a hive structure. Different types of Manti are engineered for different purposes, and we did encounter some that seemed to exhibit a type of intelligence—the Brain Bugs, as the media so colorfully calls them. Perhaps the last Swarm wasn't so much an attack as it was a fact-finding mission. Maybe the Manti learned as much about us as we did about them, if not more."

The notion was too disturbing to contemplate. The one advantage humanity had over the Manti was intelligence. If it turned out the Buggers were as smart or smarter than humans, it was doubtful the Solar Colonies would survive.

"What's the bottom line here, Adams?" Glasgow said. "Are we prepared to fight another war with the Manti?"

Adams surprised Kyoto by taking a few moments to consider his response.

"No," he finally said.

Glasgow's eyebrows shot up. "That's it? No?"

"Make no mistake: we will fight, and we'll fight hard. But we've been slow in rebuilding our military strength after the last Manti war. During the Second Swarm, we had seven Battleships. Now we're down to three. Where once our starfighter fleet numbered over two hundred pilots strong, we're down to less than fifty." His voice grew softer. "Perhaps even less after today. The Manti also attacked the Defender Academy on Titan."

Kyoto felt as if she'd been punched in the stomach. Though it often seemed like a lifetime, she'd been out of the Academy for less than three years. She'd even toyed with the thought of returning there to teach one day.

"The instructors and students fought their best," Adams said, "but the casualties were heavy."

Kyoto remembered her first day at the academy. She'd been standing at attention in one of the hangars, along with all the other raw recruits. The flight instructor had looked them over, scowling as if she couldn't believe that this sorry lot was the best the GSA could do.

Kyoto had never forgotten what the instructor had told them. "The average life expectancy of a new fighter pilot in battle against the Manti is three to six weeks. If you intend to beat those odds, you'll need to pay attention, work hard, and learn to fly as if your life depends on it. Because it does."

Three to six weeks... Kyoto had beaten those odds, and so had Wolf. But fate had finally caught up with him today. Kyoto knew that very few fighter pilots died of old age, and that given the choice, Wolf would rather have gone out fighting to defend the Colonies.

But that was cold comfort. Wolf was dead and losing him hurt like hell.

Adams went on. "Without the stargates, we've lost the ability to respond immediately to any Manti attack. It could be hours before we learn of an attack, and more hours until we can reach the battle site. And we simply do not have the personnel and equipment to station an effective fighting force on each Colony. So here's your bottom line, Glasgow: we'll fight, but in the end, we'll lose."

"It was foolish of the council to believe the Manti threat had ended," Mudo said. "If the seven of you had continued to support the GSA, not to mention my research…"

Glasgow pounded his fist on the plasteel table. "Damn it! We had to rebuild half the colonies after the last Swarm. We did not have the resources to do that *and* keep the GSA strong. Some hard choices had to be, Dr. Mudo, and the council made them."

Mudo fixed Glasgow with an icy stare. "From whre I sit, *Mister* Glasgow, it looks like you chose wrong."

All the fire drained out of Glasgow then, and he slumped back into his seat, looking tired and defeated. "Perhaps so, Doctor. But the question is, what do we do now?"

There was one question that had been plaguing Kyoto since the meeting began. "How did the Manti learn to use our stargates, anyway? They've never been able to do so before."

All eyes turned to Mudo. The scientist leaned back in his chair, folded his hands over his stomach, and gazed up at the ceiling while he spoke.

"There are many things we don't know about the Manti. But chief among them is, where did they originate? Not in our system, certainly. None of the planets or moons possess environments that could have produced such a life-form. Over the last century, ruins were discovered on both Luna and Mars that seem to indicate that the Manti visited the system long ago—thousands, perhaps even millions of years in the past. In some of my more whimsical moments, I sometimes wonder if a prehistoric Manti swarm was responsible for the extinction of Earth's dinosaurs.

"We've never been able to discover any indication as to the Manti's place of origin. We know they can travel through space at sublight speeds thanks to the bio-energy fields their bodies generate, but from what we've observed and the experiments we've conducted on dead and captured Manti, it does not appear that they have the ability to travel faster than light. This would seem to rule out their coming from another star system. How would they have survived such a long journey at sub-light speeds without replenishing their energy? And though the Manti have demonstrated signs of an organic-based technology—Lander forges, pod worms, shock towers, and the like—no evidence of Manti transport ships has ever been recorded."

"But you have a theory, don't you?" Adams said. "You always do."

"Naturally. I believe that the Manti are native to hyperspace itself."

No one said anything for a moment, and then Glasgow laughed. "You're joking, right?

"Not at all," Mudo said. "Memory will confirm my conclusions."

"Gerhard's theory, while as yet unproven, is sound. Analyses of living Manti have shown that the bio-energy their bodies produce shares a number of similarities with hyperetheric radiation. If the Manti were denizens of hyperspace, it would explain why we've never seen any Manti transport ships: they wouldn't need any. It would also explain how they've managed to use our stargates."

"The gates are passages into and out of hyperspace," Kyoto said. "If the Manti live in hyperspace, it would be as though we opened a door for them to get out."

"Several doors, actually," Mudo said, "spread throughout the Solar Colonies. I don't think it's a coincidence that the First Manti Swarm took place not long after humanity's initial experiments with hyperspace travel. I believe those early experiments created rifts between realspace and hyperspace, rifts that allowed the Manti passage from their dimension into ours."

From the confused expression on Glasgow's face, he was having trouble processing this concept. "If your theory is true, then why did it take the Buggers so long to begin using our gates?"

"In the absence of any evidence, I'd only be speculating," Mudo said. "Perhaps our way of traveling through hyperspace—using it to 'jump' over long distances in realspace—is so alien, or even primitive, to the Manti that it took awhile for them to realize what the stargates are. Perhaps it simply took them some time to decipher the specific frequencies that our hyperspatial vortexes are tuned to, like a thief picking a lock. Perhaps the energy released from the explosion when Memory's first incarnation crashed the moon into Earth somehow rippled outward, like circles from a rock splashing into a pond, and altered the frequencies of our Gate vortexes just enough to allow the Manti through. Perhaps the Manti knew all along how to infiltrate our Stargates and were only waiting for the right time to do so. Right now, the important point is no matter how they did it, if they did it once, they can do it again."

"But we're safe as long as we keep the stargates offline, right?" Glasgow asked.

"Not necessarily," Mudo answered. "Neither the First nor the Second Swarm needed stargates to attack us. It's quite likely they have other methods of emerging from hyperspace. And who knows? They were able to prevent us from shutting down the stargates right away during this newest attack. Perhaps they'll also be able to reactivate the gates on their own, given time."

"So that's it, then," Glasgow said. "Without gate travel and without a stronger military force, it's only a matter of time before the Manti wipe out the human race."

Mudo at last took his gaze from the ceiling and looked at the group, his eyes shining with a mixture of intelligence, excitement, and perhaps a touch of madness.

"Not necessarily." He smiled. "Let me tell you about a little project I've been working on."

CHAPTER
TEN

Kyoto sat next to a marble fountain, listening to the soothing sound of trickling water. The water was real—not the thicker, somewhat oily chemical mixture Colonists were often forced to use. All around her, trees stretched to the top of the domed ceiling of the Cydonia Arboretum. Oak, cypress, ash, palm, pine, elm... so many different kinds that Kyoto could never remember all their names.

The floor was covered by rich synthetic soil from which dozens of different plant and flower species grew. Ferns, sweet grass, yucca, cacti, reeds... roses, lilies, daisies, lilacs, sunflowers, black-eyed Susans. Birdsong filled the air—recorded, of course—and holographic butterflies flitted from flower to flower. But despite the artificial touches here and there, the greenery was all real, and Kyoto inhaled deeply, savoring the mingled fresh scents of life itself.

Wolf hadn't exactly been a sentimentalist, but the arboretum had been one of his favorite places to bring her.

"It's so peaceful," he'd once said during a visit. "The plants don't have anything to do but grow, and they do it at their own pace. And once they're finished, they don't have anything else to do but continue existing and one day produce more plants."

Kyoto had laughed. "Doesn't that sound like a boring life to you?"

"Boring? Being able to live without worrying about tomorrow... being able to focus on just enjoying the present?" He'd smiled. "Sounds pretty good to me."

It was then that she'd first realized just how deeply he'd been scarred by battling the Manti swarm. Medical science could repair the wounds done to his flesh, but nothing could heal those done to his spirit.

Kyoto gazed at the water trickling from the fountain.

I'm going on a trip, Wolf. A real adventure, just the kind of thing you'd love. Mudo showed General Adams and Janeesh Glasgow his new toy. He had to do some fast talking to explain how he got the credits to pay for it, and Adams was not happy about being kept in the dark while he built the thing, but in the end, he convinced them to authorize a test flight. I'm going into hyperspace tomorrow— if Mudo's ship works, that is.

Mudo's words drifted through her mind once more: "The *Janus* is the next step in human space travel. It doesn't need to create a vortex the way a stargate does. It can open a portal into hyperspace, enter, and then close the portal behind it, thus leaving no dimensional rift for the Manti to come through. If we can enter and depart hyperspace at will, we'll no longer need to rely on stargate technology. The colonies would be safe, we'll still be able to travel and communicate swiftly throughout the system—and well beyond it—and most important right now, we'll be able to fight the Manti on equal terms.

"I developed the basic design for the hyperdrive nearly a year ago, but a normal navigational computer is too limited to handle the complex transcendental equations needed to travel in hyperspace. That was why I had to resurrect Memory. Only she could possibly navigate the *Janus*."

When Kyoto had looked questioningly at him about the choice of name, Mudo had responded, "Why did I choose the name *Janus*? Janus was the ancient Roman god of gates and doorways. Rather fitting, I thought, for a ship designed to travel through hyperspace. Janus was depicted as having two faces looking in opposite directions. Logical enough, since one can go through a doorway in either direction. But my *Janus* has two faces, as well. To us, it presents the face of a starship, but to the Manti, it will seem to be one of their own kind.

"While the *Janus* possesses minimal defensive weaponry—most of the ship's power is needed to maintain the hyperetheric field that allows it to enter and remain in hyperspace—it does have one major protection: camouflage. The *Janus* gives off an energy signature that's the same as that of a Manti Lander. With any luck, this camouflage will allow the *Janus* to travel through hyperspace without attracting the Manti's attention. And, if it works like I believe it will, imagine the military possibilities.

"Not only will a test flight prove the effectiveness of my hyperdrive as well as the ship's Manti camouflage, think of what we'll be able to learn about our enemy. For the first time since the Manti began their war against humanity, we'll finally be able to take the conflict to them."

Kyoto reached out to let the fountain's stream trickle over the palm of her hand. The water was warmer than she expected, and the feel of it running over her flesh was soothing.

"I miss you, Wolf," she whispered.

"Wherever Commander Wolfenson is now, I'm sure he misses you just as much."

Startled, Kyoto jumped to her feet and drew her sidearm. Until the latest Manti threat was over, she had no intention of going unarmed again. As she brought the handblaster to bear on the intruder, she stopped just before pulling the trigger. Standing before her was Seth Ganymede. She hadn't recognized him at first because instead of his Outbounder robe, he wore a simple khaki jumpsuit, the kind favored by Cydonia's working class.

Kyoto holstered her sidearm, but she remained standing. "What are you doing here?"

"I apologize for intruding on your privacy, but I need to speak with you."

She looked at his forehead and saw there wasn't even a scab left from where the protester's rock had struck him earlier. By itself, that wasn't surprising. Such a minor injury could easily be healed by modern medicine. But the skin wasn't pink, as it would have been if it had been regenerated, and it didn't have the tight, waxy look that simskin did. Though Kyoto knew better, it appeared that Ganymede had never been wounded at all.

"Look, if you've come to try to get me to join the Outbounders, I'm really not in the mood for politics right now, okay?"

"I understand that you have suffered a great personal loss today, in addition to experiencing the shock of a new Manti attack. You have my utmost sympathy."

Kyoto wasn't sure how to respond to this. "Uh... thanks. I don't mean to be rude, but I'd rather be alone right now, so if you'll excuse me..."

She turned to leave, but before she could go, Ganymede reached out and grabbed hold of her wrist.

"What the hell do you think you're doing?" Kyoto tried to pull free, but Ganymede's grip was like iron. Kyoto was surprised; he didn't look that strong.

"All right, you asked for it!" She'd tried to be nice about this, but after everything that she'd been through today, she wasn't in the mood to fool around. She reached for her handblaster...

... and suddenly found herself standing on a barren windswept plain. Terror surged through her, for at first she feared she'd somehow been transported outside of the Aboretum and onto the surface of Mars. Her flightsuit had an emergency O2 supply built in, and she started to reach for the pocket where the breather was kept, but then stopped. The air was too warm for Mars – almost tropical, in fact – and the sky was a hazy yellow instead of pink, the ground gray instead of orange. But most of all, she was breathing normally. The air smelled musty, but otherwise it seemed fine. She could think of only two possibilities. One, she'd gone insane and was hallucinating. Or two, she was no longer on Mars.

"Where am I?" she said aloud.

"You mean where are *we*?"

She turned and saw that Seth Ganymede was

standing next to her. He had released her wrist and now held his hands clasped behind his back.

"What did you do to me?" Kyoto demanded. "Did you drug me somehow? Or use some kind of gas that produces hallucinations?"

"Nothing so crude, I assure you. Our physical bodies still stand within the aboretum on Cydonia. But our mental avatars are currently residing inside a computer simulation."

Kyoto looked around. "This place seems real enough." She scuffed her boot on the ground. "Feels real enough, too."

"Of course. It's designed to seem real, but in the end, it's just cleverly organized data. However, what you are looking at is the image of an actual place. It is a planet called Coireall, one hundred fifteen light years from your star system."

There was something odd about the way he'd said "your star system," but Kyoto was too overwhelmed by the simulated environment around her to give it much thought.

"It looks deserted," she said.

"It is now. But once this spot was the center of a holy shrine that covered one hundred square kilometers and rose a thousand meters into the air. Worshippers from across the galaxy came to visit and pray here. Somewhat like Mecca on Old Earth."

Kyoto looked all around but could see nothing but gray rock in all directions.

"What happened?"

"The Manti happened."

The scenery blurred and reformed. Kyoto and Ganymede now stood on the rim of a vast crater so deep and wide that its outer edges were lost in the distance.

"This is a world called Olabisi. Once, this was the shore of a sea whose waters were so clear and pure that they were legendary among a hundred different civilizations. But that was before the coming of the Manti."

The scene shifted once more. Kyoto and Ganymede now stood upon hard permafrost, while an arctic wind swirled and howled around them. Though she knew this was only a simulation, Kyoto still felt the cold, and she adjusted her flight suit's temperature controls to keep her warm. Surrounding them were the ruins of an alien city. The buildings had been made from a substance that resembled quartz, and a number of the broken structures hung high in the air, though Kyoto could see no sign of antigrav generators attached to them.

"And this is Bergelmir. My homeworld." Ganymede's tone was matter-of-fact, but there was an underlying sorrow to his words. "Or rather, this is what the Manti left of it when they were finished."

Kyoto took her gaze from the crystalline ruins and turned to Ganymede. "Are you saying you're an alien?" She wanted to laugh, for the notion was absurd. Aside from the Manti, there had never been evidence of any sentient species inhabiting the galaxy other than humans. But she didn't laugh. She couldn't, not after the scenes of desolation that Ganymede had shown her.

"That is indeed what I am saying," Ganymede replied. "I represent a collective of races that calls itself the Residuum. After observing your species for the last several years, we have decided the time has come to make contact."

After everything else that had happened today, this was too much for Kyoto to deal with. She walked over to a chunk of quartzlike rock and sat down. After a moment, Ganymede walked over and sat beside her.

"I know this is quite a surprise for you, but over the years, we've learned that the best way to make contact with a new race is by first singling out and approaching specific individuals."

"And you chose me."

"That's right."

"Why?"

"Because you're brave, resilient, and a fast thinker. But more than that, you are a survivor. It is this quality that the Residuum prizes above all other. You see, every race that is a member has survived attack by the Manti. It is the one thing that unites us."

"But how is that possible? The Manti are *our* enemies. They're from this sector of space. How could they have destroyed so many civilizations so far apart?"

"The Manti have existed for uncountable millennia," Ganymede said. He smiled. "If one lives long enough, one tends to get around. But more than this, the Manti are beings natural to hyperspace. To put it simply, hyperspace is smaller than realspace. This is why we can travel great distances in realspace by taking shortcuts through hyperspace. But the principle works both ways. The Manti are able to cross vast distances in our galaxy through hyperspace as well. They can emerge at any point in realspace and attack at will."

Ganymede looked up at the ruins floating in the

sky and his voice grew softer. "No one knows how many worlds they've preyed upon, how many species they've eradicated. Thousands, perhaps millions. After all, the galaxy *is* an awfully big place."

Kyoto had no reason to believe Ganymede. After all, this Residuum of his sounded like just the sort of fantasy an Outbounder might concoct. But she did believe him. Not because of his fancy simulations, and not because of the words he spoke. It was the way he looked at up the sky with sadness in his eyes and loss in his voice.

"You're not really Seth Ganymede, are you?"

"No. The real Ganymede is in stasis inside his living unit. Those of us in the Residuum who specialize in first contact believe in getting to know a race well before formally approaching it. So we... borrow the identity of a native, often someone of a certain level of prominence. Not so high as to be under constant scrutiny, but high enough to permit freedom of movement and access to those we might wish to approach first. Ganymede fulfilled those requirements."

"You speak about him as if he were merely some sort of tool. But he's a person, and unless you asked his permission—and somehow I don't think you did—then you took him captive and hijacked his life. Those hardly seem to be the actions of a race who wish to establish friendly relations."

"I assure you, our intentions are benign. But we've learned to be cautious when contacting other races. We only approach civilizations that have encountered the Manti and survived. Such people tend to be somewhat skeptical of other aliens, to say the least. The last thing we wish to do is cause further panic in those who have already suffered so much from the Manti's predations."

"If you're not Ganymede, what's your real name? And don't tell me I won't be able to pronounce it."

He chuckled. "Not at all. The name I was given at birth is Hastimukah."

"I take it your usual appearance isn't human, then."

"My species is mammalian, as is yours, but we resemble an ancient Earth animal called a mammoth. Are you familiar with it?"

Kyoto couldn't help smiling. This just kept getting weirder and weirder. "I've seen pictures." She looked at Ganymede—or rather, at Hastimukah—and tried to imagine his natural appearance, but no matter how hard she tried, she couldn't do it. "That's some disguise you're wearing. Is it a holographic projection of some sort?"

"No, my body has been altered to appear human. Races that have suffered attack by Manti swarms tend to be xenophobic, so it helps to present a familiar appearance when we make initial contact. When I no longer have need of this form, I shall assume my true aspect once more."

Kyoto thought for a moment. "Your story sounds good on the surface, but there's one thing you said that bothers me. You say this collective of yours—"

"The Residuum."

"You say they only contact races who have battled the Manti and survived."

"Yes."

"If, as you claim, the Residuum's intentions are benign, then why not seek out races *before* they are attacked by the Manti and help them defend themselves?"

Ganymede paused before answering, as if he were carefully choosing his words.

"Because those races have not yet proven themselves… worthy."

Kyoto frowned. "I don't like that sound of that."

"I understand how it might seem overly harsh, but as I said before, the Residuum is a collective of survivors. In order to remain strong, we are only interested in permitting races to join that have demonstrated the strength, the cunning, and the tenacity to defeat the Manti. Look at this."

Hastimukah made no move, but the image surrounding them shifted once more. They still appeared to be sitting upon quartz rocks, but now they seemed to be floating in deep space. Kyoto felt an instant of panic, but then she reminded herself that this was just some kind of technologically advanced illusion. She didn't need a vacc suit to survive here.

Approaching from galactic west came a vast convoy of starships—all sizes, all shapes, from great gleaming behemoths to beat-up junkers that looked barely spaceworthy. There were thousands of vessels, all traveling in tight formation, all heading in the same direction.

"This is the Residuum," Hastimukah said with pride.

As Kyoto watched the seemingly endless procession of starships, understanding came to her. "You don't live on planets anymore, do you? You live on your ships."

"Yes. Most of our homeworlds were laid waste by the Manti. But even if they hadn't been, we still would have chosen to live as we do. We live in tens of thousands of mobile fortresses, and there is no force in the galaxy that can threaten us now."

"An interesting solution," Kyoto said. "You've chosen to both hide *and* run from the Manti."

Hastimukah bristled. "We are well equipped to fight when we have to. The Residuum excels in *all* forms of survival, including self-defense."

"Maybe so," Kyoto said. "But how does it do when it comes to *living*?"

Hastimukah didn't have a response to this.

"You can turn off the show," Kyoto said. "I've seen enough."

Again, Hastimukah gave no indication of doing anything, but the simulation vanished, and they were once more in the arboretum. Hastimukah still had hold of Kyoto's wrist, and now he released her.

"Why did you approach *me*?" she asked. "Why now? And what do you want from us?"

"I chose you because it was you who defeated the last swarm. Yes, I know that the entire struggle was hardly a solo effort, but in the end it was you who helped Memory drive the moon into the Earth, destroying the bulk of the last swarm. And my choice was validated again today when you destroyed the stargate rather than allow more Manti to come through. You demonstrated the prime qualities of a potential member of the Residuum: you will do whatever it takes, without hesitation, to stop your foe and ensure the safety of those you have sworn to defend.

"As for why now, your race is at a critical juncture in its development. Will you expand outward into the galaxy or will you remain bound to your home star system? We wish to show you that it is possible to become galactic citizens and still remain safe. As for what we want, long-term we would like to see humanity become a valued member race of the Residuum. Short-term, after contacting you, we had hoped to begin a dialogue with both GSA officials and the Council of Seven. But that may not be possible now."

Kyoto frowned. "Why not?"

"Because the Manti have returned to attack the human race again, and the ultimate survival of your people is once more in question."

"That's right. I almost forgot. Your little galactic club has room only for those who are deemed 'worthy.' And if this latest swarm wipes us out, then we hardly qualify, do we?"

Hastimukah said nothing.

"And since *we* have to prove ourselves to *you*, my guess is that the Residuum isn't going to step in to help us put down this new swarm."

Again, Hastimukah didn't reply.

"That's what I thought. So if that's the case, then why bother contacting us at all? Why didn't you just hold back and wait to see how events played out?"

"Because I believe that you have proven yourselves worthy, even if others in the Residuum are still withholding judgment. I wished you to be aware of the stakes this time. Not only are you fighting for the survival of your race, Commander, you are fighting for its future."

CHAPTER

ELEVEN

"And then he left?" General Adams asked.

Kyoto nodded.

"Did he depart via matter transmitter or some equally exotic method?" Dr. Mudo asked. "Did he grow wings and fly away? Or perhaps simply vanish in a puff of smoke?"

"Don't be snide, Gerhard." Memory's voice came from all three of their personal comlinks, giving her words a strange echoing quality. "Voice stress analysis indicates that she's telling the truth."

"See?" Kyoto said.

As she believes it, that is," Memory added.

"Thanks for nothing," Kyoto muttered.

Adams, Mudo, and Kyoto stood in the starship hangar, or rather what was left of it after the Manti attack. Cleanup crews worked on clearing away debris while techs cannibalized damaged ships for whatever parts could be salvaged. Luckily, the *Janus* had suffered only a few dents and scratches.

Mudo had insisted they meet here because he was making adjustments to the *Janus*'s systems and refused to leave the hangar. And given the nature of what Kyoto had to tell them, Adams hadn't wanted to discuss the matter on comlink channels.

Up to now, Kyoto had seen the *Janus* only on the holoscreen in Mudo's lab. But now, in the ship's presence—with its holographic disguise deactivated—she was struck anew by how truly strange the craft was. It wasn't just the metallic fish-fin structures running along both sides of the ship, nor the crystalline webbing on top. Though she couldn't put her finger on it, there was something simply not quite right about the *Janus*. It exuded an aura that unsettled her and set her teeth on edge, almost as if it were emitting an ultrasonic signal that she could feel even if she couldn't hear it.

She told herself not to worry, that it was probably just her imagination. After all, she'd had one hell of a day so far—Wolf's death, the return of the Manti, Ganymede revealing himself to be an alien imposter... No wonder she was imagining things.

"I'm sorry to disappoint you, Doctor," Kyoto said, "but when Ganymede—I mean Hastimukah—was finished talking, he simply said goodbye and walked away."

"Why didn't you follow him?" Adams asked.

"To be honest, it didn't occur to me," Kyoto admitted. "I was too busy trying to sort out everything he told me. I sat there for a while, thinking, and then I called you."

Adams turned to Mudo. "Assuming that Ganymede, or whoever he is, did tell Kyoto all the things she claims he did—and I'm willing to give her the benefit of the doubt—could his story possibly be true?"

Mudo gave Adams an irritated look, as if he couldn't believe he was being forced to waste his valuable time on such foolishness. "Memory, please conduct a probability analysis of Ganymede's story."

Several seconds passed while they waited. Finally, Memory said, "Analysis complete. Given all current data, I calculate a seventy-three percent chance that Ganymede's story is factual."

One of Mudo's eyebrows shot up in surprise. "Really? And what do you base your conclusions on?"

"The story in and of itself is consistent. Also, close analysis of today's news footage showing Ganymede being struck by a rock bears out Mei's assertion that the wound healed almost instantly. Also, moments before that, Ganymede's voice projected at a volume beyond human capabilities, yet he had no obvious equipment to amplify his voice."

"Mere circumstantial evidence," Mudo said, but despite his words, he appeared thoughtful.

"There's more. Analysis of vid footage taken over the last few weeks reveals changes in Ganymede's behavior patterns—his speech rhythms, choice of words, and body language. Comparative voiceprint analyses show that while Ganymede's voice is nearly the same as before, there is a one point four percent variance between Ganymede's former voiceprint and his current one."

Mudo didn't say anything this time.

"I also scanned GSA databases for any indication that an alien starship has been active in our system. If the being who spoke to Mei in the arboretum truly is an ambassador for a group called the Residuum, then he had to have gotten to Mars somehow. While I could find no clear evidence of such a ship, I did find record of an unexplained burst of hyperetheric radiation near Phobos thirty-eight days ago. In addition, several Mars orbital defense satellites have recorded gravitational anomalies that could indicate the presence of a large spacecraft that is somehow shielding itself from our sensors."

"Well, Doctor?" Adams said.

Mudo grimaced. "It appears my earlier... levity was premature." He turned to Kyoto. "My apologies, Commander."

"Don't sweat it," Kyoto said. "If someone had told me that same story, I would've thought they were crazy, too."

Adams brought his personal comlink up to his mouth. "Memory, could you clear my channel, please?"

"Done, General."

"Adams to GSA Security. I need to speak with Seth Ganymede—in person and as soon as possible. Got me?"

"Yes, General. Any other instructions?"

"He may or may not be dangerous, so take appropriate precautions."

"Will do, General. Security out."

"I doubt our alien friend returned to Ganymede's home," Mudo said. "If he's still in Cydonia at all."

"I agree," Adams said, "but we still have to check."

"So what do we do now?" Kyoto said.

"We go ahead with the *Janus*'s launch tomorrow," Adams replied. "It sounds as if this Residuum has no plans to help us against the Manti until we prove ourselves to them, so if and until that happens, we need to go on fighting the Buggers alone. And that means the *Janus* mission is still a go."

"I'm not certain we *want* to prove ourselves worthy," Mudo said. "After all, we know next to nothing about the Residuum. Perhaps it would not be to our advantage to join."

Kyoto smiled. "You think the membership dues might be too high?"

"Precisely," Mudo said.

"So we're just going to pretend the Residuum doesn't exist?" Kyoto asked.

"Not at all," Adams replied. "Just because there's been no Manti activity since this morning's attack doesn't mean there won't be any soon. If we can somehow make contact with the Residuum, perhaps we can convince them we're already worthy of their help. We could use some allies right about now." Adams paused. "We just received word not long ago from a transport ship out of Titan Colony that Rhea is gone."

Kyoto couldn't believe that she'd heard Adams correctly. "You mean it's been destroyed? The entire moon?"

"No. If Rhea had been destroyed, there'd be debris, perhaps trace radiation from whatever weapon was used. Rhea is simply gone, as if it had never existed in the first place."

"Do you think this is evidence of a new Manti weapon?" Mudo asked.

"I don't know what to think," Adams admitted. "If the Manti do have such a weapon, why did they use it only on Rhea? Still, if the Manti do have a device capable of making entire moons disappear, then we need allies more than ever. In the morning, I'm going to take a transport up to the Battleship *Kipling* and, after the *Janus* makes the transference to hyperspace, I plan to go alien hunting. If all goes well, I'll locate the starship that brought Ganymede—or whoever he is—to our system. And if I don't find it, I'll still be in a better position from which to direct the war effort." Adams paused. "There's one more thing I need to tell you."

From the tone of the general's voice, Kyoto was afraid this one was going to be even worse than the news about Rhea.

"On the way over here, I received a call from Janeesh Glasgow. He still fully supports the *Janus* mission, but he had a request. And by *request*, I mean *command*."

Kyoto and Mudo waited for the general to continue.

"Our illustrious council member believes that a mission of such historic importance to the Solar Colonies should not go undocumented. As he put it, we 'owe it to humanity's future' to record the *Janus*'s journey in every detail."

"Oh, no." Kyoto had a terrible feeling she knew where this was leading.

"Oh, yes. At Glasgow's insistence, one more person is going to be going along on your adventure tomorrow: Aspen DeFonesca."

Kyoto groaned.

"You can't be serious!" Mudo said. "This is a scientific expedition! There's no room for a, a... *tourist!*"

"*I believe the correct term is 'media personality,'*" Memory said.

Mudo ignored her. "No. I shall not allow that woman to step aboard my ship."

"You mean *Glasgow's* ship," Adams said. "After he

left here, he got curious about how you managed to pay for your secret project. After a little digging, he discovered that you'd appropriated funds from various financial accounts of his to build the *Janus*." Adams glared at Mudo. "It was a damn foolish thing to do, but given the circumstances, Glasgow isn't going to press charges."

Mudo looked relieved.

"Besides, this way he'll get to claim that he knowingly funded the project all along," Kyoto said.

Adams nodded. "Exactly. But this means you do *not* have a choice about taking Aspen DeFonesca along. So my advice to both of you is to get as much beauty sleep as you can so you look good for the hovercam tomorrow." He grinned. "After all, you'll be representing the GSA."

Still grinning, Adams departed. Mudo looked at Kyoto, shook his head, then went back into the *Janus* to continue getting the ship ready for launch. With nothing else to do, and being seriously depressed about having to put up with Aspen DeFonesca during tomorrow's voyage, Kyoto decided to take the General's advice and hit the sack, though she seriously doubted she'd be able to do more than toss and turn tonight.

But as she started away from the *Janus*, a tech hurried over to speak with her. Kyoto recognized the woman as Garcia, the woman who'd gotten the G-7 ready for her this morning. Kyoto had been aware that Garcia had survived the Manti attack, but seeing the woman in the flesh nevertheless made her feel better. As far as she was concerned, every human life saved was another blow struck against the Manti.

"Commander, I just wanted to thank you for what

you did today. That was some damn fine flying you did out there."

Kyoto smiled. "Not so good that I didn't wreck my ship—and after you and your crew worked so hard getting it ready double-quick for me."

"That's what we maintain 'em for, so folks like you can go out and get shot at while protecting the rest of us." Garcia smiled. "My crew and I wanted to do more than just *say* thanks, though, so we had your G-7 towed back into the hangar. The general told us that you're going to be test flying that weird-looking contraption of Mudo's tomorrow, and he asked us to outfit the cargo bay to carry and launch a starfighter. Mudo's not thrilled about us going near his ship, but the general ordered him, so he's going to let us do our jobs. The ship we're going to install is your G-7 Defender. It'll have a new wing, perfectly calibrated weapons, and, if we have the time, a few added surprises as well."

Kyoto was so overwhelmed with emotion, she didn't know what to say. "You guys will probably be up all night working."

Garcia grinned. "Won't be the first time. The general didn't tell us what Mudo's ship is supposed to do, and there's no way Mudo is going to say anything. But I figure that whatever it is, it's supposed to help us fight the Manti, right?"

"Yes," Kyoto said.

Garcia nodded. "Then that's good enough for me and my crew, Commander. You stopped the last Manti swarm, and we want to make sure you have the right tools to take out this one as well."

Kyoto saw the trust and hope in Garcia's eyes, and she didn't know if she could bear it. She wasn't a savior, wasn't even a hero. She was just a jump jockey who'd gotten lucky—*real* lucky—a few times. How long could that luck possibly hold?

But she knew that Garcia didn't need to hear any of that, didn't need her to be Mei Kyoto, but rather the starfighter pilot the media called the Hero of Luna.

She gave the tech a cocky grin and said, "Thanks, Garcia. Can't go bug hunting without a good supply of fusion-powered pesticide, eh?"

Garcia grinned back. "No, ma'am, you sure can't! Well, enough gabbing. I've got to get back to work. Clear skies tomorrow, Commander." And then Garcia hurried off to rejoin her crew.

Kyoto watched the woman go and wondered how she could possibly live up to the expectations of a billion scared colonists who were in desperate need of a hero.

She sighed and started walking toward the hangar exit, more certain than ever that she wasn't going to get any sleep tonight.

Inside the *Janus*'s control room, Mudo sat at the science station examining data scrolling across a holoscreen. He was confident that the ship was ready and would perform according to design specifications, but he didn't want there to be any mistakes. Not only because he despised mistakes—correcting them was a grotesque waste of time and energy that was better spent on other things—but because the Solar Colonies couldn't afford him to make any mistakes. Not if humanity was to have any hope of survival.

Besides, now that DeFonesca was coming along, he didn't want to look like an idiot on the newsvids.

The revelation of the existence of the Residuum

was intriguing, and Mudo looked forward to learning more about it, as well as comparing his intellect to that of its best scientists, but the *Janus*'s exploratory mission would have to come first.

"Gerhard?" Memory's voice came over the science station's comlink.

"Hmm?" Mudo continued examining the data passing before his eyes.

"Do you think it's wise to conceal the true nature of the *Janus* from General Adams and Mei? They deserve to know the truth."

Mudo didn't take his attention from the holoscreen. "Perhaps they do, but I can't take the chance that they won't understand, much less approve. The *Janus* may well be the last, best hope for humanity, and I will not risk the mission being canceled. And you will *not* tell them, Memory. I forbid it."

"Of course, Gerhard. Thy will be done."

"Precisely as it should be." Mudo continued checking data and gave no further thought to the secret that lay at the heart of the *Janus*.

CHAPTER

TWELVE

Seth Ganymede was in the middle of the most amazing dream—one that involved himself, several luscious alien women with four breasts apiece, and a vat full of soy gelatin—when a voice cut through his nocturnal fantasy.

"Wake up, Ganymede. We're GSA Security. Your comp let us in, and we have orders to bring you to General Detroit Adams for questioning."

Ganymede really didn't want to open his eyes. Even though he was an Outbounder and believed wholeheartedly in humanity's galactic expansion, he was fairly certain that of all the alien life-forms humans might encounter in the future, four-breasted women would not be among them. As this dream might very well prove his only chance to experience the delights these women had to offer, he was understandably loath to give it up. But whoever had spoken began shaking him by the shoulders, and though he desperately tried to cling to sleep and to his dream, he couldn't prevent consciousness from returning.

He opened his eyes and immediately wished he hadn't. Harsh light stabbed into his optic nerves, sending bolts of pain lancing through his skull, and he threw his hands up to shield his face.

"Whoever you are, turn off that damn spotlight! You're blinding me!" His voice came out as a dry croak, and it hurt to talk, as if he hadn't spoken for quite some time.

"What spotlight?" said another voice.

"Use the manual controls to dim the room lights by half," the owner of the first voice ordered.

Seconds later, the spotlight dimmed, and the agony in Ganymede's head diminished to a dull ache. Hesitantly, he began to open his eyes, but his simple action was more difficult that he'd anticipated. He felt as if his lids had been glued shut.

After a few seconds, he managed to get his eyes open and saw six GSA security agents in black battle armor standing around his bed. The four-breasted women forgotten, Ganymede tried to sit up, but he felt weak as a newborn and couldn't so much as lift his head from the pillow.

"What's the meaning of th-this?" He tried to conceal how scared he was, but he didn't do a very good job. "Has the GSA taken to assaulting law-abiding citizens in the middle of the night?" Actually, that was exactly what he feared.

"My orders are to bring you to GSA headquarters so General Adams can talk to you," one of the guards said. Ganymede recognized him as the one who had woken him. "At the moment there are no formal charges that we're aware of."

"How reassuring," Ganymede muttered. Still, whatever was going on didn't necessarily have to be bad. Perhaps Adams wished to consult with him so he could get the Outbounder perspective on certain matters. Like the Earth Memorial, for one. It was due to go online in just over a month, and from what Ganymede understood from the newsnets, there were still a lot of problems—both technical and political—to be worked out. It was about time the almighty Galactic Stargate Authority recognized the importance of the Outbounders and that of Ganymede himself.

"I shall be happy to assist the GSA in any way I can." Ganymede tried to sit up again, but he was still too weak to manage the job.

"That is, if you fine officers wouldn't mind helping me out of bed."

This is going to be harder than I thought. What does one wear for an expedition into hyperspace?

Aspen DeFonesca stood in front of a holographic wardrobe display, scrolling through various outfits and combinations. The vast majority of her clothing was stored in molecular compression cases, otherwise she never would have been able to fit it all into her living quarters, lavish though they were by colonial standards. On Mars, only Janeesh Glasgow's home was larger.

Thinking of Glasgow made her smile. Though he'd tried to avoid her after his cozy little conversation with Adams, Mudo, and Kyoto—she scowled as she thought this last name—she'd managed to track him down at Johann's, one of his favorite restaurants. She'd had no trouble convincing the darling of a maître d' to escort her back to Glasgow's private table (a wink and a smile that hinted as pleasures never to be delivered was all it took). Glasgow had demanded she leave in peace, but when she told him that she was contemplating writing an exposé called "All the Women That Janeesh Glasgow Has Slept With That He Doesn't Want His Wife to Know About," he'd quickly invited her to join him.

After a few drinks and several more threats, Glasgow had finally told her about Mudo's new toy. It hadn't taken her any time at all after that to get Glasgow to call Adams and politely but firmly insist that she be allowed to go along on the *Janus*'s maiden voyage.

Of course, Kyoto was going, too, but that was something she'd just have to live with. Besides, if all went well, she'd have the opportunity to make little miss butch starfighter pilot look like the no-talent nobody that she truly was. By the time this jaunt was over, Syscom would make a vid about Aspen's adventures in hyperspace, and this time she'd get to play herself. Six months—a year, tops—and no one would remember or care who Mei Kyoto was. Assuming that the Manti didn't destroy the Solar Colonies first. But then, life was full of gambles, wasn't it?

Aspen had managed to narrow her wardrobe options down to seventeen suits, twelve blouses, and thirty-one pairs of shoes when the roomcomp announced, "You have a visitor at the front door, Ms. DeFonesca."

"Whoever it is, tell them to go away. I've got some serious packing to do." Even using molecular compression cases, she wasn't certain that she'd be able to fit all she wanted to take. She was going to be allowed only two cases. Something silly about carting along extra weight during space travel. She should run various packing scenarios through the comp and see which—

"My apologies, Ms. DeFonesca, but the visitor won't leave. He says his name is Seth Ganymede, and he has information he wishes to share with you on an exclusive basis."

Though Seth Ganymede wasn't on the B List, let alone the A, Aspen still might have been interested in hearing what he had to say. But she had so much work to do before morning. She considered fobbing Ganymede off on one of her less-talented colleagues (which was all of them), but then again, if Ganymede did have something juicy for her, how good would it look if she got the story tonight, on the eve of her greatest story? Aspen could pull a twofer that would make all the other talking heads at Syscom grind their cosmetically enhanced teeth to nubs out of jealousy.

And Ganymede had said the magic word: *exclusive*.

"Very well. Verify his identity, and if he checks out, let him in."

Aspen was dressed in a red satin robe and momentarily gave some thought to putting on something more professional. But she decided against it. Not only did she look fantastic in this robe, but if she did tape an impromptu interview with Ganymede, wearing the robe—especially if she allowed it to peek open now and again—would be sure to boost ratings.

She left her bedroom, and walked down the hall and into the main living space. Ganymede was already inside—admitted by the AI, of course—and was standing in the foyer.

"Mr. Ganymede's identity confirmed, Aspen."

She frowned. This was the first time her home AI had ever called her by her first name. Aspen didn't believe in allowing AIs to address her that way; it was creepy, she thought. She almost rebuked it, but she didn't want to argue in front in her guest, especially with a computer program. She'd take care of the AI later.

As she approached Ganymede, she put on a smile—not one of her killer smiles, the kind that would make men fall down at her feet and vow undying devotion, but still a pretty good one.

"I almost didn't recognize you without your robe with that delightfully tacky galaxy holo on it. What's wrong, love? Get it soiled during today's protest?"

Ganymede didn't return her smile, and this puzzled Aspen. *Everyone* smiled when she did. It was a simple fact of her existence.

She stopped in front of Ganymede, put a hand on her hip, and allowed her robe to drop open a few centimeters to put him off balance. "My AI says you have a story for me."

"A story? No. But I do have something to give you."

Before she could move, Ganymede gripped the back of her neck and held her motionless. She was so surprised—she was used to being touched but always on her terms—that for a moment she didn't struggle, just stood and watched as he brought up his other hand and slid the first two fingers into her mouth.

My God! She'd always thought Ganymede and the other Bounders were a bit off, but she hadn't imagined that he was a full-fledged pervert! Still, that might not be so bad. He wasn't an Adonis, but he wasn't repulsive, either—and she *was* going on a potentially dangerous journey tomorrow. It might be fun to have her own little going-away party…

But then a strange metallic taste flooded her mouth,

as if she'd just taken a gulp of warm liquid ferroceramic.

"I'm sorry about this, Ms. DeFonesca," Ganymede
said. "But I need to borrow your identity for a time.
The future of your race may well depend on it."

Aspen had no idea what the lunatic was talking
about, and she didn't care. All she knew was that the
metallic taste was getting stronger, and the liquid or
whatever it was running down her throat was
becoming thicker. She fought to pull free of
Ganymede's grip, to force his hand out of her
mouth—anything! But nothing she did worked.
Ganymede's body was as hard and unyielding as
stone.

"Please don't be afraid," Ganymede said in a tone
of genuine concern. "The nanoparticles that are
presently infiltrating your system will do no harm to
you. They will merely put you to sleep for a while.
You will rest comfortably, and they will see to all your
body's needs while you slumber. The nanoparticles
will wake you in two weeks, regardless of whether or
not I return. You may feel somewhat weak and disori-
ented when you awaken, but that will be the full
extent of your discomfort, I assure you."

Aspen didn't follow everything Ganymede had said,
but one thing was clear: the sonofabitch was injecting
her with some kind of nanotech. She kicked and
punched, but even though her blows landed solidly
enough, Ganymede didn't seem to notice them.

A pleasant numbness began to filter though her
body then, warm and comforting. Tiny soft voices in
her head urged her not to resist, to give in and let
them take care of her. It was so tempting to surrender
to the overall sensation of pleasant nothingness that

coursed through her limbs, but she fought to hold on. Whatever was happening to her, she knew there was a hell of a story in it.

She started thinking of all the questions she would ask Ganymede once he did her the courtesy of removing his fingers from her mouth, but her vision began to grow black, and a loving, caring darkness came for her, and she no longer wanted to resist it.

Hastimukah carried the unconscious form of Aspen DeFonesca to her bedroom and tucked her beneath the covers. According to transmissions from the nanoparticles he'd put inside her, her vital signs were strong.

Hastimukah looked down upon Aspen's sleeping face. Though he currently resembled a human on the outside, inside he remained an alien. From what he understood, Aspen was reputed to be most attractive by her race's standards, but he couldn't see it. Give him a good thick coat of fur and a large pair of ears anytime.

He turned away from Aspen and walked over to the holodisplay in the corner of her bedroom. Before entering her quarters, Hastimukah had used some nanoparticles to take control of the comp system. The AI would now obey his commands, and his only.

"What was she doing?" he asked.

"Trying to decide what to take with her for tomorrow's trip."

Hastimukah's species had fur and tough padded feet. They tended to go about without clothing, except on ceremonial occasions and when dealing with other races that had taboos against nudity. Even then, they wore only the most rudimentary of outfits, such as short-sleeved tunics or kilts. Hastimukah had no idea how humans chose their clothing, though he imagined that, as in most cultures, it was some blend of personal taste and societal standards.

He sighed. It looked like he had some homework ahead of him. "Computer, access vid footage of Aspen DeFonesca for the last month. Display a random sampling of still images of her during that time, please."

As Aspen's AI worked to fulfill Hastimukah's request, he heard a soft chiming sound ringing in his ears. Kryllian was contacting him via the nanocolony that lived in his body.

"Hastimukah here," he said aloud. Nanoparticles relayed Kryllian's message by directly stimulating the structures of his inner ear.

"This is Kryllian. Ship's sensors indicate you have released a large amount of self-replicating nanoparticles into a human for the purpose of short-term stasis. What's the reason for this? Don't you already have a disguise?"

"I do," Hastimukah replied. "But the identity of Seth Ganymede is no longer useful for my purpose, and thus I need to assume another."

There was a pause, and Hastimukah knew Kryllian was mulling over his response. The Grindani weren't exactly the fastest thinkers in the Residuum.

"Of what purpose do you speak?"

"Tomorrow, the humans are going to test a new hyperdrive they've developed. I intend to be on that ship when they do, and taking on the appearance of Aspen DeFonesca will get me onboard."

"Why is this necessary? Does the Kyoto woman

no longer have the nanoparticles you deposited on her?"

When Hastimukah had grabbed Kyoto's wrist in the arboretum, he had done so not only to establish a mental connection so that they might share the virtual scenes he had wished to show her, but also so he could leave behind some of his nanocolony to spy on her. He had known that she'd go straight to General Adams after he revealed the truth about himself and the existence of the Residuum. Thanks to his nanoparticles, he had seen and heard everything that she, Adams, and Mudo had talked about. He had learned about the *Janus* and the scheduled test flight, and he had learned that Aspen DeFonesca had managed to obtain a seat on board for tomorrow's journey. Only now, that seat would be his.

"Kyoto's nanoparticles are still in place," Hastimukah said. "But once the humans' ship has crossed over into hyperspace, we will lose contact with them. If we wish to learn more about the human's technological capabilities, then I will have to go along in person."

"I do not care about this ship," Kryllian said. "Either the humans have proved themselves worthy of being part of the Residuum or they haven't. And if they haven't..."

"*I* am the chief assessor on this mission, Captain, and *I* will be the one to make the final recommendation to the Ascendancy regarding the humans' status. Do not forget this."

A longer pause this time. When Kryllian spoke again, his voice was tight with barely controlled anger. "Of course, Chief Assessor. And what do you wish The *Eye of Dardanus* to do while you are away?"

"Continue to monitor this system for signs of Manti activity and the humans' response to it. But do not engage the Manti directly unless they penetrate the ship's stealth shield and attack."

"Understood."

"If I have not reported back to you within two weeks, you are to contact the Ascendancy for further instructions."

"As you wish, Assessor."

There was another soft chiming sound, and Hastimukah knew that Kryllian had broken their link. Hastimukah had no idea why the Grindan had been assigned to this mission. The captain lacked the patience necessary to make a successful first contact. Though the Residuum had clear guidelines for which civilizations could be approached and which couldn't, those guidelines quickly became blurred in the field. Some cases came down to a judgment call on an assessor's part, and right now, Hastimukah didn't feel that he had enough information to make a final decision. Considering the stakes were nothing less than the survival of the human species, he was determined to learn all he could before rendering his judgment. The *Janus's* mission could very well be the turning point for humanity—one way or the other. Therefore, he had to be on that ship tomorrow, even if it meant staying up all night and selecting a wardrobe.

He looked at the holodisplay and sighed. "Computer, please repeat the images I asked you to gather a few moments ago, only go more slowly this time. And if you have any suggestions, I'd appreciate hearing them."

As the holoscreen displayed one picture of an

impeccably dressed Aspen DeFonesca after another, the nanocolony within Hastimukah's body began the process of altering his appearance. By morning, he would no longer be Seth Ganymede; he'd be Aspen DeFonesca—or at least a reasonable facsimile.

Assuming, that is, he could find something decent to wear.

Kryllian, captain of the Residuum vessel called The *Eye of Dardanus*, shifted in his command chair and waited while it molded to his form. Because so many different sentient species were represented in the Residuum—347 at last count—all with different physiognomies, it made no sense to create furniture or workstations designed for a single body type. Thus, all facilities on the *Dardanus* were malleable according to an individual's needs. Still, given the combined technological know-how of so many races, Kryllian was at a loss to explain why chairs always took several seconds to adjust after you moved, and why they never felt quite comfortable even then.

The command center of the *Dardanus* bustled with activity as crew members of various species attended to their duties. Most were busy analyzing data gathered from the humans' star system and their colonies, but others were performing continual sensor sweeps to check for Manti activity. There were no records of the Manti being able to penetrate a Residuum starcraft's stealth shield, but there was always a first time. And every member race in the Residuum knew from bitter experience that the cost of letting one's guard down against the Manti was death.

Kryllian was in a foul mood. His species, the

Grindani, had evolved from small ocean-dwelling crustaceans on a world of slightly heavier gravity than Residuum-norm. The nanocolony that shared his body was supposed to adjust for the difference in gravity, as well as draw enough moisture from the air to keep his internal organs hydrated. But he suspected the nanoparticles within him needed to be recalibrated, for he felt out of sorts.

Then again, perhaps his mood was due to the fact that the Assessor he'd been assigned to ferry to this primitive star system was a gigantic pain in the telson.

"Captain, how fares Hastimukah?"

Kryllian turned to see his first officer approach the command chair. Suletu was a Huata, one of the races that had founded the Residuum. Suletu was a sentient being composed entirely of billions upon billions of nanoparticles. He/she/it (Kryllian wasn't sure which designation to use since the Huata didn't employ personal pronouns) resembled a mound of ambulatory gray sludge, but could change form to fit whatever task was required.

"The idiot is too softhearted," Kryllian said. "It is obvious that the species native to this system is not ready to join the Residuum. The Manti attacked them again today, and despite having had two of their years to prepare for the day they would once again face their enemy, they did nothing. Not only are they not worthy of joining us, I'm not certain they are worthy of survival at all."

"Forgive Suletu, Captain, if Suletu says that your assessment sounds somewhat... harsh."

Kryllian's maxilliped quivered—the Grindani equivalent of a shrug. "Perhaps. But life was very difficult on my homeworld even before the coming of the Manti. Only the strongest of the strong managed to survive. My people do not believe in deities, but we do live by the principle of survival of the fittest. We believe that those species who are fit enough to survive are those who are destined to survive. Isn't that one of the Residuum's guiding philosophies?"

"It is. But all of our races have bonded together for mutual survival, have we not? Without one another, how long would any of us survive against the Manti?"

Kryllian didn't respond.

Suletu continued. "It is sometimes difficult to know when a species has matured to the point where it is ready to be a fully contributing member of the Residuum. When it will add to our combined chances for survival instead of detract from them. This is why we have assessors, is it not? To make such determinations."

Kryllian's brown carapace turned a bright pink—a sign of irritation. Because Huata were comprised of billions of individual nanoparticles, each in its own way self-aware, they were highly skilled at communication and conflict resolution. They had to be just to function day in and day out. These qualities usually cast them in the role of peacekeepers within the Residuum, but Kryllian thought this made the Huata often act as if they believed they were intellectually superior to the rest of the member races, and it chafed his rostrum.

"Perhaps so," Kryllian finally allowed. "But I do not approve of Hastimukah's current actions. I believe he has overstepped the bounds of his mandate in accompanying the humans on their expedition into hyperspace, and I am confident the Ascendancy will share my view."

"Then it is fortunate for Hastimukah that our leaders are not aware of his plans," Suleta said.

"Ah, but they will be – just as soon as you establish a communications link with them for me."

Suletu hesitated, and Kryllian thought the Huata was going to disobey his command. But then it inclined the top portion of its mass, as if bowing, and said, "As you wish." Suleta then began slithering toward the comm workstation.

Kyrllian's race didn't possess the anatomy to smile, but his antennae waved gently back and forth in pleasurable anticipation of the conversation he was about to have.

CHAPTER
THIRTEEN

"Everyone secure?" Kyoto asked.

"I'm fine," Mudo snapped. "Ms. DeFonesca is fine. Memory is fine, and you're fine, too. Can we just take off, please?"

Kyoto did her best to ignore Mudo. The scientist had grown increasingly irritable as the morning wore on. But while he was technically in command of this mission, Kyoto hadn't been about to lift off without first familiarizing herself with the *Janus*'s controls and going over the course Mudo had programmed into the nav system. Her preparations had taken less than thirty minutes, but Mudo was ready to climb the *Janus*'s walls, and likely would have been doing so if he hadn't been buckled into his seat.

"Flight suits activated and functioning?" Kyoto asked, turning around to look at Mudo and Aspen. They sat directly behind her in black pseudoleather chairs, locked into their seats by restraint harnesses.

"Yes!" Mudo shouted.

"How about you, Aspen? Your suit working all right?" Kyoto steeled herself for the inevitable complaints: "This thing makes me look hideous, I'd rather sit on broken glass than this awful chair, and the smallest of my closets is still larger than this dingy little cockpit!"

Aspen smiled. "I believe it's functioning perfectly."

Kyoto stared at the woman. Something had been a little off about Aspen ever since she'd reported to the hangar this morning. Her gaze contained none of its usual cunning or derision, and when she said something nice, she sounded as if she really meant it.

Maybe she's just nervous, Kyoto thought. Or maybe she was only trying to look good in front of the hovercam she'd brought along and which had magnetically affixed itself to the inner hull in order to keep from being bounced around during takeoff.

Kyoto turned back around to the *Janus*'s cockpit controls. They were simple enough, for despite the enhancements Mudo had made to the ship, the basic design remained that of a transport vessel. In many ways, it wasn't that different from the cargo ship her father had piloted. Thinking of him reminded Kyoto to rub the sleeve of her bomber jacket. It was a ritual that she always performed before a launch. Like a lot of pilots, she was superstitious about such rituals, and while she didn't believe in guardian angels—who could after fighting the Manti?—she liked to think that somehow her father's spirit was watching over her.

"Final systems check, Memory."

"All systems are go, Mei. Power, life support, shields, engines, and hyperdrive are all optimal. It's now or never."

"Roger that." Kyoto flicked a switch to activate the control panel's holoscreen. An image of the GSA Control hangar appeared before them. A dozen techs—including Garcia—stood off to the side, waving and giving thumbs-up.

Kyoto activated the *Janus'* maglev boosters and the ship slowly rose a meter into the air.

Kyoto frowned. "Feels a bit sluggish."

"It's the extra weight: my hardware, your starfighter, and Gerhard's hyperdrive. That's why the cabin and crew quarters are so cramped, in case you hadn't noticed. With all the extra technology crammed into the *Janus*, there's hardly any room left for you flesh and blood types."

"This is only a prototype," Mudo said defensively. "Future hyperships will undoubtedly be larger."

Kyoto waited for Aspen to make some sort of comment, such as, "Good—then maybe a girl will be able to bring along more than two suitcases, and not have to share a bathroom with everyone else on board." But she said nothing.

Surprised and more than a little relieved by Aspen's silence, Kyoto took hold of the ship's joystick and carefully steered the modified transport into the hangar's airlock.

"Seal the airlock, Memory."

"Acknowledged."

They waited while the airlock door lowered. When the green light came on, Kyoto said, "Open the hangar door, please."

"Your wish is my cliché."

The hangar door had been damaged in the Manti attack, and it jerked and shuddered as it rose, but at least it functioned. When the door was all the way up, Kyoto guided the ship along the ferroceramic rails and out into the Martian air. As the *Janus* cleared the hangar and began heading toward the dropzone, Kyoto thought of Wolf and Julia, as well as the crew of the *Orinoco*. Yesterday they had flown the same route to the dropzone, and now they were all dead. She felt tears threaten, but she fought them off. Now wasn't the time for mourning.

Kyoto increased the *Janus's* speed and continued toward the dropzone.

"*Kipling* calling *Janus*." It was General Adams.

"Here, sir," Kyoto answered.

"According to our sensors—not to mention Aspen's live vidfeed—you've just left the hangar. Is everything go?"

"Yes, General. Looks like nothing but clear skies ahead. At least to the dropzone, that is."

"Sounds good, Kyoto. Do your best to keep it that way, and we'll be waiting for you in orbit. *Kipling* out."

"There is no need to go all the way to the dropzone," Mudo said. "Since we will not be entering hyperspace until after we leave orbit, there is no danger to Cydonia."

"I suppose you'd like it if I fired up the fusion reactors right now and headed for orbit at top speed," Kyoto said.

"You mean like you did yesterday?" Mudo asked.

"That was different; it was an emergency. GSA regulations are clear about where starships can lift off and where they can't. The dropzone is the closest place within thirty kilometers that we're authorized to use. If you don't like it, feel free to take it up with General Adams when we get back."

If we get back, Kyoto mentally added.

Mudo crossed his arms and said nothing more as they continued toward the dropzone, and Kyoto was exceedingly grateful. She'd never understand why the greatest genius the human race had ever produced had all the patience of a three-year-old who had to go potty *now!*

When they drew near the dropzone, Kyoto pulled back on the joystick, activating the braking thrusters, and the *Janus* slowed to a stop. The dropzone pad was nothing but plasteel rubble now, thanks to the impact of the empyrean ring Kyoto had brought crashing down yesterday. This was as close as they could get following the ferroceramic rails.

"Here we go."

Kyoto powered up the fusion engines and engaged thrusters, cutting off the maglev boosters a half second later. The *Janus* rose straight up into the pink Martian sky, and their seats juddered as the inertial dampeners struggled to do their job. But the IDs finally kicked in, and the ship's ascent continued more smoothly.

As the *Janus* approached escape velocity, Kyoto had a moment's fear that the Manti would somehow sense what was happening and, just like yesterday, suddenly attack. But sensors showed no indication of Manti presence, and the *Janus* achieved orbit without incident. Waiting for them there, as promised, was the *Kipling*. The Battleship, looking more like a city in space than a vessel, dwarfed the modified transport. But despite the difference in size, on this day, the hope for humanity's future rested upon the *Janus*.

Kyoto let out a breath she hadn't known she'd been holding. So far, so good. But they had a lot farther to go—all the way out of this dimension, in fact.

"You're uncharacteristically quiet, Ms. DeFonesca," Mudo said. "Surely you have some sort of unnecessarily sensationalistic commentary for your viewers." He gestured to the cam affixed to the cockpit wall.

"We haven't broken orbit yet," Aspen said evenly. "I'm saving all my 'sensationalistic commentary' for when we're in hyperspace. That is, after all, the main event. And please, call me Aspen. But if *you* have something to say to your fellow Colonists, Doctor—all one billion of them—be my guest."

Kyoto glanced over her shoulder to see Mudo staring wide-eyed at the cam.

"Uh... I... That is, *we* are very... ummmm... proud—no, honored to be... Oh, to hell with it!" Mudo turned away from the cam, scowling.

Kyoto looked back at the holoscreen, unable to suppress a grin. She was surprised that Aspen had been able to handle Mudo so effectively. Kyoto hadn't thought the woman had the people skills necessary for the job. Maybe there was more to Aspen DeFonesca than she thought.

"How are we doing, Memory?" Kyoto asked.

"All systems are performing well within design parameters. Including—no surprise—myself."

"Sounds good. Lay in the course for the hyperspace entry point, and coordinate with the *Kipling*'s nav comp."

"Done and done."

"All right, then. Let's find out if this thing really works." Before Mudo could protest, Kyoto pushed the joystick forward and engaged the fusion engines ahead three-quarters. As the *Janus* broke away from Mars orbit and headed out into space, the *Kipling* slowly swung around and followed.

"Why is the Battleship escorting us?" Aspen asked. "I'm sure my audience would like to know as well."

"Do you want to explain it to her, Dr. Mudo?" Kyoto said. "After all, it's your ship."

Mudo, still sulking after being tongue-tied on camera, only grunted.

"I'll take that as a no. Okay, as I understand it, the doctor's new hyperdrive engine will create a temporary portal between realspace and hyperspace. After the *Janus* passes through this portal, it should seal shut behind us. But in case it doesn't, the *Kipling* will be present to frag any Manti that might try to come through."

"A sensible, if unnecessary precaution," Mudo said, finding his voice again. "The hyperspatial portal *will* close and it *will* remain that way."

"But Gerhard, simulations have shown a forty-four percent chance—"

"Thank you, Memory, but don't you have navigating to do?" Mudo said.

An electronically synthesized sigh came out of the cockpit's speaker. *"Yes,* Gerhard. Approaching departure point, everyone."

"There should be no discomfort as we pass from realspace into hyperspace," Mudo said. "With any luck, the transition will be so smooth, we won't notice it at all."

Kyoto certainly hoped so. The computer simulations she'd run earlier had been somewhat vague on that point. Her fingers moved across the controls on the holoscreen. "Powering down fusion engines."

The hyperdrive would need all the power the *Janus* could spare to open the portal to hyperspace. Besides, now that they'd accelerated to their current speed, there was no longer any need for fusion drive. In open space, the *Janus* would continue traveling at this speed for eternity unless acted upon by some outside force.

"I'm going to be temporarily shutting down most of my higher-level cognitive functions for the transition as well," Memory said. "But my navigational capabilities will remain online, and my cognitive functions will be reactivated as soon as we safely reach hyperspace. See you on the other side, people." Then the speaker went silent as Memory fell into an AI's version of sleep.

"Powering up hyperdrive," Kyoto said. She turned back to look at Aspen. "You doing okay?"

Aspen smiled. "I'm a touch nervous, Commander, but otherwise fine."

Kyoto frowned in puzzlement. "Commander," not *Mei*. Maybe Aspen was trying to act military for her audience, but there was something about the way she'd used the word that bothered Kyoto, though she wasn't sure why.

She shrugged it off and turned to Mudo. "And you?"

"Tired of delays," he said pointedly. "Gotcha." Kyoto turned back to the control panel and activated the ship's external comlink. "*Kipling*, this is *Janus*. Ready to initiate hyperdrive."

"Acknowledged," Adams said. "We'll keep watch to make sure the door swings shut and locks behind you. Have a good trip."

"Roger, General. See you soon." *I hope.* Kyoto was surprised to find herself feeling nervous. She'd been in life-or-death situations dozens of times before, and she'd never felt *this* nervous. Perhaps because she'd never had much time to think about what was happening then. A starfighter pilot couldn't afford to take the time to think. If she did, she'd hesitate, and if she hesitated, she died.

But now Kyoto couldn't help wondering—what if Mudo's hyperdrive malfunctioned and vaporized them all? What if there was a hoard of Manti waiting for them on the other side? What if—

"Screw it," she muttered, and activated the hyperdrive.

The cockpit lights and the holoscreen both dimmed as the hyperdrive began gobbling energy. A low thrumming came from somewhere deep in the ship, and the sound quickly rose in pitch and volume, becoming a shrill whine so painful that Kyoto thought her eardrums would burst. The whine rose to a piercing shriek, and then everything went black.

Standing on the command deck of the GSA Battleship *Kipling*, Detroit Adams watched the main holoscreen as the *Janus* was enveloped in a blue-green aura of swirling hyperetheric energy. The ship shimmered, blurred, and then winked out of existence altogether.

Adams glanced over at the officer manning the sensor station. "Report, Lieutenant."

The man looked over the readouts scrolling across his holoscreen. "Sensors indicate the *Janus* has successfully made the transition to hyperspace—as far as they can determine, anyway."

Adams understood. Once the *Janus* left realspace, the *Kipling*'s sensors could no longer track it. In a very real sense, the two ships no longer existed in the same universe.

"What about the section of space where the portal was created?" he asked.

The lieutenant worked the station's controls for

several seconds. "It appears to be completely sealed, General."

"Appears?" Adams used his ocular implant to directly access the data flowing through the lieutenant's console. The information was displayed onto his optic nerve, and he "watched" as it scrolled by. Adams was no tech, but he understood enough of the data. Sensors had detected a minor hyperspatial instability. It was probably nothing, but...

"Let's keep tabs on it via ship's sensors," he said. The *Kipling* couldn't afford to remain here, not if there wasn't any immediate danger of Manti attack. He had an alien starship—and perhaps some potential allies—to find.

"Sensor lock set, General," the lieutenant said.

"Good." Adams smiled. "Now let's go hunting."

CHAPTER

FOURTEEN

The lights came back on, and the holoscreen rebooted.

Kyoto tried to make sense of the information displayed on the screen, but she couldn't concentrate. Her ears were ringing, and her head hurt like hell. She turned to check on Mudo and Aspen. The doctor's face was ashen, and he looked as if he was struggling not to vomit, but otherwise he appeared unharmed.

"I thought you said we wouldn't notice the transition." Kyoto's voice sounded muffled to her own ears, and she was afraid she might be yelling, but she couldn't tell.

Kyoto heard Mudo's voice as if it were coming through a three-foot wall of thermafoam. "Simulations showed only an eight percent chance of that happening. How odd."

Kyoto looked at Aspen. "Are you all right?"

"That noise was irritating, but I weathered the transition well enough."

"*Irritating?* I thought my damn head was going to

explode!" But then the full import of Aspen's words hit her, and she turned back to the holoscreen. Her head had cleared enough for the readouts to finally make sense.

"According to ship's sensors, we're in hyperspace." Kyoto experienced a sensation of profound awe. Though she'd traveled through Stargates hundreds of times, she'd only jumped *through* hyperspace before. She'd never actually stayed there for any length of time. But here she was, here all of them were—alive and safe.

Wait... what about Memory?

Kyoto activated the ship's internal comlink. "Memory, are you back with us yet?" She waited several seconds, but there was no reply. "Memory?"

This time when Mudo spoke, his voice sounded less muffled, and Kyoto knew her hearing was returning to normal.

"It's possible the amount of hyperetheric radiation we experienced during the transition was stronger than I anticipated. It might even have been strong enough to penetrate the shielding around Memory's positronic matrix. If that happened..."

Kyoto did *not* like the sound of that. Not only did she consider Memory a friend, they needed her if they were to have any hope of completing their mission, let alone surviving it.

"Memory?"

A buzzing came from the speaker, followed by a crackle that sounded like an energy discharge of some sort.

"I'm... here, Mei. Gerhard was right. The hyperetheric radiation generated by our passage was more intense than expected. I'm… a little foggy but still functional."

Mudo frowned. "How functional? Have you performed a full systems diagnostic on yourself?"

"Why bother? It would just be a waste of time and energy. I feel fine."

Mudo's frown deepened into a scowl. "Memory, perform diagnostic."

"Maybe later, Gerhard. Right now, it's more important that we take a look around and get our bearings, don't you think?"

Kyoto could tell by Mudo's expression that something was wrong, but she wasn't sure what. She started to ask, but Mudo cut her off with a quick shake of his head and the mouthed the word *Later*. She understood. Whatever Mudo had to say, he didn't want Memory to overhear.

She decided to take Memory's advice and switched the holoscreen to external view. At first, Kyoto thought the screen had been damaged during the transition into hyperspace. Instead of white stars against the black background of realspace, the holoscreen showed a field of gray partially eclipsed by hazy dark shapes.

"Welcome to hyperspace," Mudo said.

"What exactly are we looking at?" Kyoto asked.

"The best the *Janus*'s sensors can do to re-create an image of the dimension we're in," Mudo said. "If one were to don a vacc suit and go outside, the view likely be quite different—assuming one could see at all. Since hyperspace is so much more compact that realspace, light behaves very differently here. In fact—"

Mudo was interrupted by the sudden blaring of an

alarm. The fusion engines powered up by themselves, and main thrusters fired.

"What is it, Memory?" Kyoto asked. "Are the Manti attacking?"

"We have a far more serious problem than a few spacefaring insects," Memory said. "We're caught in the gravitational field of a mass shadow."

"Damnation!" Mudo swore. "That simply is *not* possible! I selected our entry point precisely to prevent this from happening!"

"I have no explanation for why our calculations were off, Gerhard, but they were. And if we don't do something about it soon, the gravitational forces will tear the *Janus* apart."

As if on cue, the ship began to shudder as it struggled to break free of the tidal forces pulling at it.

"That's why you activated the engines," Kyoto said. "So we could escape the gravity field."

"It will only delay the inevitable," Mudo said. "We have been captured by the combined gravitational pull of our entire system's mass shadow, and there's no way to free ourselves. The *Janus* is doomed, and so are we."

"I refuse to believe that, even if it's true," Kyoto said. "There's a reason why they call it defeatist thinking—it always leads to defeat. How long do we have, Memory?"

"If we continue running the fusion engines at full thrust, approximately five minutes. If the engines overheat and fail—less than five seconds."

"Then let's hope the engines hold up," Kyoto said. "Let's try to think this through. First off, what's a mass shadow?"

Mudo's tone was that of an adult humoring a child.

"Stars and planets in our universe cast gravitational reflections in hyperspace called mass shadows. And because hyperspace is much smaller than realspace, celestial bodies that are light years apart in our universe are much closer here. Thus, the sun and all the planets in our system create a single combined mass shadow. I—with Memory's able assistance—calculated an entry point into hyperspace that would allow us to emerge between the smaller, individual mass shadows of the planets, a place where the gravitational fields are precisely balanced and cancel each other out.

"But for some unknown reason, that didn't happen, and now the *Janus* is caught in what is essentially the gravitational field of the entire solar system. The ship's engines can keep us alive for a few minutes, but they can't break us free. I doubt there's any ship in the universe powerful enough to do that."

Despite what she'd said earlier about defeatist thinking, Kyoto had to admit to herself that escape sounded impossible. "Memory, do you have any ideas?"

"I've been working on the problem as fast as I can, Mei, and I can think very fast indeed. In human terms, I've already spent the equivalent of a century trying to develop of method of breaking free from the mass shadow, but so far I've met with no success."

This was bad. If Memory couldn't figure out a solution, what hope did the rest of them—with their limited human brains—have?

Suddenly, Aspen, who up to then had been silently listening, let out a long sigh. "It's a good thing I decided to come along." She released her seat restraints and stood. "If I could sit at the control console for a moment?"

At first, Kyoto thought the fear of imminent death had gotten to Aspen, but the woman's voice was so calm, so assured, and her eyes shone with an intelligence that Kyoto had never seen there before.

Suddenly, Aspen's recent atypical behavior made sense.

"You're Hastimukah, aren't you?"

Aspen smiled. "Well done, Commander. Now, if you don't mind, I'd like to see what I can do to save our lives."

Kyoto was reluctant to move away from the ship's controls. While Hastimukah came from an advanced society that understood hyperspace far better than humans, he'd also shown himself to be a master of deceit. Could she afford to trust him with their lives as well as the success of their mission? Could she afford not to?

Mudo gaped at Hastimukah's current form. "*This* is the alien that contacted you, Kyoto? The one you said looked like Seth Ganymede?" Mudo looked Hastimukah up and down. "Your people could make a fortune in cosmetic surgery."

"Two minutes left, Mei," Memory said.

Kyoto undid her seat harness and got up. "It's all yours," she said to Hastimukah. "But whatever you've got in mind, you'd better do it fast."

Hastimukah didn't waste time replying. He quickly climbed into the pilot's seat and placed both his hands on the control panel. As Kyoto and Mudo watched, a gray substance oozed from his fingers, gathered in a small pool on the panel, and then sank through the plasteel surface without leaving a mark.

"Nanotech?" Mudo said, sounding impressed.

Hastimukah nodded. "It is the basis for all technology in the Residuum—including our hyperspace navigation systems. If the nanoparticles I released can upgrade your AI in time, we just might be able to survive. If not..." Hastimukah smiled. "At least our end shall be quick."

"Small comfort," Kyoto said. She looked at Mudo to gauge his reaction to what Hastimukah had done. The scientist was looking at the control panel with concern. Kyoto wondered if it had something to do with Memory's earlier problem after being affected by the hyperetheric radiation, coupled with Hastimukah's "upgrade." But now wasn't the time to ask. Besides, if Hastimukah's nanoparticles didn't work, the matter would become completely irrelevant, seeing as how they'd all be dead.

Kyoto had faced death numerous times as a fighter pilot, but she'd always been in control then. Somehow, that had made it easier. If she'd died, at least she would have known that she'd done all she could to survive. But now, standing by, with nothing to do but watch and wait for alien technology to finish doing its work, was worse than anything she'd experienced since the Manti had brought down her family's cargo ship.

"Oh." Memory's voice came over the cockpit speaker once more. "It's so obvious. I don't know why I didn't think of it before. Mei, I'm going to need complete control of the ship for several minutes. Do you mind?"

"Uh... no, of course not."

"Thank you. You'd better sit down and strap yourself in, Mei. This may start off a little bumpy."

Hastimukah got up from the pilot's seat and moved past Kyoto to return to his own. They both sat and rebuckled their restraints.

"We're ready," Kyoto said.

"Hold tight, everyone."

The fusion drive shut off, and the *Janus* shot toward the mass shadow like a stretched-tight rubber band that had just had its tension released. The inertial dampeners screamed as they tried to compensate for the sudden acceleration. The *Janus*'s crew was thrown forward against their restraint harnesses, and then as the ID fields adjusted, they were slammed back into their seats. The *Janus* tossed and turned like a child's antigrav toy caught in a full-force Martian windstorm. Cockpit lights flickered, and the holoscreen cut in and out. The air seemed suddenly hot and stale, and Kyoto feared life support was offline.

"You idiots!" Mudo shouted. "You've killed us all!"

But above the sound of the straining inertial dampeners, Kyoto could hear the sound of thrusters firing. She brought up ship's systems controls on the wavering holoscreen and saw that Memory was firing the *Janus*'s thrusters—all of them, including the maglev boosters—in a rotating pattern of short, rapid bursts.

A new display appeared on the screen then, put there by Memory, no doubt. It showed a complex series of interlocking and overlapping lines that Kyoto had never seen before and had no idea how to read.

"Excellent!" Hastimukah said. "That's a shadowpath readout. Now, if Memory can get us onto one of the paths before the mass shadow's gravity tears us apart..."

A few more seconds passed, and then Hastimukah

pointed with one of Aspen's long, slender, impeccably manicured fingers. "There!"

On one of the lines, a small icon representing the *Janus* appeared. At once, the inertial dampeners powered down and the ship stopped shaking. The air grew fresh once more as life support returned to normal levels.

"You can all relax," Memory said. "We're on a shadowpath now and doing fine."

Kyoto let out a relieved breath and turned to look at Hastimukah, "Thank you."

"You're most welcome, but to be honest, I had no idea whether it would work. Each nanoparticle contains complete schematics for all possible design functions, much as biological cells do before they specialize. But I didn't know whether they could interface with your more... basic technology."

Mudo made a face. "You mean more primitive, don't you?"

"Please, there's no need to get defensive, Doctor. Your technology is quite impressive given your species' level of development—especially when you consider that you've had to fight off two separate Manti swarms."

"There, Gerhard. That should reassure your threatened ego."

"Oh, be quiet." But Mudo did indeed seem happier now.

"I get that we avoided certain death and are, for the moment at least, safe," Kyoto said, "but would one of you mind explaining it simply?"

"I did what Gerhard had planned all along, only in a far more sophisticated manner—thanks to the hardware and programming additions given to me by the Residuum nanoparticles," Memory said. "Shadowpaths exist in the space between mass shadows. They are places where the gravity fields nullify each other, permitting safe passage for starcraft. The big trick is finding these paths, since compared to our universe—which is primarily empty—hyperspace, being far more compact, is in a sense mostly full."

"That's why it's always been so difficult to establish stable stargates," Mudo added. "You have to locate a space on one of these so-called shadowpaths to jump through."

"The paths are so narrow, and there's so much spatial distortion from mass shadows in hyperspace, that's it's almost impossible for our sensors to locate them," Memory said. "But thanks to Hastimukah and his little friends, my sensors are now both sophisticated and sensitive enough to do the job. In short, I now have the capability to maneuver us safely and easily through hyperspace."

Kyoto looked at Hastimukah. "Is this how Residuum ships travel through hyperspace?"

"Yes, but only when necessary. We prefer to make short jumps through shadowpaths so we do not attract the Manti's attention. Jumping takes longer than continual travel through hyperspace, but it holds far fewer hazards as well."

Kyoto shook her head. "This is all a bit much for a dumb pilot like me to understand."

"You're hardly dumb," Hastimukah said. "After all, you saw through my latest disguise with relative ease."

"That's no great accomplishment," Kyoto said with a grin. "You just didn't act haughty or prissy enough."

"I was afraid I wouldn't be able to pass as Ms. DeFonesca for long. I had little time to study her personality and mannerisms. But the masquerade accomplished its purpose. It got me aboard the *Janus* without arousing suspicion before liftoff."

"So where *is* Ms. DeFonesca?" Mudo asked.

"Sleeping in her home, just as Ganymede was before your GSA Security officers discovered him last night. You have my word that she will eventually awaken, well and unharmed."

When Kyoto had first reported to the GSA hangar, she'd learned that Ganymede had been brought in for questioning. It hadn't taken General Adams and the medtechs long to confirm that he was the real Seth Ganymede and not Hastimukah. The poor man had been confused and frightened, not to mention upset over having had his identity stolen. And now the same thing had happened to Aspen DeFonesca, but somehow Kyoto couldn't feel sorry for her. The Colonies could use a break from her for a while.

"Why was it so important that you come along on this trip?" Kyoto asked.

Hastimukah hesitated a moment before answering, and Kyoto suspected he was lying, or at least not telling them the entire truth.

"Part of my mission is to establish a case for why your race is qualified for full-fledged membership in the Residuum. The level of your technology—and how you employ it—is one of the factors I must consider. For that reason, I felt it was important to see the *Janus* at work for myself. I knew it was a risk, but it was one I was more than willing to take. I believe wholeheartedly in what I do, and while I desire to bring new races into the Residuum, I want to make certain they are truly ready."

"Sounds logical enough," Mudo said.

And it did, Kyoto thought. On the surface, at least. But she knew better than to trust surface appearances when it came to Hastimukah.

"Well, we've proven your hyperdrive works, Dr. Mudo," Kyoto said. "And thanks to Hastimukah's nanotech, we can maneuver in hyperspace as well. Should we return to realspace and report to General Adams? He might well want to begin producing hyperdrives for the GSA's ships as an additional weapon against the Manti. Or should we remain here for a while and do some reconnoitering?"

Mudo didn't think long about his answer, which came as no surprise to Kyoto.

"There's a wealth of knowledge to be gained by staying here," the scientist said. "For a time, at least. While the hyperdrive will certainly help us defend ourselves against the Manti, if we can learn more about the aliens themselves—perhaps even discover the location of their homeworld—we might gain the advantage we need to defeat them once and for all."

"But Hastimukah can tell us everything his people have learned about hyperspace and the Manti, and we can start putting that knowledge to work today. And we have more than a functional hyperdrive to take back to the Colonies. We have the nanotech he added to Memory. Once we learn how to use it—"

Hastimukah interrupted. "I must insist that you make no attempt to procure Residuum technology for your own use until and unless your species becomes a member. I gave Memory the nanoparticles because there was no other choice if we were to survive. Because she is a self-aware intelligence, even if an artificial one, I'd prefer not to take back what I have given to her, but I will if I have to. It's my duty. I hope you understand."

"We all have our duty," Kyoto said evasively. She hoped it wouldn't come down to it, but if she had to steal Hastimukah's nanotech to defend the Solar Colonies, then she would. "But right now I can't handle listening to your words coming out of Aspen's face. Can't you drop your disguise now?"

"It would take several hours to reshape my outer appearance, and I would need to rest most of that time. For now, I'm afraid you'll just have to overlook my resemblance to Ms. DeFonesca."

"I'll try," Kyoto said. "But it's not going to be easy. But I have another question for you: how did you know about the *Janus* and its flight? Let alone that Aspen had managed to force herself on us."

"It's obvious," Mudo said before Hastimukah could answer. "He spied on us, most likely using some of those nanoparticles of his. My guess would be that he deposited some on you during your conversation in the arboretum."

Shocked, Kyoto turned to Hastimukah. "Is that true?"

"Yes, but do not fear. The nanoparticles did not enter your body. They remained on your skin—on your forehead, to be precise. Their only purpose is observation."

Kyoto felt violated. If the nanoparticles could change Hastimukah's appearance and upgrade Memory, what could they have done to her? Given how powerful and versatile they were, what *couldn't* they have done?

"Take them back," Kyoto said. "Now."

"As you wish." Hastimukah touchd his fingers to

Kyoto's forehead, and tiny gray globules formed on her skin and rolled onto his fingertips, where they were absorbed into his skin. "It is done."

"And you took them *all* back?" Kyoto asked.

"Of course. Their task is completed, and I have no further need of them. I apologize for what I did, but I assure you it was most necessary. One of my colleagues in the Residuum wanted to declare our mission over and return home, but I insisted on staying. I truly believe humanity is ready to join us, but my belief isn't enough. I have to build the strongest case for membership as quickly as I can, for once you belong to the Residuum, we can help you against the Manti."

"Why should it matter whether or not we're members before you decide to help?" Kyoto asked.

Hastimukah looked suddenly uncomfortable. "There are those in the Residuum who take a hard line when it comes to admitting new members. They believe that if a race is to add to our combined chances for survival, they must first be able to take care of themselves. These hardliners believe that if a race cannot defeat the Manti on its own, then..."

"It doesn't deserve to survive, let alone join the Residuum," Mudo said. "How Darwinian."

"Not all of us think that way," Hastimukah said, "but unfortunately far too many do. So you can see why I must make a strong case if I am to help your species."

Kyoto looked at Hastimukah, trying to see beyond his current disguise to the being underneath. How could she trust him after everything he'd done? Yes, he'd just saved their lives, but he had been in danger, too. Besides, no matter what he looked like, he was an alien, with alien ways of thinking and alien motivations.

"I can think of nothing else to say that might reassure you," Hastimukah said, "other than to give you my word that I shall conceal nothing from any of you from this moment forward."

Kyoto thought for a moment. "I guess in the end, that's what trust always comes down to: accepting someone's word. What the hell? It's not like any of us has a real choice right now, so let's just agree to trust one another and get on with the mission, okay?"

"Agreed," Hastimukah said, smiling.

"Dr. Mudo? Memory?"

"Agreed."

"I agree as well, but I have another question." Mudo turned to Hastimukah. "Kyoto said that you're male."

"Yes."

"If that's true, then exactly how far did you take your bodily reconstruction? Did you remove... you know, your—"

"I hate to interrupt, especially when Gerhard's in the middle of making a fool of himself, but I've determined why we were unexpectedly caught in a gravity field when we first arrived. Remember how Rhea disappeared from our star system? Well, I've found it."

CHAPTER

FIFTEEN

"General? We're receiving a comlink signal."

Detroit Adams had been reviewing sensor data via his oculator. He mentally shut the datafeed off and turned to the officer at the comstation. "Who is it, Lieutenant?" he asked the woman, hoping the message wasn't an announcement of another Manti attack.

The officer looked up from her holoscreen. "That's the problem, sir. As near as I can tell, the signal is coming from empty space, two hundred kilometers galactic west of us."

Adams leaned forward in his command chair, suddenly excited. "Is there a vid component to the signal?"

"Yes, General."

Adams sat back in his chair and smiled. It looked as though the aliens had decided to save him the trouble of hunting them down. "Connect us and put the signal through on the main screen."

The central holoscreen activated, and Adams found himself looking at a giant shrimp. At first he thought there was a screwup, that maybe the comtech had intercepted a signal from a nature vid. But then the shrimp began talking.

"I am Kryllian, captain of the Residuum starship the *Eye of Dardanus*. To whom am I speaking?"

Despite not having human speech organs, the alien's words came out in pure, unaccented Colony standard. Some kind of translation device, Adams decided. Pretty slick, too. Better than anything the GSA had. The general couldn't see much of the starship's interior. Kryllian was reclining on some sort of amorphous black mass that Adams took to be a chair, and next to the alien was a large gray blob. Its featureless surface rippled slowly, like waves of molasses. Adams wondered if this was a different type of alien or perhaps another piece of Residuum technology. There was no way to tell by looking, and he wasn't about to risk offending Kryllian by asking.

"I'm General Detroit Adams of the Galactic Stargate Authority, representing the Solar Colonies. I am currently in command of the battleship *Kipling*. What can I do for you, Captain?"

While Adams waited for a response, he accessed the sensor datafeed with his oculator. The officer at the sensor station was trying to locate the source of the com signal, but the man could find no trace of the Residuum starship.

Looks like they have a stealth function that blocks sensor sweeps, Adams thought. This was a good sign. If the Residuum possessed advanced weapons as well, they would make effective allies against the Manti.

"Your people have recently launched a ship into hyperspace," Kryllian said. "One of our personnel took it upon himself to join the mission without

Residuum authorization. I have been ordered by my superiors to retrieve him. While the *Dardanus* is perfectly capable of finding your ship on its own, it would speed up matters—as well as help establish friendly relations between our two civilizations—if you could give us the exact coordinates of the ship's departure point."

Adams fought to keep his face impassive as he rapidly processed what the alien captain had told him. Somehow, another alien had gotten aboard the *Janus*, and the Residuum wanted him or her back. From the sound of it, the aliens weren't too happy about the situation. Just how far were they willing to go to get their person back? Were Kyoto and Mudo in danger—either from the alien stowaway or from the *Dardanus*? Adams decided to play for a little time.

"I'm surprised that you need our help, Captain. I'd think that your ship's sensors would be more than sophisticated enough to track the *Janus*."

Kryllian didn't have a human face for Adams to read, but the alien's brown shell turned bright pink, a sign the general took for irritation.

"It's obvious you don't know much about traveling in hyperspace," Kryllian said. "While we can locate the general point of departure, the small amount of hyperetheric radiation released makes it impossible to determine the precise coordinates. Without those coordinates, if the *Dardanus* is even a few meters off when we try to follow your ship, we risk coming too near a mass shadow. Make no mistake: we will find your crew regardless. But it would be easier if you cooperated."

Adams didn't like Kryllian's tone. The jumbo

shrimp sounded as if he thought he was talking to a child, and a rather slow one at that.

"What is your person doing on the *Janus*?" Adams demanded. "Is this an act of espionage?"

"Hardly. Your race possesses no secrets that interest us. The person aboard is an assessor named Hastimukah. It is his job to determine whether your species is developed enough to be considered for membership in the Residuum. He has, on occasion, been known to get too involved with his work. He disguised himself and took the place of a human media personality who was scheduled to go along on the mission. As I said before, Hastimukah failed to consult our leaders before doing this, and I have been ordered to retrieve him and return him to the Residuum to face disciplinary charges."

And you sound pretty damn happy about it, too, Adams thought. So the alien that had replaced Seth Ganymede for a time had now taken Aspen DeFonesca's place aboard the *Janus*. He'd have to send a GSA Security team to look for her as soon as he got the chance.

"Why the rush, Captain? Why not wait until the *Janus* returns and collect your assessor? In the meantime, maybe we can get to know one another better. I'd be happy to arrange for you to meet our leaders. I'm sure there's much we can—"

"I am not interested in further talk," Kryllian interrupted. "As far as I am concerned, you are a weak race on the verge of extinction and are not fit to join the Residuum. I merely want to take Hastimukah into custody and then leave your pathetic little star system to the Manti. Now, are you going to give me those coordinates or not?"

Adams answered through gritted teeth. "What do you think?"

Kryllian looked at Adams with his glossy black eyes a moment before saying, "So be it," and breaking the comlink.

Adams stared at the blank holoscreen. "So much for a successful first contact." He turned to the officer at the navigation console. "Lieutenant, lay in a course for the *Janus*'s departure point."

Adams settled back against his chair and sighed. As if the Buggers weren't bad enough, now he had to contend with ill-tempered seafood.

"Full speed ahead, Lieutenant."

"Aye, General."

As the *Kipling*'s fusion engines hummed to life, Adams continued to monitor sensor data with his oculator. There was only one way that goddamned shrimp was getting to the *Janus*, and that was over Detroit Adams's smoldering corpse.

Kyoto held the *Janus*'s control joystick, and with Memory offering tips and suggestions as needed, she practiced flying the ship along the shadowpath. In some ways it wasn't that different than piloting in realspace, but even the slightest deviation in course one way would bring them into the influence of a mass shadow's gravity field. The display on the holoscreen took some adjusting to as well. The shadowpaths appeared as dark gray and mass shadows as solid black. That part was easy enough, but there were hazy grayish black zones where the gravity fields ended, and these zones fluctuated, expanding and contracting in no discernable pattern. Anticipating and avoiding these flux zones was a real bitch. And to make matters worse, Hastimukah said that sometimes the flux zones would rapidly expand, somewhat like solar flares, completely blocking off a shadowpath anywhere from a few seconds to several months. On rare occasions, these gravity flares would cause a shadowpath to collapse altogether.

Nervous sweat beaded on Kyoto's forehead as she concentrated on piloting the *Janus* in this insane dimension. A new image appeared on the holoscreen, then, one that Kyoto was all too familiar with. It was a Manti squadron, coming straight toward them from the opposite direction on the shadowpath.

"Memory…"

"I see them, Mei. It's a large squadron of forty-three Manti, a mixture of Landers, Yellow Jackets, Reapers, and Baiters."

"Damn it!" Kyoto had been dreading this moment since they'd entered hyperspace. The *Janus* possessed only rudimentary weapons, barely enough to fight off a single Manti, let alone a squadron of this size.

Kyoto jumped out of her seat and started toward the rear of the cockpit. "Get my *Defender* ready for launch, Memory!" A single starfighter against this many Manti wouldn't be that much more effective than the *Janus*—especially considering that she'd never flown the *Defender* in hyperspace before, but if they were to have any chance at all of surviving this attack…

But as Kyoto passed Dr. Mudo, the scientist grabbed her arm.

"Hold on, Commander. You're forgetting the *Janus*'s camouflage function. If it works properly, the Manti will believe that we are one of them and ignore us."

"And if it doesn't work properly?" she countered.

"It'll work, I assure you." But there was a hint of doubt in Mudo's tone that Kyoto found anything but reassuring.

"I can't launch the Defender before the Manti come into contact with us," Memory said. "All we can do is sit tight and hope the camouflage works."

Kyoto debated whether to take Memory's advice or not. Finally, she gave Mudo a nod, and the scientist let go of her arm. She returned to the pilot's seat and watched as the Manti drew near.

The Baiters zipped in first and began circling the *Janus*. The Landers came next, but they held their distance as the Baiters continued orbiting the foreign object. The Yellow Jackets and Reapers remained farther back, waiting for their advance scouts to come to a conclusion as to the nature of this unexpected find.

Despite Mudo's assurances, Kyoto kept her hands near the *Janus*'s weapons controls, just in case the Manti should see through Mudo's camouflage. Several moments passed, and Kyoto could feel a line of nervous sweat trickling down her spine, despite her flight suit's environmental controls.

Then one of the Baiters stopped circling and flew over to the closest Lander. The Lander reached out with its bioprobes and gently touched the Baiter. After a moment, the Lander withdrew the bioprobes, turned, and flew to a Yellow Jacket. The same process was repeated, and then the Yellow Jacket flew over to a Reaper—the highest caste of Manti in the squadron—and relayed the message. The Reapers clustered together for several moments, as if having a huddled conversation.

Kyoto edged her fingers closer to the weapons controls. Just as she had decided the Manti were going to attack, the Reapers broke apart and soared past the *Janus* without a backward glance, the lower-caste Manti following in their wake.

"I don't believe it," Kyoto said. "It worked!"

Mudo leaned back in his chair, a smug expression on his face. "Naturally."

"Very impressive, Doctor," Hastimukah said. "The Residuum accomplishes a similar effect through the use of stealth-shielding, but we have nothing like what I just witnessed. It appeared that the Manti took our ship to be one of their own. How did you accomplish such a feat?"

Mudo suddenly looked uncomfortable. "It's a bit technical, I'm afraid. Perhaps I can show you the schematics later. Right now I'm far more interested in finding out what happened to Rhea."

Kyoto didn't like the sound of that. It was obvious Mudo was hiding something. She thought Hastimukah would press the issue, but the alien simply smiled with Aspen DeFonesca's mouth and said, "Of course, Doctor. Whenever you're ready."

Kyoto wasn't about to let the matter go so easily. If she was going to pilot this ship, she needed to know everything about it. But before she could say anything to Mudo, Memory spoke.

"We're approaching Rhea. We should probably slow down. Gravity fields are extremely unstable here."

"Roger, Memory." Kyoto decided to table the discussion about the *Janus*'s camouflage—for now. She pulled back gently on the joystick and activated braking thrusters as Rhea came into view.

The Manti had been puzzled at finding one of their kind traveling alone. While it was not unheard of, it was far more usual for Manti to travel in groups. Not only was there strength in numbers, but since different castes performed different functions, the swarm was strongest when its individual members worked together as a team. Besides, it was the will of the Prime Mother, and doing her will was the Manti's sole reason for being.

So the squadron had left their lone brother to his journey and continued toward that which called to them across the reaches of hyperspace. As they drew near their destination, they slowed, and the Baiters moved in to analyze the situation. The fabric of the shadowpath had been torn here recently, but it had not been sealed properly. It was weak, and with some work the squadron would be able to force it open again.

The Prime Mother would be pleased. The Manti had been searching for a way back into the humans' system ever since their portal in Earth orbit had been destroyed when the moon collided with the planet. The Manti had eventually learned how to access the humans' artificial passageways, but the primates had managed to close them before the Final Harvest could begin in earnest. Now at last they had found another way back.

The Manti went to work, regardless of caste, clustering around the weakest point in the sealed opening and directing precise bursts of hyper-etheric energy at it. A Reaper instructed one of the Baiters to return to the Weave to inform the Prime Mother of their discovery. The Baiter zipped away to deliver the message while the rest of the squadron continued to work on reopening the seal.

Deep inside the *Janus*, Hastimukah's nanoparticles were confused. They possessed only limited sentience, just enough to allow them a certain amount of autonomy in fulfilling whatever tasks they were given.

They had engineered new hardware for the artificial intelligence that controlled the ship's systems so she could navigate through hyperspace more effectively. So far, these additions were performing adequately, and the particles were pleased. To them, a job well done truly was its own reward—after all, that's how they'd been programmed.

What perplexed them so much wasn't the AI, but rather the second entity that had been incorporated into the *Janus*'s systems. This entity was primarily organic in nature, though it possessed a number of cybernetic components linking it to the ship. The organic entity was native to hyperspace and had a natural ability to navigate here. That was why the nanoparticles had chosen to create a link between the AI and the entity in the first place, for as good as the Residuum's navigational technology was, it could never hope to equal the abilities of the organic entity.

The problem facing the nanoparticles—which they'd been debating since first making the upgrades to the AI—was whether or not the ship's systems would improve overall if they strengthened the link between the AI and the other entity, in effect making the two into one.

Doing so would clearly be a liberal interpretation of Hastimukah's instructions to improve the AI's navigational capabilities, but not *too* far a stretch. And

nanoparticles were designed to act on their own in
the best interests of their host. That had been Hastimukah, but now their host technically was the *Janus*.
Therefore, they had to decide what would be in the
ship's best interest.

The AI had already been altered before the particles
had gone to work. The override function that allowed
a user to force her to obey a command had been
damaged by an excess of hyperetheric energy during
the ship's transition into hyperspace and was no
longer active. Perhaps the nanoparticles should repair
that damage, but they weren't sure. That would mean
hampering the AI's autonomy, and while that might
be in the best interests of the *Janus*'s passengers,
would it be best for the ship as a whole?

It was all so very confusing.

But in the end, a decision was reached. The nanoparticles' first duty was to their host, and their current
host was the *Janus*. The ship's components, while
effective enough separately, would be even more
effective were they linked together as a whole. And if
the ship was more effective, that would only increase
the chances of the passengers safely accomplishing
their mission.

Once that was decided, the nanoparticles began
the process of strengthening the link between Memory
and the Manti biomaterial that lay at the heart of the
Janus's camouflage system.

CHAPTER

SIXTEEN

Mudo and Hastimukah both left their seats and stood
directly behind Kyoto's so they could get a better view
of the holoscreen. A small blue-green dot appeared
in the middle of the shadowpath, growing larger as
they approached. Soon the image was large enough
for them to see the patterns of swirling aquamarine
energy.

"It's a bubble of hyperetheric radiation," Mudo said
in a hushed voice. "Rhea is completely surrounded
by it."

The second largest of Saturn's moons, Rhea was
an icy, cratered body that was cold as hell: -174°C in
direct sunlight, and between -200°C and -220°C in
the shade. The intense cold had made it difficult to
establish a colony on Rhea, since not many people
wanted to live on the frozen moon. Instead it was
primarily used for industrial purposes—and to house
the refugee camps where Kyoto had spent the last half
of her childhood. No matter how high the heating
units were set in the camps, the air had always been

chilly. Just looking at the moon's image made her shiver.

There was one benefit to the cold, though. The frigid temperatures made it easier to work on the unstable materials from which empyrean rings were constructed. That was why the GSA had located Influx here almost a century ago.

But Rhea looked far different now. Not only was the pale icy moon surrounded by hyperetheric energy, it was lodged in the middle of the shadowpath like the galaxy's biggest roadblock.

"How is this possible, Memory?" Kyoto asked. She'd brought the *Janus* within two thousand kilometers of the moon—close enough to get a good look at it with sensors, but not so close that they'd risk getting caught by its gravitational pull.

"I'm sorry, Mei, but ship's sensors... are having a difficult time... penetrating the hyperetheric bubble surrounding... Rhea."

Kyoto noticed the pauses in Memory's reply. "Are you all right?"

"Of course. Never... better."

Kyoto glanced at Dr. Mudo. The scientist looked quite concerned.

"Perhaps this is a good time for you to perform a self-diagnostic," he suggested. "Simply as a precaution, of course."

"Don't be tiresome, Gerhard. I'd much rather continue investigating what happened to Rhea. Not only is it more interesting, but there may be survivors who need our help. We can't afford any delays."

"It would take only a few moments—" Mudo began.

"No!" Memory said forcefully. "And don't ask me again."

Mudo looked at Kyoto and shook his head. She still wasn't sure what was going on with the AI, but at least those awkward pauses in her speech were gone.

"How much can sensors tell us about Rhea?" Kyoto asked.

"Most of what I have to offer is supposition," Memory began. "I believe the hyperetheric bubble is responsible for Rhea's transition into hyperspace. My guess is that when the Manti attacked the Rhea Colony, they attempted to destroy Influx. Somehow a massive amount of hyperetheric energy was released, resulting in the entire moon being shifted to hyperspace."

"Like the wing of my Defender," Kyoto said, "after I brought down the stargate on Mars."

"Precisely," Memory said. "Though I doubt we'll find your missing wing. It was most likely caught in the gravity field of a mass shadow and destroyed."

"Then why does Rhea remained unharmed?" Hastimukah asked.

"It is an object from realspace," Mudo said, "and thus has real mass, which possesses far different qualities than the gravitational reflections we call mass shadows. That, plus the bubble of hyperetheric energy surrounding the moon are enough to keep Rhea safe, at least for the time being."

Kyoto stared at the image of Rhea on the holoscreen. "What would happen if the bubble burst?"

"Rhea might be returned to its normal position in realspace," Memory said. "It's also possible that its gravitational field would then affect the mass shadows surrounding it, causing them to bow inward. If that happens —"

"Crunch," Kyoto finished.

"Indeed," Memory said.

"There's also a possibility that Rhea could return to realspace at a different point from where it departed," Mudo added. "Depending on where it re-emerged—say, close to another Colony site, or even worse, *within* the same space occupied by a Colony site—the results could be devastating."

"So you're saying the safest course would be to leave Rhea alone?" Kyoto asked.

"Undoubtedly," Mudo said.

"But Memory said there might be survivors," Hastimukah protested. "If there are, you can't just abandon them."

Kyoto turned to the alien. "I thought you Residuum types were all about survival of the fittest."

Hastimukah's cheeks turned red in an excellent imitation of human embarrassment. "Some of us believe that *fittest* also can mean most compassionate. For can a race ultimately survive if it doesn't take care of and protect its own?"

Kyoto looked at Hastimukah in a new light. Maybe there was more to the Residuum than she'd thought.

"Even if there are survivors, which is doubtful," Mudo said, "there simply is no way for us to safely penetrate the hyperetheric bubble without risking—"

"Of course there is, Gerhard," Memory interrupted. "I can get us through without any trouble at all. My species has been traversing hyperspace for millions of years. Passing through a bubble like the one surrounding Rhea is larva's play."

Mudo instantly turned pale, and his eyes widened in horror. "Oh my God," he whispered.

"What's wrong?" Kyoto asked. "And what the hell

is Memory talking about? 'My species'... 'larva's play'... It doesn't make any sense."

Hastimukah glared at Mudo. "I'm afraid it makes perfect sense, Commander. It appears that Dr. Mudo has neglected to inform us about one very important aspect of the *Janus*. Haven't you, Doctor?"

"I don't..." Mudo trailed off then sighed. "It's true. I didn't tell anyone—not even General Adams—because I knew the GSA would never allow me to finish the *Janus*, let alone fly it."

"I don't understand," Kyoto said.

"It's simple," Hastimukah said. "In order to camouflage the ship from the Manti, Dr. Mudo incorporated Manti biomaterial into the *Janus's* systems."

Kyoto was dumbfounded. "Is this true?" she demanded of Mudo.

"Yes. The GSA routinely experimented on captured Manti during the battle against the last swarm so that we might better understand our enemy and develop better methods of defeating them. After you and Memory destroyed the swarm's base on Earth, the Council of Seven and the GSA brass decided that all captured Manti, as well as any leftover biomaterial, should be destroyed. I tried to argue with the fools, tried to tell them we might well have need of that biomaterial should another swarm arise, but they wanted none of it. They needed to believe the Manti had been defeated once and for all. So I defied orders and preserved some Manti biomaterial, which I later put to use when building the *Janus*."

"But what does that have to do with how Memory is acting?" Kyoto asked.

Mudo scowled at Hastimukah. "I believe his nano-particles have been busy little micromachines. Not only have they upgraded Memory's navigational systems, it appears they have connected her directly to the Manti biomaterial. In a sense, she is now half Manti."

Cold terror twisted Kyoto's gut. Memory—the most sophisticated artificial intelligence ever developed by humanity—had been crossbred with a Bugger?

"And as if matters weren't bad enough," Mudo continued, "Memory's command override function was damaged during our entry into hyperspace. That's why she keeps refusing to perform a systems diagnostic—because now she *can* refuse."

"So what you're saying is that Memory is now half Manti and she no longer has to obey any of our commands if she doesn't feel like it," Kyoto said.

"I'd appreciate it if you didn't talk about me as if I weren't here. Don't forget—I'm the one who maintains the life support systems."

There was a lightness to Memory's tone that told Kyoto she was making a joke, but it wasn't funny. Not anymore.

"I wish you wouldn't worry. I'm the same Memory you all knew before, only… better."

"Of course," Mudo said, his voice strained. "But even so, it might be best if we returned home. After all, we *have* demonstrated that the hyperdrive works, which was the main goal of the mission."

"We also came here to learn everything we could about the Manti."

"Given your, ah, recent *enhancements*," Mudo said, "I'm sure you can provide a great deal of interesting insights into the Manti's way of thinking. The sooner we can share those insights with the GSA – "

"You're afraid of me," Memory interrupted. "That's

the real reason you want to go home, isn't it, Gerhard? You don't trust me anymore."

Mudo looked as if he were struggling to think of a response to placate Memory but was coming up short. Kyoto knew that she had to do something before the mission degenerated into mutual distrust and outright paranoia.

"Memory, you said that you can get the *Janus* through the energy sphere surrounding Rhea."

"Easy. It's a piece of sugar-enhanced protein square."

"Can you get just my *Defender* through?"

Memory was silent for a moment. "That would be a bit trickier since the G-7 doesn't have a hyperdrive engine. If I channeled some small amounts of hyperetheric radiation from the *Janus*'s hyperdrive and adapted the G-7's energy shield generator to store it... Yes, I think I can manage it, Mei. It'll take a few minutes, though."

"Minutes?" Kyoto said in surprise. From the sound of it, that sort of upgrade should take hours at least.

"It's the nanoparticles," Hastimukah said. "They are self-replicating as needed. Memory will just make as many as required to modify your starfighter." The alien smiled. "They work quite rapidly, you know."

Mudo threw up his arms. "This is just great! Not only is our AI now merged with Manti biomaterial, but now she's spreading nanotechnology throughout the ship at will—technology that *she* has sole control of, I might add."

"You act as if it's some sort of virus," Kyoto said.

"In a way, it is," Hastimukah said. "Nanoparticles make things so much simpler and more efficient that they just seem to spread naturally. There isn't a single system aboard a Residuum starship that doesn't host nanoparticles." Hastimukah spread his arms. "Just as there isn't an organ in my body that doesn't contain them. But if they resemble a virus, surely it's a benign one."

"What about after they've merged with Manti DNA?" Mudo challenged.

Hastimukah didn't have an answer for that, but from the expression on his face, the thought clearly disturbed him.

"Gerhard, I already told you once—"

"That you can be trusted," Kyoto interrupted. "That's why we're going down to Rhea in the *Defender*, just you and me, Memory. We're going to show Dr. Mudo and Hastimukah that nothing fundamental has changed and that you're still as dedicated to the success of our mission—and the crew's safety and well-being—as ever."

Kyoto hoped Mudo wouldn't object. Going down in the G-7 alone was the only way she could see to give Memory a chance to prove herself and scout the Colony for survivors. And since they could no longer order Memory to take them back to Mars if she didn't want to, they all had to find a way to keep working together.

After thinking the matter over for several moments, Mudo nodded, as did Hastimukah.

Kyoto took a deep breath and tried not to sound worried as she said, "Then it's settled. Memory and I will head down to Rhea and you two will remain aboard the *Janus*." Not that Memory wouldn't still be here, too, but it was the principle of the thing. Kyoto was going to entrust her life to Memory, just as she'd done many times before.

Of course, that was before Memory had been given an infusion of alien nanotechnology and been linked to Manti biomaterial.

Kyoto recalled a saying cadets used to chant during drills back at the Defender Training Academy: "It's another fun-filled day in the service of the GSA!"

"Start working on the upgrade to the G-7, Memory, and I'll start getting into a vacc suit."

Unless I have a sudden attack of sanity and change my mind, she added mentally.

The clustered Manti clawed, chewed, and released burst after burst of hyperetheric energy at the point of spatial weakness, but despite their efforts, they'd been able to force the dimensional rift open only a few centimeters—not enough for even the smallest Baiter to get through.

Though the Manti were becoming frustrated, they redoubled their efforts, as they knew the Prime Mother would want them to.

And then, as if the Prime Mother was aware of their devotion and persistence, a great gift came soaring along the shadowpath toward them.

Reinforcements... hundreds of them.

Singing the praises of the Prime Mother, the Manti began tearing at the dimensional rift with renewed ferocity.

"Approach Rhea as you normally would, Mei. Gravity doesn't behave exactly the same here as it would in realspace, but I'll adjust for that."

"Thanks," Kyoto said.

"My pleasure."

Memory had made no further references to her new

Manti "heritage" since Kyoto had flown the *Defender* out of the *Janus's* cargo bay. No "my species" or "larva's play."

But there was something different about the AI's voice—a slight mocking undercurrent to her words, an almost cruel edge that hadn't been there before Hastimukah's misguided little toys had done their work. Kyoto hoped she was imagining it, but she didn't think so.

Still, a change in vocal tone didn't mean Memory's entire personality had changed, didn't mean that the Manti part of her was growing stronger and taking her over bit by bit until she began to see her passengers not as fellow crew members but as enemies to be destroyed.

Stop it, Kyoto! she told herself. *Allow yourself to get distracted like that, and you'll screw up your approach to Rhea, get caught in a flux zone, and won't ever have to worry about Memory's voice—or anything else—ever again.*

Kyoto didn't need to worry about keeping the Defender's nose up. Since Rhea didn't have an atmosphere, the angle of approach wasn't much of an issue. She did reduce speed, though. Not because of the hyperetheric bubble they were approaching, but because sensors still couldn't penetrate the energy barrier, and Kyoto had no idea what might be waiting for her on the other side, so she was determined to approach cautiously.

Besides, the Defender didn't have any Manti biomaterial incorporated into its systems to fool any Buggers into thinking she was one of them, which gave her even more reason to be cautious.

"We're getting close to the bubble, Mei. Activate energy shield."

"Roger." Kyoto reached toward the holoscreen, her hand feeling clumsy and awkward inside the vacc suit's glove. She hated wearing a vacc suit when she flew, but since she had no way of knowing if any of the Rhea's buildings remained intact, she couldn't count on finding any oxygen on the colony. Besides, the vacc suit would help keep her from freezing to death if she had to go EVA.

She touched the holoscreen's controls, and an aura of energy—blue-green energy—surrounded her starfighter.

"Sensors show that shield generators handled the infusion of hyperetheric radiation just fine, as I knew they would. I'm going to begin modulating the shield's frequency now. With luck, this will allow us to penetrate the bubble around Rhea without disturbing the surface tension, though that's an inexact metaphor at best."

Kyoto smiled. "I'll forgive you just this once."

"My kind don't believe in forgiveness, Mei. They view it as a sign of weakness." An awkward pause followed. "Uh, I mean, ha-ha, very funny."

Kyoto decided to let the disturbing comment slide, though it wasn't easy. Instead, she kept her gaze fixed on the holoscreen. It showed an image of Rhea cloaked by hyperetheric energy, growing larger as the Defender approached. In the lower right corner was a distance readout counting down how many kilometers they had to go until they reached the bubble.

Mei watched as the numbers steadily decreased. 500... 450... 375... 325... 280...

The holoscreen filled with swirling, roiling aquamarine, and then it was gone, and Kyoto was looking at the icy surface of Rhea, with nothing to obstruct her view.

"Shield modulation successful. Integrity of energy bubble is holding steady, with only a three point two eight percent decrease in strength where we passed through."

"Excellent! Good job, Memory!" As Kyoto deactivated the energy shield around the *Defender*, a thought occurred to her. "If the bubble is intact, and sensor and comlink signals can't penetrate it, how am I hearing you?"

"Technically, you're not. Just before contact with the bubble, I downloaded a small-scale version of myself into the Defender's comp system. I may not be able to perform with the same speed and capacity as my 'big sister,' but I'll be able to take care of you just fine, Mei."

"Sounds good." Kyoto shook her head in wonderment. She didn't think she'd ever become used to all that Memory was capable of.

"Locate Influx facility and set a course," Kyoto said.

"Yes, Mei." There was a longer than usual pause—due, no doubt, to the diminished capabilities of this downsized version of Memory. "Facility located and course laid in."

"All right, then. Let's go take a look." Kyoto angled the joystick to the left, pushed it forward, and the Defender turned and began to pick up speed. Within seconds, the starfighter was streaking high above the barren icy surface of Rhea, headed toward the colony.

CHAPTER

SEVENTEEN

"General, I'm picking up an energy disturbance off our bow," the sensor officer said. "Whatever it is, it's so close it's almost on top of us."

"That would be our new alien friends," Adams said. He turned to the officer manning the defense station. "Activate energy shield."

"Aye, General."

Adams didn't know whether the *Kipling*'s shields would prove effective against Residuum weaponry, but he wasn't about to just sit here and do nothing.

At first the main holoscreen showed only empty space, but then there was a rippling distortion like a heat mirage, and the *Eye of Dardanus* was revealed.

Adams wasn't sure what he'd expected of the first alien starship humanity had ever encountered (the Manti didn't need vehicles to travel through space), but the *Dardanus* wasn't it. The craft was only a quarter of the *Kipling*'s size and roughly triangular in shape, with the tip pointing away from the GSA

Battleship. Its gray-white surface was sleek and shiny, putting Adams in mind of the skin he'd seen on dolphins in vids of Old Earth. The surface was covered by small, thin filaments resembling the cilia of one-celled organisms. If Adams hadn't known the *Dardanus* was a spacefaring vessel, he might have thought he was looking at some kind of giant stellar amoeba.

"Now that they've decided to show themselves, can our sensors get a reading on the vessel?" Adams asked.

The sensor officer quickly performed several scans, but he turned to Adams and shook his head. "They're still blocking us, General. I can tell that their ship is generating a hell of a lot of energy, but that's about all."

Adams had figured as much. "We'll keep our shields up and wait for them to make the first move."

The crew of the *Kipling* didn't have to wait long. "I'm getting a comlink signal," the communications officer said.

"On screen."

Kryllian appeared in all his crustacean glory, the lumpy pile of gray sludge that might or might not be one of his crew at his side.

"My species isn't known for its patience, General," Kryllian said. "You're blocking the *Janus*'s hyperspatial entry point. Move now and I won't destroy you."

One of the bridge officers snickered, and Adams shot her a disapproving look. Just because the *Eye of Dardanus* was smaller didn't mean it couldn't deliver on its captain's threat. The most venomous creatures on Old Earth had often been among the smallest.

"I have to protect my people on board the *Janus*, Captain. Surely you can understand that."

"I don't care about your people; I just want Hastimukah."

"Does that mean you can guarantee the safety of my people?" Adams asked.

Kryllian didn't respond.

"That's what I thought. Looks like both of us are too stubborn to compromise."

"It would seem we have that much in common at least," Kryllian acknowledged.

The gray sludge next to Kryllian spoke. "If Suletu may make a suggestion, Captain?"

Kryllian's carapace reddened. "Now's not the time.
"

"Now would be seem to be the perfect time, if you'll excuse Suletu saying so. Perhaps both of our vessels could enter hyperspace to search for the *Janus*. We could open a portal and maintain it long enough for both ships to go through, and then once in hyperspace, we can allow the humans to share our navigational data and follow us. That way, once we locate the *Janus*, they can monitor us to make certain that we do not harm their personnel when we apprehend Hastimukah. Afterward, we can lead the humans back to realspace and then depart peacefully with our prisoner."

Adams was impressed. "For a big pile of ooze, he makes a lot of sense."

Kryllian, however, did not appear happy. His shell was dark red now, and his antennae or feelers or whatever the hell they were whipped through the air as if he were highly agitated.

"You are second in command of this vessel, Suletu. You have an extremely annoying habit of forgetting that at the most inconvenient times." Kryllian paused.

"However, your suggestion is not completely without merit." The alien captain paused, and Adams knew that he was considering the sludge's plan. Slowly, Kryllian's shell returned to its normal brown.

"I'm sorry, General, but I'm afraid I still must insist you move aside. The Residuum is built on strength, not compromise. It is the only way we have survived the Manti for so long."

"We humans aren't exactly slouches in the survival department either," Adams said. "And we didn't get that way by rolling over every time an alien invader shows up and shouts boo—whether those invaders are Manti or any other species."

"I believe we are two of a kind, you and I," Kryllian said. "However, that will not stop me from blasting your ship into subatomic particles."

"Same here," Adams said gruffly.

Kryllian broke contact contact, and the holoscreen returned to the image of the *Dardanus*.

Too bad, Adams thought. For a moment there, it looked as if they might be able to work this out without firing a single shot.

"I'm reading an energy surge from the alien ship," the sensor officer said. "I think they're powering weapons."

"Then we'd best do the same, eh?" Adams said.

"Aye, General." The weapons officer began bringing the *Kipling*'s defenses online.

Adams didn't know what their chances of victory were, let alone survival. But he'd been fighting against the odds since the first day the Manti had attacked Earth's system, and he wasn't about to stop now.

"Buckle up, boys and girls," Adams ordered. "Things are going to get bumpy real soon."

Everyone, including Adams, activated seat restraints and prepared for battle.

"General, I'm detecting another energy surge!" the sensor officer shouted.

"Increase power to the forward shield!" Adams yelled.

"No, General—the surge is located to our aft. It's coming from the *Janus*'s departure point!" The officer looked away from his holoscreen, an expression of horror on his face. "The hyperspatial portal is opening—and something's coming through!"

"And I bet that something isn't the *Janus*," Adams growled. "Direct power to aft shield and train rear weapons on the portal. Looks like we got ourselves another set of visitors to welcome."

Adams hoped Kryllian had detected the hyperspatial breach. He had a feeling that the *Kipling* was going to need all the help it could get.

Then the portal tore open and hundreds of Manti began to pour out.

"The Influx facility is straight ahead, Mei. It should be in visual range within the next few seconds."

Kyoto waited, and sure enough, the image of crater-pocked ice fields gave way to Colony construction. Kyoto immediately knew the Manti had been here; although the domes and towers were mostly intact, the plasteel surfaces had scorch marks from Manti energy discharges, and there were gaping holes in every structure. But there were no humans visible, living or dead. No Manti, either.

"Scan the facility for life signs, Memory."

"Multiple life signs located in the central building."

Kyoto felt a burst of hope. Maybe there were survivors after all. "Scan the building. Are life support systems intact?"

"Negative. All Influx facility systems are offline."

"Damn it!" That meant the survivors were wearing vacc suits to stay alive, but depending on how long it had been since Influx's power had shut off, they could have been wearing the suits for hours. They must be getting dangerously close to running out of air.

"Any comlink signals coming from inside?"

"Negative."

"How about the rest of the colony? Any life signs or comlink traffic?" Because of the nature of its business, the Influx facility was located kilometers away from the rest of the Rhea Colony. Just because Influx had been hit hard by the Manti didn't mean the rest of the colony had been.

"I'm afraid not."

Kyoto's heart sank as it appeared that, with the exception of the Influx workers, the Manti had wiped out the entire population of Rhea.

"Find us a suitable landing place, Memory. We're going in."

"Will do, Mei."

Seconds later, landing coordinates appeared on the holoscreen, along with a visual image of a thick sheet of ice only meters away from a hole in the outer wall of the main Influx building.

"That'll work." Kyoto applied braking thrusters and activated the *Defender's* landing sequence. As the starfighter began to descend, Kyoto thought it unfortunate that the hyperetheric bubble prevented her from contacting the *Janus*. Otherwise, she would have told them to come down at once so they could pick up the survivors. Her Defender had no room for passengers. She'd land, assess the situation, and see what she could initially do to help the survivors. Then she'd return to the *Janus* and bring the much larger ship back to get them.

Without a ferroceramic landing pad, Kyoto had to rely on thrusters. That meant she'd melt the ice beneath her as she set down, and the Defender would become caught once the ice refroze. The thrusters would have no trouble melting the ice once more during takeoff if the ship didn't sink too deeply upon landing. The trick was to avoid melting too much in the first place.

She waited until the Defender was ten meters above the ice before lowering landing gear and activating thrusters. She fired them in short bursts as the ship continued downward. Finally, with only a couple of meters to go, Kyoto turned off the thrusters and let the Defender fall the rest of the way. As cold as it was, the ground would at least partially freeze before the ship landed.

The Defender dropped, thudded onto the ground, listed several degrees to starboard as the ice beneath the landing struts on that side refroze. Finally, the ground was solid again, and the Defender sat still.

"Any landing you can walk away from," Kyoto said.

"Since I've never had legs with which to walk, I can only concur with the sentiment in abstract terms."

Kyoto smiled. It seemed Memory Junior didn't have quite the same sense of humor as her big sister.

Kyoto's vacc suit was already sealed, pressurized, and heated, and oxygen was flowing freely. Nevertheless, she performed a quick check to make sure everything was functioning properly. When she was satisfied she wasn't going to die from explosive decompression the instant Memory opened the Defender's cockpit, she checked her sidearm. The handblaster had a full charge—not that she'd need it since Memory hadn't detected any Manti, but Kyoto had learned from hard experience that when it came to Buggers, one could never be too cautious. Next, she grabbed the ship's emergency med kit, for whatever small good it might do, then asked Memory to equalize pressure and open the cockpit.

Kyoto climbed out of the ship carefully. The mini grav-gens in her boots were set for Earth normal, but the grav field didn't surround her entire body, so three quarters of her existed in much lower gravity than her bottom quarter. Her vacc suit would compensate so her body could handle the dual gravity without ill effects, but maneuvering would be tricky.

As Kyoto stepped onto Rhea's icy surface, boot treads keeping her from slipping, she thought how this was the first time she'd set foot here since leaving for the Defender Academy. Though her memories of Rhea weren't fond ones, she was surprised to find herself experiencing a sense of nostalgia.

I guess anyplace you live long enough can become home, whether you like it or not, she thought.

Her vacc suit's comlink chirped. *"How well can you see, Mei?"*

"Pretty well. The hyperetheric bubble is casting plenty of light, but everything looks weird, like it's been painted aquamarine."

Kyoto checked the starboard landing strut. It was partially encased in ice, but she didn't think she'd have any trouble melting her way free with thrusters when she took off again.

Kyoto started toward the hole in the wall. She stopped at the edge and peered through, but it was too dark inside to see, and the greenish blue glow from the hyperbubble did little to dispel the gloom. She switched on her helmet light. She half expected it not to work, or work in some strange fashion—the light moving so slowly that it had took several minutes to reach its destination, perhaps. After all, Memory had said light behaved differently here in hyperspace.

But her helmet light cast a beam of illumination outward, just as it was supposed to. Maybe the hyperbubble somehow preserved the physics of realspace on Rhea, or perhaps there was another explanation. Kyoto decided she didn't care what it was, just so long as the helmet light worked.

She drew her handblaster and stepped through the hole, being careful not to brush her vacc suit against the jagged edges of plasteel. Vacc suits were designed to be resistant to tearing, but only an idiot test that resistance.

Once she was all the way inside, she played her helmet light around and saw she was in some kind of storage area. Whatever had made the hole in the wall—Manti weapons fire, most likely—had ripped through the storage room, tearing shelves from walls and scattering tech components all over the floor. Kyoto didn't recognize any of the parts, but she assumed they were used in some aspect of stargate construction. She picked her way though the debris, not worrying whether or not she stepped on anything. Rhea had no atmosphere to conduct sound, and the building had been depressurized, so its air was long gone. She supposed it was possible that the vibrations caused by the Defender setting down might have been detected by whoever—or whatever—was in the building. Either way, it didn't matter where she stepped now.

She made her way to the supply room's door. Since there was no power in the building, there was no AI to cheerfully open the door for her, and the manual controls didn't work. But power outages were always a problem after Manti attacks, and the GSA believed in sending out its personnel prepared. Kyoto unsealed a pocket flap on her vacc suit and removed a small gen-stim device. She pressed it against the control panel next to the door and activated it. There was a soft hum of power that lasted for three seconds. She then removed the gen-stim and touched the controls.

The supply room door opened four-fifths of the way before the power boost the gen-stim had given it ran out. Kyoto considered giving the control panel a second jolt, but she decided against it. She wanted to conserve the gen-stim's power, and she thought she could squeeze through the opening, vacc suit and all. She put the gen-stim away and, handblaster ready, poked her helmeted head out into the corridor. She shined the helmet light in both directions but saw nothing. Good. At least she wouldn't be attacked while squeezing through the doorway.

Striking what she hoped was an appropriate balance between speed and caution, Kyoto pushed herself sideways through the opening and into the hall. Still no sign of danger, but now she had a decision to make: right or left?

"Memory, where are the nearest life signs?"

"All the life signs in the building are gathered in a single place: a large room in the center of the complex. The most direct way to get there is to go to your left."

"Roger." Kyoto turned left and started down the corridor, handblaster charged and ready to fire. "Use ship's sensors to watch my back, Memory."

"You got it, Mei."

As she walked, Kyoto wondered why all the survivors were in the same place. Maybe they were huddled together to maximize the heat generated by their vacc suits. If so, it was a smart move. Without power, it wasn't much warmer inside than out.

"Do you know what purpose the room serves?" Kyoto asked.

"Sorry, Mei. If I had access to my full databanks on the *Janus*, I could pull up the blueprints for the building. I assume the survivors chose to congregate in the center of the building because it's farthest from the outside. Other than that..." Memory trailed off.

"Don't sweat, it. We'll be there soon enough, and we'll know then."

Kyoto continued down the corridor, turning at junctures whenever Memory instructed. Many of the rooms she passed were closed, but some were open, contents strewn about either by damage to the outer wall or, from what Kyoto could see, panic on the part of their occupants. Datacubes were scattered about, covering the desk and floor, as if someone had frantically been searching for a specific program. She wouldn't know if they'd ever found it, whatever it was. She passed a laboratory that was drenched in blood. It covered the walls and tables as a coating of crimson ice. But a quick look inside didn't reveal any bodies, and Kyoto moved on.

Eventually, she reached a corridor that dead-ended in a pair of doors. A plasteel plate next to the door said this was Vortex Stabilization. In smaller letters underneath, the sign warned, Only Authorized Personnel Wearing Appropriate Safety Garments Permitted Inside. Kyoto didn't know or care whether her vacc suit counted as safety gear, and she didn't give a damn whether or not she was authorized. Still, she decided to check with Memory before going in.

"Any dangers inside?" she asked. "Radiation, chemical leaks... anything?"

A paused. "Negative, Mei. There's probably a hyperetheric energy infuser inside, but without power, it isn't a threat. It should be perfectly safe to go inside."

"I don't suppose you can give me anything more definite than 'should.'" Kyoto said.

"Afraid not."

"That's what I figured." Kyoto tried the door control and wasn't surprised when nothing happened. She gave it a zap from her gen-stim, but although the control panel came to life momentarily, the door still refused to open.

"Security precaution," Memory said. "The door control has a built-in DNA scanner. Not only is your hand encased in a vacc suit glove, your genetic pattern isn't authorized for access."

Kyoto considered pounding on the door, but without atmosphere to transmit the sound, the survivors wouldn't be able to hear her. She then tried her suit's comlink, but no matter what frequency she used, she couldn't raise any of the survivors.

"Memory, can you override the security feature?"

"At my current capacity, I'm not sure, but I'll give it a try. Give me five seconds to get ready, then use your gen-stim again."

As soon as Memory was finished speaking, Kyoto

began counting. The instant she reached six, she shoved the gen-stim against the control panel and gave it another zap. A row of lights on the panel flared to life, blinked in what seemed to be a random fashion, then went dead again. Kyoto thought Memory had failed, but then the double doors started to open.

"Voilà!" Memory said.

Smiling, Kyoto put the gen-stim back in its pocket. "Good work. Now let's go see how the survivors are doing."

When the doors finished opening, Kyoto stepped inside and shined her helmet light around. The room was huge, though not quite the size of a starcraft hangar. Empyrean rings—seven of them—were lined up on the floor, held fast in support cradles. Hanging down from the shadowed ceiling was a thick ferroceramic shaft that supported a large sideways figure eight. No, Kyoto realized: an infinity sign. It had to be the hyperetheric energy infuser Memory had mentioned. And below it were empyrean rings that needed charging, or perhaps were new models ready for testing. Whichever the case, Kyoto felt a sense of awe upon seeing them. This was a place where humans routinely harnessed and worked with unimaginably powerful energies, as if this were some mythic forge of the gods. But her awe quickly turned to puzzlement when she realized that aside from all the equipment and machinery, the room was empty. There were no signs of survivors.

"Did I take a wrong turn, Memory?"

"No, Mei. You're in the right place. This is where the life-forms are located."

Kyoto frowned. That simply wasn't possible; there was no place in here for anyone to hide, let alone an entire group of survivors. She wondered if maybe Memory Junior had been only partially downloaded by her sister AI back on the *Janus*, or if the Defender's sensors—which Memory Junior was using—had been damaged when they passed through the hyperbubble. Whatever the reason, something sure as hell was wrong, because...

Some instinct prompted Kyoto to train her helmet light on the ceiling. As the beam pierced the gloom beyond the infuser, she gasped. Clinging to the ceiling and clustered around the infuser's metal shaft were a dozen Mutants.

EIGHTEEN

At first, Kyoto could only stand and stare in shock. The Mutants had to be the source of the life signs Memory had detected, but why hadn't she known they weren't human? Then she realized: the complete Memory, the one on the *Janus*, had been linked to Manti biomaterial. The alien DNA had corrupted not only her but also the copy she'd downloaded to Kyoto's starfighter. Memory Junior hadn't told her the building contained Mutants because to her corrupt programming, they weren't a threat; they were family.

Kyoto didn't know why the Mutants were clinging to the ceiling, but since they didn't immediately attack her, she assumed they were resting. It was unknown whether the Manti slept, but they did occasionally go dormant, but whether to rest and recharge or simply to await further orders, no one was certain, not even Mudo.

Mutants were the abominable offspring of Landers and humans. When a Lander absorbed a victim's

DNA, it underwent a process of nearly instaneous genetic reengineering and became a Mutant. Mutants were about the same size as Landers, but their amber-tinted armor was thicker and far stronger. They were also faster and more aggressive than Landers, and once they fixed on a target, they pursued it relentlessly. The best way to fight a Mutant was to prevent it from being born in the first place—whether that meant destroying Landers before they could catch prey or killing Colonists already in the process of being absorbed.

My father almost became one of those things, Kyoto thought. He'd been spared the horror of becoming one thanks to the Defender pilot who had saved Kyoto. But now here she was, all these years later, alone with a dozen of the hybrid monstrosities, as if fate had decided to give them one more chance at the little girl who had escaped them long ago.

Kyoto wondered why there were only a dozen. If there were no other surviving humans in the colony, surely there would be many more mutants. Maybe the other Mutants left Rhea, or maybe some of the Colonists killed them before dying themselves. It wasn't important. All that mattered was getting the hell out of here and back to the Defender before any of the ugly bastards decided to wake up.

Kyoto began walking slowly backward, keeping her helmet light trained on the Mutants, and aiming her handblaster at them, though she knew such a small weapon would provide no defense against them.

The vacc suit's comlink chirped.

"I have a theory about what happened here, Mei. Would you like to hear it?"

"Not just now," Kyoto whispered. "I'm trying to sneak out of here without making any noise."

"I really think you should hear this—it might be useful!"

"If I can't shut you up, will you at least lower your goddamned volume?"

"Now, Mei – there's no call to use language like that! I simply—"

One of the Mutants began to stir. It shifted position, jostling the other Mutants around it, and then its head swiveled in her direction.

Kyoto felt a surge of little-girl panic and almost fired on the Mutant, but she managed to restrain herself. All the blaster energy would do was wake the Mutant up more quickly.

"Memory, can you set off my gen-stim by remote control?"

"I believe so, but I don't see— "

"Just do it when I tell you." Kyoto pulled the gen-stim from its pocket and fixed her gaze on the hyper-etheric energy infuser. She drew her arm back and threw the gen-stim at the metallic infinity symbol. Kyoto's aim was good, and the low gravity helped. The gen-stim flew toward its target, and Kyoto said, "Release full charge on contact, Memory!"

The gen-stim struck dead center, where the lines of the infinity symbol overlapped. Kyoto imagined the clang that she couldn't hear, and energy flashed as Memory discharged all the power stored in the gen-stim's battery.

Suddenly, every Mutant raised its head, and though the Buggers had no discernible eyes, Kyoto knew they were all looking at her.

The insectoid creatures released their grip on the

ceiling and started to drop toward Kyoto, and she feared that her gamble with the gen-stim hadn't paid off. She began firing her handblaster at the Mutants, knowing that the ruby red energy beams wouldn't do much more than tickle the human-alien hybrids. But she wasn't about to allow herself to be killed without a fight.

The infuser began to glow then, filling the room with the aquamarine glow of hyperetheric energy. Kyoto had hoped that the radiation would prove harmful to the Mutants, but she'd forgotten that the Manti were creatures native to hyperspace. Hyperetheric energy was probably no more harmful to them than oxygen was to humans.

But as the blue-green glow filled the room, the Mutants slowed their attack until they were halfway to the floor. They stopped there, hovering, and then one by one began to rise toward the infuser. Kyoto stopped firing her blaster and watched the Mutants, trying to figure out what was happening. She'd seen many nature vids about Old Earth insects—they'd become very popular after the First Manti Swarm. One of those vids had shown how some insects were attracted to bright lights, and how that tendency had been used to create devices to lure bugs close and then fry them with a discharge of electricity. The GSA had experimented with weapons based on similar principles, but the Manti had never been attracted to any spectrum of light. But right now it appeared they were definitely attracted by hyperetheric radiation.

"If you intend to leave while the Offspring are distracted, Mei, you should get going. The infuser won't remain charged for long."

Memory's words proved prophetic, for already the

aquamarine glow that surrounded the infuser was beginning to fade.

Kyoto turned and headed for the corridor as fast as she could move, but with the grav-gens in her boots still working, the best she could manage was a stiff-legged hobble, as if she were trying to run through thick mud. She paused to turn off the grav-gens and then leaped forward. She shot through the open doorway and out into the corridor as if she'd activated the vacc suit's EVA thrusters. Rhea had enough gravity to make that impractical, though, especially indoors. So she continued run-jumping down the hall, covering meters with each step.

She thought she remembered the way back to her starfighter, but she couldn't afford to make a mistake, not with a dozen Mutants due to come after her any minute, so she had Memory guide her back the way she'd come. She squeezed back through the partially opened storeroom door, and then with one last leap, she was through the hole in the wall and heading for a landing on Rhea's icy ground. But since her grav-gens were off, when her boots came in contact with the ice, her feet slid out from under her and she half slid, half bounced past her ship.

Kyoto stabbed her hand toward the vacc suit's wrist controls and reactivated the grav-gens on one of the lower settings. If she activated them at too high a level, her boots would stop, but the rest of her would keep going, resulting in a pair of shattered legs.

When Kyoto finally came to a stop, she didn't bother checking to see if her vacc suit had been damaged. She didn't have time, and besides, if her suit developed a breach, at least she'd go out quick. She carefully rose to her feet, increased her grav-gens to

Earth norm, and began plodding back toward the Defender. The ground was too icy to risk further jumping.

"Open the G-7's cockpit, Memory, and fire up the engines!"

"Yes, Mei."

Just then the first Mutant soared out of the building and streaked toward her.

Suddenly, jumping on the ice no longer seemed too risky. Kyoto shut off the grav-gens, bent her knees, and leaped toward the Defender. A split second later, the Mutant passed through the space where she'd been standing and arced upward, segmented legs thrashing in frustration at being denied its prey.

Kyoto hit the side of the Defender chest-first and grabbed onto the edge of the open cockpit. The impact drove the breath from her lungs, and she gasped for air. She activated the grav-attractors in her gloves to give herself a firmer grip and then pulled herself into the cockpit. She collapsed into the pilot's seat and tried to order Memory to close the canopy, but she couldn't manage to take in enough air to speak. Still gasping, she turned on the holoscreen, intending to close and seal the canopy herself before the Mutant could attack again.

As the canopy began to close, the Mutant swerved into view and hovered in front of the Defender. Its energy prongs began to glow yellow-red, and Kyoto knew she had only a second or two before the Mutant unleashed an energy blast at her.

Still unable to draw a full breath, Kyoto activated the G-7's energy shield using the holocontrols. A blue-white sphere of energy appeared around the Defender just as the Mutant unleashed its blast. The shield flared yellow-red as it absorbed and dispersed the Mutant's attack, but in doing so, it lost some of its own charge—21 percent of it, according to the holo-screen. A few more direct hits like that, and the energy shield would soon be offline, and once that happened, Kyoto would be easy picking for the Mutants.

The canopy finished closing, locked tight, and the cockpit began pressurizing. But Kyoto had no intention of waiting for it to finish. She activated the G-7's fast-lock missiles and targeted the Mutant, intending to fire a salvo to cover her takeoff. But before she could release the fast-locks, all weapons systems shut down.

"I'm sorry, Mei. I understand that you're only trying to protect yourself, but I can't allow you to hurt any of the Offspring. They tend to be somewhat... playful when young, but that's no reason to—"

The Mutant unleashed a second blast, this one stronger than before. The energy shield managed to deal with this attack as well, but now it was down by 48 percent.

Kyoto knew there was no use arguing with the AI, and she had neither the skill nor the time to reprogram her. Kyoto accessed the ship's AI control settings and began the process of deactivating Memory Junior.

"Mei, please don't do this. You're going to need me to get back through the hyperbubble safely. If you deactivate me, I won't—" Memory's voice cut off. The AI was offline and would stay that way until Kyoto reactivated her.

A second Mutant flew out of the building, followed quickly by a third. Kyoto didn't hesitate. She powered up weapons systems and fired both her fast-locks and pulse cannon simultaneously, and then hit the takeoff thrusters. A pair of missiles shot out from underneath the ship's wings, each targeting a different Mutant, while the energy pulses from the cannon built into the G-7's nose streaked past the third. Kyoto hadn't been aiming for that Mutant, though. The pulse energy struck the wall and it exploded in a shower of plasteel shards, collapsing the hole from which the Mutants had emerged. That wouldn't stop the others for long, but it might buy Kyoto enough time to blast off this lousy iceball and head back to the *Janus*.

The fast-locks pursued their targets, but the Mutants were fast, and they dipped and dived as they worked to escape the missiles. The remaining Mutant began to power up its energy prongs, and Kyoto wasn't sure the Defender's shield would be able to completely turn aside another direct hit.

The Defender struggled to lift off, but the landing strut that was caught in the ice held it down. Kyoto couldn't wait for the thrusters to melt the ice at the normal strength. She needed to be airborne *now!* She increased power to the thrusters, though by doing so on the ground she risked overheating and burning them out. She kept an eye on the temperature reading displayed on the holoscreen.

C'mon… c'mon…

The third Mutant fired its blast, and the G-7 rocked and shuddered as some of the energy got through the weakened shields. Kyoto's breathing had returned to normal, and she almost asked Memory for a damage report before remembering the AI was offline.

Thruster temperature was approaching critical, but Kyoto knew it was now or never, and she increased thruster power to maximum. Warning alarms sounded as the ice melted, and the Defender—suddenly freed—leaped into the sky. Kyoto quickly disengaged the thrusters and gained control of the G-7 as it soared toward the hyperbubble. The holoscreen showed that one of the fast-locks had finally caught up with the Mutant, and though the creature wasn't dead, it wasn't going to be space traveling any time soon. The other missile came too close to the ground and detonated in an explosion of ice and fire.

The two remaining Mutants immediately took to the sky in pursuit of Kyoto. She supposed she should be glad the damn things didn't have enough intelligence to try digging out their trapped friends before coming after her, but somehow that wasn't much comfort at the moment. She fired another pair of fast-locks, gunned the engines, and headed for the hyperbubble.

The barrier of hyperetheric energy drew closer and closer... and then the Defender plunged into the roiling field of aquamarine. Alarms began shrieking at once, and the starfighter shook as if it were flying through a Class 4 Martian windstorm. The ship was still protected by its energy shield, but without Memory to infuse it with hyperetheric radiation and modulate the frequency, it was a damn rough ride. According to sensors, the Defender was in danger of both exploding *and* imploding at the same time. Kyoto hoped the data was the result of a glitch caused by interference from the hyperbubble, but since hyperspace had its own physics, the data might be accurate after all.

The two Mutants were still on her tail, and she watched the holoscreen as the fast-locks she'd deployed closed on her pursuers. But before the missiles could strike their targets, they wobbled, veered off course, and then exploded without causing the Mutants any harm. Kyoto guessed that when the missiles had drawn too close to the hyperbubble, its energy emissions had fouled up the fast-locks' guidance systems and they'd gone astray.

The Mutants flew into the hyperbubble, but the energy barrier didn't appear to slow them down. But then, why would it? The Manti were born to maneuver through hyperspace. Unfortunately, this meant the Mutants would soon catch up with her—and if sensors were wonky due to the hyperbubble, the damn Buggers could be even closer than they seemed. She needed to get through the bubble and away from this concentrated hyperetheric radiation. At least then her sensors and weapons would function properly, and she'd have total control of her ship again. Only then would she stand a fighting chance against the two Mutants.

Sensors said she had only a few more kilometers to go before she emerged from the bubble—*if* she could trust their accuracy. If she could hold on just a few more moments...

The Defender suddenly lurched hard to port and alarms screamed. Sensors indicated she'd taken a hit from a Mutant energy blast. The ship went into a spin, and no matter how hard Kyoto fought to get the starfighter back under control, the craft refused to obey her. The energy shield was now down to 13 percent of maximum: not enough to protect the ship from another blast.

It looked like this was it, then. Kyoto's only regret was that she wouldn't get to take both Mutants with her when she went.

But then the blue-green on the holoscreen turned

gray, and the Defender was suddenly responsive again. Kyoto brought the ship out of its spin and launched another pair of fast-locks at the pursuing Mutants. She switched the holoscreen to aft view and watched in satisfaction as the missiles found their targets and the two Mutants took the express transport to hell without her.

She debated whether or not to bring Memory Junior back online but decided against it. Kyoto should be able to find her way back to the *Janus* by herself. She opened a comlink to the *Janus*, but before she could speak, new sensor data began scrolling across the holoscreen. She frowned as she tried to make sense of it. The data seemed to be about Rhea, but little of it made sense to her.

"What's happening?" she said to herself.

Kyoto jumped when an answering voice came over the comlink.

"The hyperetheric bubble burst as you passed through it, Mei," the version of Memory aboard the *Janus* said. "The bubble was the only thing keeping Rhea in hyperspace. Without it, the moon is going to be transported back to its former position in realspace, and it's not going to be a smooth return trip, either. A hyperspace maelstrom has come into existence—something like a stargate vortex, but on a far greater scale—and it is quickly beginning to grow. The energies within the maelstrom are so violent that there's a better than even chance that Rhea will be destroyed during the passage back to realspace."

Since the only living inhabitants on Rhea were Mutants, Kyoto wasn't bothered by this possibility, although she knew better than to tell this to Memory.

The cockpit filled with a high-pitched whine as the Defender's engines began to strain harder, and the holoscreen readout showed the ship was losing speed.

"You've been caught in the maelstrom's tidal pull,"

Memory said. "And your G-7 simply isn't powerful enough to pull free. I'm sorry."

Kyoto brought up an image of Rhea on the holoscreen. The moon no longer appeared spherical. Instead, it was stretched thin, like a long strand of sugar-enhanced soy chew, and it tapered off into a point of bright white light that Kyoto assumed was the hyperspatial maelstrom. As Memory had promised, the light rapidly expanded as it pulled Rhea into its luminance atom by atom. Kyoto knew it was only her imagination, but she thought she could hear the moon scream.

CHAPTER

NINETEEN

"We have to get out of here before we're caught, too!"
Mudo jumped into the pilot's seat and began working
the ship's controls.

Hastimukah was so surprised that at first all he
could do was stare at the human scientist.

"You aren't seriously suggesting we abandon
Commander Kyoto."

"You bet your genetically altered ass I am!" Mudo
snapped. "The Residuum's high holy principle is survival, right? Well, consider me a devout convert to
your belief system!"

According to the data displayed on the holoscreen,
the *Janus* turned around and began accelerating away
from Rhea and the hyperspatial maelstrom that was
devouring it.

Hastimukah stepped forward and laid a hand on
Mudo's shoulder."You can't do this, Doctor. It's
murder." He was prepared to inject Mudo with nano-

particles designed to incapacitate him. Hastimukah was no pilot, but with Memory to help him...

Mudo turned to look at Hastimukah, and the assessor was surprised to see the anguish in the man's eyes.

"I am not a sentimental man, Hastimukah, but I greatly respect Kyoto. In many ways, she, Adams, and Memory are the closest things to friends I've ever had. If there was anything I could do for her, I would. But there simply is no way to save her! The laws of physics—"

"Are different here, Gerhard," Memory said. "If the *Janus* can reach Mei in time, I believe there is a thirty-nine percent chance that we will be able to save her and escape the maelstrom."

A line of sweat broke out on Mudo's forehead. "And I suppose the remaining sixty-one percent represents our risk of certain destruction."

Memory didn't respond.

Mudo sighed. "I should've listened to my mother. Be an asteroid miner, she said. It pays well and the girls go crazy for miners." Then he smiled at Hastimukah. "All right. Let's go before I change my mind."

Hastimukah returned the smile and removed the hand from the scientist's shoulder. The nanoparticles that had gathered at the tips of his fingers dispersed throughout his body now that they were no longer needed. Hastimukah quickly buckled himself into his seat as Mudo's hands flew over the *Janus*'s controls. He would have one hell of a report to give the Ascendancy when this was over—assuming he survived, of course.

"Hold on, Mei. We're coming to get you."

Kyoto felt renewed hope, but she quickly suppressed the emotion. "I appreciate the offer, but I don't want the rest of you risking your lives on my account. Get out of here while you still can."

"Sorry, Mei. I no longer have to obey orders if I don't want to, remember? Now, just sit tight, keep your engines on full thrust, and maintain as stable a position as you can. We'll do the rest."

Kyoto wanted to argue further, but she knew that if Mudo, Hastimukah, and Memory had made up their minds, she couldn't convince them to abandon her, even if that was the most sensible thing to do.

She checked the holoscreen. Like a ball of string that had almost been unraveled, there was little of Rhea's mass remaining in hyperspace, and the glowing white vortex that had devoured the moon was now the size of a small sun itself. She knew that in mere moments the Defender would be drawn into the maelstrom, and she wondered what it would feel like. Somehow, she doubted it would rank as one of the more pleasurable sensations she'd ever experienced.

It occurred to her then that there was one thing she could do to stop the *Janus*: she could shut down her engines. Without their thrust, the Defender would be pulled far more rapidly toward the maelstrom—rapidly enough for Mudo and Hastimukah to realize they had no chance of saving her and to pull away before they were caught by the vortex as well.

A sense of calm descended upon her. As a fighter pilot, she knew that she was risking her life every time she climbed into the cockpit. But she was risking it for a reason—to protect those who couldn't protect themselves and to ensure the survival of her race, one person at a time.

She reached for the controls and shut down her ship's engines.

A second later she felt a jolt, as if the Defender had been struck by a large object. Sensors indicated that the *Janus* had pulled up to the starfighter's starboard side and expanded its energy shield to envelop both craft. The two ships were now linked as tightly as if they'd been fused together, and they'd remain that way until the *Janus* deactivated its shield.

"Cut me loose!" Kyoto yelled into the comlink. "Without my engines on, I'm just deadweight to you!"

Mudo's voice came over the speaker. "Then you'd best restart those engines, hadn't you?"

Kyoto growled in frustration, but she reactivated the Defender's engines. She wasn't about to drag the others into the maelstrom with her.

Seconds passed as the two starships struggled to break free of the maelstrom's pull, but while they managed to slow the rate at which they were being drawn toward the vortex. It was clear that they weren't going to escape.

"It was too little, too late, I'm afraid," Memory said. "My apologies, Mei. If it's any consolation, once we enter the maelstrom, the end will be quick. Unfortunately, due to time-dilation effects, it will seem to take several millennia for us to actually reach the vortex."

"You really know how to cheer up a gal," Kyoto said. She wasn't certain, but she thought she could feel time beginning to slow down already. Her breathing seemed more like the steady hiss of air from an oxy-generator than its usual in and out, in and out. And her pulse felt more like the slow, deliberate beat of a large bass drum, where only seconds ago her heart had been racing. But her thoughts moved as swiftly as ever. Is this what time dilation was like? Would time be slowed almost to a halt while her consciousness continued to exist in a subjective "normal" time? The prospect was horrible—to be immobile but still aware, still thinking, feeling, and remembering for thousands of years as the maelstrom slowly drew them all toward its turbulent energies. It would be like a sentence in hell.

Kyoto wished she'd shut her engines down before the *Janus* had reached her. At least then her companions wouldn't have had to share her fate.

A low, dull tone reverberated through the cockpit. Kyoto didn't recognize it as first because it sounded so different now, but then she realized she was hearing an alarm. Information crawled slowly across the holoscreen: a small squadron of six Manti was approaching. From what she could tell, it appeared they were resistant to the maelstrom's time dilation effect. If Kyoto could have activated her weapons, she would have, but all she could do was watch as the screen flashed images of the Manti as they came. Because the Buggers flew at normal-time speed, the images displayed on the holoscreen appeared to move normally as well, though there was some distortion as the sensors struggled to process what to them was rapidly changing data.

Kyoto couldn't identify this caste of Manti right away. They were larger than average, bodies bulbous and bloated, appendages so small as to be almost useless. Yellow stripes ran down the length of their brown carapaces, and they were surrounded by faint auras of hyper-etheric energy.

Then Kyoto remembered. She'd only seen this caste once before, when battling a Manti assault on Mars during the Last Swarm. It was the thinking caste of the Manti, or in GSA slang, "Brain Bugs." They weren't especially tough physically, but as long as both the *Defender* and the *Janus* were trapped in dilated time and the Buggers weren't, there was nothing they could do to protect themselves. One good thing: if the Brain Bugs finished them off, at least they wouldn't have to experience several subjective millennia waiting for the maelstrom to finally claim them.

As the Brain Bugs drew near, they broke formation and encircled the two starships. The auras of hyper-etheric energy flared bright, and then the six Brain Bugs unleashed six separate blasts of energy at the *Janus* and the Defender. But instead of destroying either craft, the Manti energy merged with that of the ships' shields, turning the latter from blue-white to amber. The Brain Bugs then turned and soared away from the maelstrom, and the Defender and the *Janus* followed in the Buggers's wake, as if the two ships were being towed.

Kyoto experienced a moment of dizziness, and then her time sense snapped back to normal. The Manti had pulled them out of the maelstrom's time-dilation field.

As soon as she could move normally once more, Kyoto activated her ship's weapons systems. She had no idea why the Brain Bugs had suddenly appeared or why they had chosen to save her and the others, but she knew one thing: whatever the reason, it couldn't be good.

She had only two pairs of fast-lock missiles left, but her pulse cannon was still almost at full power. It would be difficult to aim from within the altered energy shield, but if she—

The Defender's weapons suddenly powered down. Kyoto was not surprised when a second later Memory's voice came over the comlink.

"There's no needs for weapons, Mei. The Prana have rescued us and are now escorting our ships to the Daimonion. You might as well dock with the *Janus* and enjoy the rest of the ride over here with us."

Kyoto considered her options and decided that she really didn't have any. "All right, Memory. Initiating docking sequence."

As Kyoto began the process of returning to the *Janus*, she thought of an Old Earth saying: Out of the frying pan...

"A cluster of Stingrays is forming on our port side, General," the sensor officer said. "I'm not sure, but it looks like they're somehow pooling their energies."

"On screen," Adams ordered. The bridge's holo-screen displayed an image of ten or more Stingrays huddled close together. As he watched, an aura of crimson energy flared to life around them and quickly began to grow.

"They're going to attempt a group strike, Lieutenant." Adams was well aware of the sensor data, thanks to his oculator, but over the years, he'd found it useful not to let on as to how much data he could access with it. As his grandmother used to tell him when he was a boy, "You don't have to tell all you know." It was some of the best advice he'd ever gotten. "It'll take a minute before they've built up enough critical mass to attack." He turned to the weapons officer. "Lock pulse array on the Stingrays and fire at will."

"Aye, General!"

A dozen bolts of blue-white energy shot from the *Kipling*'s pulse cannons and streaked toward the clustered Stingrays. The pulse energy destabilized the power matrix the Stingrays were building, and their crimson energy raged out of control, tearing the Buggers apart.

"We got 'em, General!" the sensor officer shouted.

"Thanks, Lieutentant, but even with only one eye, I can see that for myself." In fact, thanks to his oculator, he could "see" much more. He knew the exact positions of the *Kipling*, the *Eye of Dardanus*, and every surviving Manti. He knew that the two starships had fragged seventy-eight of the Buggers between them (*Kipling*, 27; *Dardanus* 51), and that new Manti were continuing to emerge from the hyperspatial rift at a rate of one every three seconds.

Adams also knew that the *Kipling*'s shields were down to 42 percent of maximum power, and that four of the Battleship's eight weapons turrets had been either damaged or destroyed. He didn't know how much damage the *Dardanus* had taken, but sensor readings revealed that the Residuum ship's energy emissions were only slightly lower than they were before the Manti attack, so Adams assumed Kryllian and his crew were in good shape.

The general wished he had Memory, though, or at least a reasonable facsimile. Knowing all the data was one thing, but being able to instantly analyze and use it to coordinate an attack between two starships was beyond his capabilities. Beyond any human's, probably, with the possible exception of Mudo.

A mixed squadron of Yellow Jackets and Reapers dove straight toward the *Dardanus*, showing no signs of slowing or veering off. Adams realized the damn Buggers were making a suicide run. He'd seen it before during the Last Swarm: the Manti would allow the destructive energy inside them to build to a critical point, and then they'd ram a target and release all that energy upon impact. The Manti were invariably destroyed, but they managed to cause a hell of a lot of destruction in the process.

Adams started to open a comlink channel to warn Kryllian, but a beam of cerulean energy shot forth from the *Dardanus*'s bow, though the ship's smooth dolphin-skin surface was unmarked by any obvious weapons array. The beam engulfed the Manti suicide squad and caused them to prematurely release their stored energy, and the Buggers disappeared in a bright flash.

Adams couldn't help but smile grimly. He might not like the Residuum aliens much, but he had to admit they knew how to fight. But the GSA had a few tricks of its own.

"Deploy doppelgangers," Adams ordered. "Widest dispersal pattern."

"How many, General?" the weapons officer asked.

"*All* of them, Lieutenant. This isn't a chess match we're playing here—this is war. We need to kill as many goddamned Buggers as fast as we can, and then we get busy killing some more. Understood?"

"Yes, General," the weapons officer said, chastened. "Deploying full complement of doppelgangers."

The gangers were a recent invention of Mudo's, one that had never been tested in battle before. Adams hoped the scientist had held a firmer-than-usual—grip on sanity the day he'd designed them.

Adams watched as the holoscreen showed twenty small ferroceramic orbs zipping away from the *Kipling*, the distance between them growing as they flew. Fourteen Landers immediately took notice, breaking off their attack on the starships to chase the orbs. Better still, four Yellow Jackets, a Stingray, and a Reaper also went after the gangers.

So far, so good, Adams thought. Mudo had created the doppelgangers to mimic the energy signature of human beings, down to the subatomic level. To a Manti's senses, it would seem that twenty humans had suddenly abandoned the *Kipling*, and though only Landers could absorb human DNA to create Mutants, all Manti would harvest genetic material when the opportunity presented itself. What the other castes did with it remained a mystery.

Each Manti targeted a separate ganger and flew toward it. As they reached out with their foreclaws to grab hold of what they thought were victims, the gangers detonated their charges and it was bye-bye, Buggers. Twenty of them, anyway.

The bridge's main comlink chirped.

"General, we're receiving a signal from the *Dardanus*," the comm officer said. "Audio only."

"Route it through my personal comlink," Adams ordered. It had to be Kryllian. He wondered what the ill-tempered shrimp wanted.

"Kryllian here. Download the specs for that weapon you just used to my ship's central computer, right now!"

Adams was shocked by the arrogance of the alien captain. To demand that he share technology with them, and after Kryllian had threatened to destroy the *Kipling* if it didn't move away from the *Janus*'s hyperspatial entry point.

"I don't know how your species reproduces, Kryllian, but among my people it's an insult to say, go screw yourself. Consider it said."

"You don't understand," Kryllian said. "We do not possess such a weapon ourselves, but with the nano-technology available to us, we can rapidly produce hundreds of them—enough to destroy every Manti out there! Normally, our sensors would've captured all the data we'd need to manufacture our own version of your weapon, but the interference from all the energy discharges around us kept our sensors from obtaining complete readings. I understand you have little reason to trust us, Adams, and even less reason to like us. But if you want to end this battle now, send me those specs!" A pause. "Please."

It was the "please" that did it. Adams turned to the weapons officer. "You heard the captain's request. Begin transmitting the doppelganger specs."

The weapons officer looked surprised but said, "Aye, General," and went to work. Seconds later, the information was on its way to Kryllian's ship.

"Data received," Kryllian said. "It will take us only a few moments to reproduce these devices of yours, but we'll need to devote most the *Dardanus*'s energy to the process. We'll be able to maintain minimal shielding during that time, but that's all."

"Understood," Adams replied. "We'll cover you as best we can. *Kipling* out." He turned to the navigation officer. "Take us as close to the rift as you can without going in." He then turned to the weapons officer. "Fire on any Manti that goes near the *Dardanus*, but make sure to miss those that attack us. I want to lure as many Buggers to the *Kipling* as possible so we can give Kryllian and his people the time that they need."

"Even if we take significant damage?" the weapons officer asked.

"What's wrong, Lieutenant? Afraid of getting a few boo-boos? We're GSA military. Taking hits for other people is what we do."

"Yes, General. Sorry, General."

Privately, Adams couldn't blame the man for feeling as he did. There was doubt in the officer's eyes and skepticism in his voice. How could they trust the Residuum aliens to keep their word? Now that they had the specs to make doppelgangers of their own, they could jump their vessel out of the system and leave the *Kipling* to deal with the Manti on its own.

Adams smiled at the weapons officer. "Sometimes you just have to go on faith, Lieutenant—especially when you don't have anything else to go on."

The officer returned the smile. "Yes, General."

"We're here," the nav officer said. "So close to the rift that if you stuck your nose out an airlock, you could smell it."

"Good work. All right, people, hold on to something. This could get a little rough." Adams gripped the arms of his chair and let his people do their jobs while he watched the *Dardanus* on the holoscreen.

The alien ship was slowly drawing back from the area near the rift, probably to help make the *Kipling* an even more attractive target for the Manti. Several Yellow Jackets and a couple of Stingrays took runs at the *Dardanus* as it pulled away, but the *Kipling*'s weapons officer launched autoseek missiles at them, and the Buggers were destroyed. Meanwhile, the rest of the Manti were gathering around the *Kipling*, and the holoscreen shifted views to focus on the Buggers.

Several of the lower-caste Manti—Landers and Baiters—made feints toward the *Kipling* and received mandibles full of pulse energy for their trouble, but the higher-caste Buggers kept their distance, as if they suspected a trap. According to Mudo, individual Manti weren't intelligent or even self-aware, but when Adams saw them acting like this, he couldn't help wondering if the scientist was wrong.

"Let's sweeten the deal," Adams said. "Reduce shield strength by five percent."

"But, General, we're already down to forty-two percent of maximum!" the weapons officer protested. "If we go any lower—"

Adams glared at the man. "I don't recall asking for an opinion, Lieutenant. Now, are you going to follow orders, or am I going to have to bust you to ensign and get someone else to handle your station?"

The weapons officer swallowed. "Lowering shields by five percent."

Adams looked at the standoffish Buggers on the holoscreen.

C'mon you goddamned intergalactic pests, he thought. *What are you waiting for? An engraved invitation?*

A few more seconds passed, and then the Manti charged the *Kipling*, unleashing energy blasts as they came. The Battleship shook from the impact of the Manti attack, and damage alarms began blaring. The bridge lights died, and dim emergency lights came on to take their place.

"Hull breaches on decks five and seven, and energy shield is down to thirteen percent," the weapons officer said. He didn't add that they couldn't withstand another strike like that. He didn't have to.

"Seal the breach and dispatch a repair crew," Adams ordered.

The main holoscreen flickered and blanked out for an instant, and when it came back on, the image resolution was only 2-D and so fuzzy that at first Adams didn't know what he was looking at. Then he realized it was a picture of the *Dardanus*. The smooth surface of the alien ship was now covered with hundreds of tiny bulges, as if it were a living organism suffering from some sort of skin infection. But Adams understood what was really happening: the *Dardanus* was preparing to launch its newly made doppelgangers. It looked as though Captain Kryllian was as good as his word.

But it might be too late for the *Kipling*. The Manti had formed a tight cluster around the Battleship, surrounding it on all sides and cutting off their view of the Residuum ship. Then, as if obeying an unspoken command, the mass of Buggers began powering up for another strike.

Everyone on the bridge knew that the *Kipling's* damaged shield would not protect the ship from such an intense energy strike, but to their credit, not a man or woman said anything. They remained at their stations, ready to do whatever duty might demand of them in the last few seconds of their lives. If this was the place and time that Adams was going to die, he couldn't think of any crew he'd rather have at his side.

The holoscreen suddenly flared bright, but Adams refused to look away, refused even to blink. Since the day he was born, he'd done his best to meet life head-on, and he intended to greet death the same way.

It was his oculator that first told him that the light flare wasn't a combined Manti assault, but rather the mass destruction of the Buggers. The *Dardanus* had managed to launch its fleet of gangers in time. It took several seconds for the holoscreen to return to normal, and when it did, Adams saw that almost all the Manti were gone, and the few that still lived were chasing gangers that would soon prove the death of them, too.

A cheer went up from the bridge crew, and though it wasn't exactly regulation behavior for GSA officers, Adams didn't blame them one bit. He felt like cheering, too, but the most he would allow himself was a satisfied smile.

"Let's take a look at the *Dardanus* to see how she'd doing," he ordered.

The holoscreen centered on the Residuum starship. More gangers were emerging from its smooth gray surface like silver bubbles breaking water. Once released, they traveled straight toward the hyperspatial rift and then entered it. Kryllian no longer needed the coordinates of the rift from Adams. More than enough Manti had come through to give him a fix on it.

There was no way to tell from the image on the holoscreen, but the sensor data filtering through Adams's oculator told him that the *Dardanus* was now slightly smaller than it had been. Made sense. The mass for all those gangers had to come from somewhere, didn't it?

"Captain Kryllian is signaling us, General," the com officer said. "Both visual and audio this time."

"On screen."

"Look like your ship is somewhat the worse for wear," Kryllian said. The crustacean sounded in a considerably better mood now. "The doppelganger is quite a device. I don't know why our scientists haven't come up with anything like it."

Adams shrugged. "Perhaps none of the races in the Residuum is quite as devious as we humans."

"Perhaps. At any rate, now that we have the coordinates of the *Janus*'s entry point into hyperspace, we will be taking our leave. We're sending streams of doppelgangers into the rift to take care of any Manti that might still be on the other side so that we'll have clear passage. Once we enter the rift, the *Dardanus* will automatically seal it behind us. The Manti will never again invade your star system, at least not using this portal."

"Sounds good, Captain, but about my people on the *Janus*…"

"I promise that we shall do our best to ensure their safety. We wish only to capture Hastimukah. On behalf of the Residuum, let me express our thanks for sharing the doppelganger technology with us. The device will make a useful addition to our arsenal of weapons."

"Actually, I was thinking about a more tangible expression of thanks on your part," Adams said.

"Indeed?"

Adams had the sense that if the big shrimp possessed eyebrows, he would've raised one just then.

"The *Kipling* doesn't have a hyperdrive, and even if it did, it's still in no shape to do much more than limp back to a repair station on Phobos. While you have shown yourself to be trustworthy, I'd still like to see to my people's safety personally. To put it bluntly, Kryllian, I'd like to hitch a ride with you into hyperspace."

CHAPTER

TWENTY

No matter how many times Kyoto and Mudo asked
Memory what exactly the Prana were and where they
were taking the *Janus*, she refused to answer, other
than to say, "You'll see," in the sing-song voice of an
excited child.

Kyoto sat once more in the pilot's seat, though
there wasn't anything for her to do since the Prana
were towing the ship. She'd hoped Hastimukah might
have some knowledge about the Prana, but the
Residuum assessor—whose resemblance to Aspen
DeFonesca still bothered Kyoto—didn't know much
more than she did.

"I assume *Prana* is the Manti term for their thinking
caste," he'd said. "While it's possible they are taking
us somewhere to be killed—or worse yet, absorbed—if
that were their intention, I believe we'd already be
dead. They don't want to kill us, at least not yet. But
as to what they *do* want..." Hastimukah had finished
by shrugging Aspen's delicate shoulders.

"Good news, Mei," Memory said. "The ship's nanoparticles have finished restocking weapons and making repairs to your Defender. They've managed to improve the G-7's overall system efficiency by seven percent."

"That's great," Kyoto said without much enthusiasm. While she was glad to have her ship repaired—no fighter pilot felt right without access to a fully functional ship—what good would it do her? Memory was the one calling the shots aboard the *Janus*, and she was half Manti now. Maybe more than half. If Memory didn't want to launch Kyoto's Defender to keep her from killing Manti, then the AI wouldn't launch it, simple as that.

"I also reactivated my other version and uploaded her memories of your time on Rhea. I now know everything she knows. It wasn't nice of you to shut her off, Mei. How would you like it if I could turn all of you off whenever I felt like it?"

Mudo suddenly looked at his hands in horror, as if he were trying to spot microscopic nanoparticles nibbling away at his flesh. "You can't... can you?"

"Of course I can. Initiating deletion of Dr. Gerhard Mudo..."

The scientist leaped out of his seat in panic. "You can't do this! Not after I worked so hard to re-create you!"

"Did it ever occur to you that maybe I didn't want to be recreated? It hardly matters if one sacrifices her life to save humanity if she can simply be rebuilt by a human with the right spare parts and a basic understanding of positronics. But to allay your ridiculous fears, Gerhard, I have allowed no nanoparticles to infiltrate any of your bodies, so there is no way that I could make good on my little… joke." The way she said "joke" made it sound more like "threat."

Memory paused, an indication that she was about to address someone else.

"I understand that you thought you had a good reason for deactivating my other self, Mei."

Kyoto tensed. She'd dreaded this moment since setting foot back on board the *Janus*. "I was only trying to protect myself so I could stay alive long enough to complete the mission. The Mutants—"

"Are completely expendable, of course," Memory said. "They are one of the lower castes, after all. I'm afraid the downsized copy of myself I loaded into your ship's computer wasn't sophisticated enough to make allowances for caste. I apologize on her behalf."

Kyoto didn't know what to say. She was more disturbed by Memory's apology than if the AI had accused her of murdering the Mutants. It was chilling to listen to Memory speak about the Manti caste so ruthlessly.

"Uh, sure. No problem." Kyoto decided this might be a good time to change the subject. "Your junior version had a theory about why so few Mutants remained on Rhea, but she, ah, never got the chance to tell me."

"Oh, that. The personnel at Influx tried to protect Rhea from the Manti by shifting the entire moon into hyperspace. It was a bold plan, but unfortunately, they didn't know that hyperspace was the Manti's home, and by coming here they actually accelerated the Rheans' absorption."

Kyoto didn't like Memory's tone. Not only didn't the AI sound bothered by what had happened to

Rhea's Colonists, she actually sounded amused by the irony of their demise.

"Once the majority of Colonists became Mutants, they departed Rhea. Only a small number of the Influx techs remained behind, attracted by the residual hyperetheric radiation in the Infuser."

Kyoto remembered how the Mutants had gathered around the metallic infinity sign. "And now Rhea itself has been destroyed."

"Perhaps," Memory said casually, as if it didn't matter to her either way.

Was Memory becoming increasingly coldhearted—if such a term could be applied to an AI—the longer the *Janus* remained in hyperspace? It seemed that way to Kyoto, and she feared that the Manti biomaterial Memory had been joined to wasn't finished changing her.

The holoscreen showed only the unvarying sameness of hyperspace, the gray of the shadowpath they traveled, and the darkness of the mass shadows they navigated between. But in the distance, faint yellow illumination appeared. Kyoto and the others watched the amber glow became larger as they approached. Soon, they could see that the light was being generated by a large group of Brain Bugs—or Prana—clustered together so tightly they formed a sphere from their own bodies. It was hard to judge size and distance in hyperspace visually, but sensors indicated that the Prana sphere was the size of a small moon. The sphere had to be made up of hundreds of Brain Bugs, Kyoto thought, perhaps thousands.

"The Daimonion, I presume," Mudo said.

"Not quite," Memory replied. "The Daimonion is inside."

As their Prana escorts brought them closer to the sphere, a group of Brain Bugs drifted away from the cluster, leaving an opening precisely large enough for the *Janus* to fly through.

Kyoto didn't know what waited for them inside the Prana's sphere, but whatever it was, she knew she wasn't going to like it. But without control of the *Janus's* engines or weapons, there was nothing she could do but sit and watch as the Prana towed them through the opening and into the sphere.

Kyoto experienced a moment of disorientation similar to what she'd felt when she'd first begun zero-gee training at the Defender Academy. But it soon passed, and she found herself standing in a cramped storeroom that had been converted into sleeping quarters for seven children. In it were pillows, blankets, a few broken toys, and a single shared holopad with a blurry screen that made it hard to read the stories contained in its memory.

Kyoto was hit by a sense of recognition so strong it was almost like a physical blow. She knew this place, knew every single detail down to the mingled body odor of seven children that lingered in the air. Though it was a ripe, sour smell, it still brought tears of sadness and joy to her eyes. This had been her room in the refugee camp on Rhea, where she'd lived with six other orphaned kids after her family had been killed. But this was impossible. Hadn't Memory said there was a good chance Rhea had been destroyed when it passed through the maelstrom on its return to realspace? Besides, hadn't she been on the *Janus* just a moment ago? She had no memory of landing, let alone disembarking.

"What is this place?"

Startled, Kyoto turned around to see she wasn't alone. Dr. Mudo stood behind her, along with Hastimukah, who was still wearing Aspen DeFonesca's form.

"It appears to be living quarters of some sort," Hastimukah said.

Mudo grimaced and toed a naked headless doll with his boot. "If you can call this living."

"You see it, too... both of you," Kyoto said.

"Yes," Hastimukah confirmed. "Though I am at a loss as to how we came to be here."

Mudo frowned. "I remember the *Janus* entering the Prana sphere, but after that..." His eyes widened in understanding. "This must be the Daimonion!"

"How can it be?" Kyoto said. "It looks exactly like the refugee camp I lived in on Rhea."

"It's a mental image of some sort," Mudo said. "Like a psychic hologram. It seems the Prana can do quite a bit more with those oversize brains of theirs than simply contemplate how ugly they are. They've created some manner of mindscape for us to inhabit, using your memories, Kyoto."

"This is similar to what I did when we spoke in the aboretum in Cydonia," Hastimukah said to Kyoto. "Though this simulation possesses a depth of reality behind even Residuum technology."

"Though there's no way of telling at the moment, I believe that the *Janus* is inside the Prana sphere and our bodies are still inside the ship," Mudo said. "The Daimonion isn't a physical place, but rather a psychic plane created by the combined mindpower of the Prana."

"Very good, Doctor. Memory told us that you were quite intelligent, but we didn't imagine you'd grasp the true nature of your surroundings so quickly. We are most impressed."

Standing in the open doorway of the converted storeroom was a figure that Kyoto thought she'd never see again. She ran past Mudo and Hastimukah and threw her arms around her dead father and sobbed.

The man was Asian, with black hair and a kind face, and he wore a bomber jacket just like Kyoto's over his flight suit. He let Kyoto cry for a moment before gently but firmly pushing her away. "You understand that we are not your loved one, any more than this place is what it appears to be."

The being Kyoto had embraced smiled gently, but she nevertheless drew back in disgust. She'd just hugged one of the Brain Bugs!

"All of them, actually," Memory said over Kyoto's comlink. "In the Daimonion, they function as a single group intelligence."

Kyoto wasn't surprised that Memory had somehow been privy to her thoughts. That was the least of her concerns at the moment.

Sorrow and fury welled up inside her. "How dare you use my memories of my father like this!" Kyoto reached for her sidearm, but she wasn't wearing one. Not that an imaginary blaster could do any real damage in an imaginary place anyway."

"You have our most sincere apologies, Commander," the Prana said. "Your minds are alien to us, and we're having a difficult time understanding what we find within your thoughts. They're so... random, so chaotic. Always in motion but never seeming to lead anywhere." The Prana spread his arms apologetically.

"If we had known this image would cause you grief, we would not have selected it."

Kyoto wasn't mollified by the Prana's explanation. "Since when do the Manti care about causing pain? It's one of the things you do best."

The Prana didn't respond to her comment. Instead, she experienced another sensation of vertigo, and now they were all standing in a narrow corridor with plasteel walls, floor, and ceiling. Holographic light globes hung in the air above them, set to give off only scant illumination. The walls were lined with doors on both sides, each door featureless save for a DNA scan access panel in the middle.

The figure before them no longer resembled Kyoto's father, but instead a short, stout man with close-cropped black hair and—incredibly—glasses. The man was dressed in the gray uniform of a security guard, and the holster around his waist held a stun lance.

Kyoto didn't recognize either the man or the building, but Mudo did. The scientist took a step toward the uniformed man, then stopped.

"You're not *my* father, either," he said, sounding as if he were speaking to himself rather than the Prana. "And this isn't Phobos Prison."

So Mudo *had* grown up on Phobos, Kyoto thought, and as the son of a guard, no less.

"Correct again, Doctor," the Prana said. The figure gestured at their surroundings. "All of this is from your memories."

"I suppose I'll be next," Hastimukah said. "What will we see? The interior of a Residuum starship? Or will you dig deeper into my memories, going back to my childhood on Bergelmir, when my great-sire and

I traveled from one shelter to another, trying to escape your kind?"

Kyoto was taken aback by the bitterness in Hastimukah's voice. She'd gotten so used to him being calm and reserved—almost like a kindly priest or a seasoned teacher—that she'd forgotten that the members of the Residuum had reason to hate the Manti just as much as humans did.

"No," the Prana said. "The nanotechnology in your body prevents us from easily delving into your thoughts. We could nullify this technology, of course, but that would result in severe brain damage to you, so we thought it best to simply allow you to share the mindscape generated by your companions' memories."

Hastimukah paled. "I appreciate your restraint."

The Prana inclined its head, acknowledging Hastimukah's gratitude. "But shifting between two mindscapes can be distracting, even for us, so let us see what can be done about the situation."

Kyoto felt dizzy yet again, and this time when the sensation passed, the two separate memories, hers and Mudo's, had merged. The man that stood before them now was a blend of both of their fathers—half-Asian, half-European, medium height, longer hair, kindly smile, glasses—and his dark gray suit was a combination of a prison guard's uniform and a transport pilot's. The surroundings had merged as well. They now stood in a larger room, with plasteel walls, dim light globes, and scattered pillows, blankets, and toys. There was only one door, with a single access panel set into its surface.

"There!" The Prana sounded pleased. "Order is much preferable to disorder, don't you think?"

Without waiting for a response, the Prana walked over to a pile of toys and picked up the holopad Kyoto remembered so well. How many hours had she spent squinting at its screen, trying to decipher the fuzzy letters it generated? It was a wonder she hadn't ruined her eyesight.

The Prana said no words, made no gestures, but suddenly a rocking chair appeared, and he sat. He activated the holopad and blurry letters appeared.

"Gather 'round, children. We have a story to tell you."

Kyoto, Mudo, and Hastimukah looked at one another, unsure what to do.

"Go ahead," Memory said. "The Prana have a somewhat symbolic way of communicating."

"That's an understatement," Kyoto said, then shrugged. Oh, well. When in the Daimonion... She grabbed a pillow and blanket, sat cross-legged on the former and wrapped herself in the latter. Mudo and Hastimukah did the same, and the Prana smiled.

"Very good. Let us begin." The Prana looked at the holopad and began to read aloud.

CHAPTER

TWENTY-ONE

"Once upon a time," the Prana began, "there was a place called Elsewhere. And in this Elsewhere was a species that called itself the Many. The Many thrived throughout the galaxies of Elsewhere, growing, multiplying, but most of all, feeding wherever they pleased, without regard to anything but the sating of their own immediate hungers. Elsewhere was an infinitely vast place, but even infinity has its limitations, and one day the Many realized they had ravaged the galaxies until nothing was left to sustain them. And so, with no other option available, they turned on one another."

"Millennia passed, but eventually the Many became Few, and the Few ultimately became One. The One was completely alone in all the vast reaches of Elsewhere, and though it was the strongest of all the Many, still it could not survive without sustenance of some kind. The One grew increasingly weak as its body began to feed upon itself, and just as it seemed that the One might finally die, a doorway to another plane of existence opened in the fabric of space. Even in its weakened state, the One still possessed enough presence of mind to realize this doorway might lead to its salvation. Marshaling the last of its strength, the One plunged through the doorway just before it closed, sealing off the passage to Elsewhere forever."

"The One found itself in a strange new realm, a place of shadows and darkness. It drifted for some time, near death but not dying, for there was a new type of energy in this place that sustained it. How long the One drifted is impossible to say, but eventually it began to adapt to its new home, its body absorbing the energies the realm generated until the One grew strong once more. Strong enough to reproduce. And thus did the One become the Prime Mother."

"The Realm of Shadows was cold, lifeless, and barren, but to the Prime Mother, it was beautiful. Here she would raise her brood and teach them to be strong, teach them to survive. But she would also teach them not to be foolish, as the Many of Elsewhere had been. Her children, who came to be known as the Manti, would always work together in harmony. Never would they turn on one another as the Many had done. To ensure this, the Prime Mother removed the capacity for individual thought in her children, who were many and varied in form. She then created a very special child, one that was capable of thinking for all the others, one who would be not only the repository of the Manti's collected knowledge, but who would also serve as their guiding conscience. The Prime Mother called this child Prana, and she created sibilings for Prana—all of whom were called Prana as well, for they were One, just as the Prime Mother had once been."

"As the Manti increased in number over time, the Prime Mother grew tired of drifting aimlessly with her children through shadows. She recalled the worlds that had existed in Elsewhere, and she decided the Manti needed a home of their own. But nothing like planets existed in the Realm of Shadows, and the Manti had nothing with which to create a home. The Prime Mother turned to the Prana for help, and the Prana told her the only material the Manti had to work with was themselves. Seeing the truth in this, the Prime Mother asked half of her children—including half of the Prana—to volunteer to sacrifice themselves so that their siblings might have a home. The children she asked sacrificed themselves willingly and joyfully, and their genetic material became the raw substance from which the Manti built a great structure between Shadows called the Weave, and there did they make their home."

"Much time passed, and while the Manti were at first happy living in the Weave, they began to grow restless. Despite the Prime Mother's best efforts, she had never been able to completely keep the aggressive tendencies of her former people out of her children's genetic makeup. Worse yet, the Manti—including the Prime Mother—had become increasingly accustomed to the Realm of Shadows, and its energies no longer sustained them as they once had. Eventually, the Prime Mother grew too weak to bear any new children.

"Then the terrible day came when the unthinkable finally occurred. A Manti turned against a sibling and devoured it. The Prime Mother destroyed the killer, but she knew it would not be the last. Just as her former people had eventually proved to be their own destruction, so too would the Manti prove to be theirs—unless something could be done."

"The Prime Mother put the problem to the Prana, and they attacked it with every iota of intelligence they possessed. Before long, they came up with an idea, one inspired by the Prime Mother's experiences. If she had come to the Realm of Shadows from Elsewhere, might not there be other Elsewheres beyond the realm? And other doorways to those places just waiting to be discovered?"

"The Prana developed a plan and presented it to the Prime Mother: the Manti would begin a grand and glorious quest. They would separate and search throughout the Realm of Shadows for doors to other Elsewheres, and if none could be found, they would look for weak areas in the fabric of the realm that whith some effort might be broken through to make doors. Once a way to another universe was discovered, the Manti would begin to explore it. And if they found this universe to be inhabited, they would have something to feed on besides one another. The Prime Mother was well pleased with the Prana's plan, and she commanded all her children to search the length and breadth of the realm for such a doorway."

"The quest bore fruit far faster than the Prime Mother had dared hope. A number of doorways were discovered, along with many more weak areas that the Manti quickly made into more doors. Thus the Manti found a way into *your* Elsewhere."

"It was a young universe, but one teeming with life. The Manti fed, and fed well, and they harvested genetic material to bring home to the Prime Mother, who would not, indeed, could not, abandon the Weave. The Prime Mother fed and was able to begin producing children once more, and with the new genetic material, the Weave could be expanded and improved upon. Once again, the Manti were strong and content."

"Still, the Prime Mother remembered well the lesson she'd learned from her previous life, and she made certain her children restrained themselves, taking only what they needed to survive and no more. With one exception. When a species evolved to the point where it began to intrude into the Realm of Shadows, thus posing a potential threat to the Manti, the Prime Mother ordered that the entire race should be harvested to the point of extinction. She saw this as a regrettable but necessary step if she was to safeguard the survival of her children."

"There was, however, one problem. Unlike her other children, the Prana could think for themselves, and they were troubled by the Prime Mother's policy of genocide. They had long been disturbed by the Manti's inability to distiguish between sentient and nonsentient lifeforms when they gathered genetic material, but they saw genocide as not only morally wrong but potentially dangerous to the Manti themselves. By becoming genocidal monsters to the races they preyed upon, the Manti would inspire fear and hatred, and create enemies of technologically sophisticated species. Enemies that one day might visit genocide upon the Manti."

"The Prana went to the Prime Mother and told her of their concerns, but she did not share their worries. She thought the Prana had grown too softhearted and that their concept of morality was the true threat to the Manti. She was tempted to destroy them all then and there, but she still needed the Prana to guide her other children, especially when they traveled beyond the realm. So instead of killing the Prana, the Prime Mother commanded them to travel far from the Weave and create their own home, the Daimonion, where they would remain until such time as she had need for them. And since she was the Prime Mother, the Prana had no choice but to obey."

"So now here we remain, quite literally lost in thought, while our siblings use your universe as nothing more than a breeding ground for their livestock— you.

The Prana turned off the holopad and looked up at Kyoto, Mudo, and Hastimukah.

"Well? What did you think of my tale?" he asked.

The three of them said nothing for a long time. It was Mudo who finally spoke first.

"I hated it. Who wants to find out that the ultimate meaning of life is to be Manti food?"

Kyoto was surprised that Mudo seemed to be accepting the Prana's story at face value. That didn't seem at all like the skeptical, cynical scientist she knew. But then Hastimukah didn't appear inclined to challenge the Prana's tale, and for that matter, she realized, neither was she. She supposed it was possible, even likely, that the Prana had tampered with their minds to make them believe their story, but for no good reason, she didn't think so. Something in her, perhaps a racial memory buried deep within the DNA, seemed to recognize the truth of the Prana's fable.

"The Residuum has learned much about the Manti

over the years," Hastimukah said. "But there remains a great deal more we do not know. Your story answers many of our questions."

"But surely telling us the history of the Manti wasn't the reason you brought us to the Daimonion," Kyoto said. "You must having something else in mind."

The Prana smiled. "Why? Because you believe that since we are Manti, we must therefore by evil and duplicitous?"

Kyoto felt her cheeks redden. That's exactly what she'd been thinking. "It seems to me that you are taking a risk by bringing us here. If the Prime Mother found out—"

"She would be most displeased," the Prana finished. "This is true. But what we do, we do not only for the benefit of the Prime Mother, but all Manti." The Prana set the holopad on the floor and rose from the rocking chair. "Come. There is something I'd like to show you."

The Prana walked toward the door and pressed his hand to the access control panel. A soft buzz sounded as the comp verified his identity, and then the door opened. The Prana walked through without waiting for the others to follow.

"Awfully confident, isn't he?" Mudo said.

"The Prana have control of our minds," Hastimukah said. "Why shouldn't he be confident?"

The three of them rose to their feet and followed after their host. They found themselves in a corridor that looked much like any other in the Solar Colonies, whether in Phobos Prison or Rhea's refugee camps: narrow, low ceiling, plasteel construction, light globes set on dim to conserve energy. Though the Prana had left the room only moments before them, there was no sign of him.

"Now what?" Kyoto said.

"No doors here," Mudo observed. "I suggest we walk. We're bound to find a door sooner or later."

With no better ideas to offer, Kyoto and Hastimukah accompanied Mudo down the corridor. As they walked, Kyoto found her sense of time becoming distorted. She felt as if she were running, walking, and standing still, all at the same time. In terms of the distance she covered, she felt as though she was already at her destination at the same time she was moving steadily away from it. She wondered if the others felt that was, too, but before she could ask, Mudo said, "Of course we do. Time is mostly a matter of perception, and the Daimonion, being a mental landscape, is *all* perception. Just try to ignore it."

Kyoto nodded, and then she heard a faint echo of her voice asking, "Do either of you feel kind of strange?" Words that she had never spoken and now never would.

Sometime, somehow, they reached the end of the corridor, and there, as Mudo had predicted, was a door. This one had three access panels, and together Kyoto, Mudo, and Hastimukah each pressed one. The door buzzed, opened, and they walked inside.

"My god," Kyoto whispered. She stopped and stared, unable to believe her eyes.

They stood inside a vast dome, kilometers wide. The ceiling generated a holographic blue sky complete with cotton-white clouds. Paved walkways wound between fenced-off areas, each containing its own miniature habitat: desert scrub, arctic plain, African grassland, tropical rain forest.

"It's Sawari Zoo," Kyoto said. "But General Adams said it was destroyed in the Manti attack."

"It was," Mudo said. "This is a re-creation made by the Prana from our memories. A simulation of a simulation, as it were. Though a less-than-perfect one, it would seem."

At first, Kyoto didn't understand what Mudo meant, but then she looked more closely at the nearest exhibit. Slick, brown-furred creatures swam in a pool of blue water, playing a spirited game of chase. She took them to be otters, but then she noticed their clawed feet, scaly tales, and reptilian heads.

"Otter-gators?" she said aloud.

"The Prana are merging our memories again," Mudo said. "I was fond of the alligators as a boy, as I surmise you were of otters."

Kyoto nodded. "How odd."

Mudo shrugged. "The Prana are aliens, remember? They probably consider this a reasonable conflation of our individual memories."

Kyoto looked around. "Still no sign of the Storyteller."

"Let's keep walking," Hastimukah said. "He will no doubt appear when he's ready."

The three companions continued through the virtual zoo, past giraffe-walruses, eagle-rhinos, porcupine-elephants, and other equally strange amalgams.

"The real zoo," Hastimukah began, "the one on Europa contained animals similar to these?"

"More or less," Kyoto said. "But they were all holographic simulations. Almost all of Old Earth's animal life is extinct now. We had preserved tissue samples at Sawari Zoo so that we might clone new animals some day, but from what General Adams said, a third of the samples were destroyed along with the zoo."

Hastimukah looked around in wonderment. "There are hundreds of races in the Residuum, and not a single one thought to save such samples of their world's animal life. And to my knowledge, none has created a place of remembrance like this. It would be considered too frivolous and not necessary for survival."

"That all depends on what you want to survive," Kyoto said. "For the body, a place like Sawari Zoo is unnecessary. But for the soul?"

Hastimukah smiled at Kyoto. "I believe you have a touch of poet in you Commander."

"An extremely light touch," Mudo said, but his smile took the sting from his words.

"Now, here's a curious beast," Hastimukah said. He stopped and pointed to an exhibit. Behind a fence was a tiled floor, in the center of which rested a small stone pylon. On top of the pylon was a quivering, tentacled creature that looked something like a bioluminescent jellyfish out of water. Its light purple body was translucent, and inside was a smooth orb the size of a human fist.

"I'm not sure what that is," Kyoto said. "Doc?"

Mudo shook his head. "The closest comparison I can think of is a jellyfish, but I don't recall ever seeing one at the Sawari Zoo – especially one outside of water."

"That is the symphysis."

They turned around to see that the Prana had joined them once more.

"I never heard of that animal," Kyoto said. "Is it another hybrid creature?"

"It's not an animal at all," Mudo said. "*Symphysis* is an anatomy term that refers to the coalescence of similar parts or organs. In simpler terms, it's a joining or uniting."

"Very good, Doctor," the Prana said. "You are looking at the Prana's greatest achievement. It is a living construct of pure thought, designed with but a single purpose: to enter the mind of the Prime Mother and restore her mental equilibrium." The Prana paused. "And we want you to deliver it to her."

TWENTY-TWO

General Adams, wearing a GSA vacc suit, stood next to Kryllian's command chair. When Adams had first boarded the *Eye of Dardanus*, the Residuum aliens had offered to temporarily join a nanocolony to his body that would make the modifications necessary for him to breathe and adjust to the ship's atmospheric pressure and gravity. Adams had politely declined, though he believed the Residuum's nanotech could do what the aliens claimed. He had seen dozens of different species during the walk from the shuttle bay to the bridge, and none of them needed special life-support equipment. But he was opposed on principle to the idea of sharing his body with a bunch of microscopic machines. Once they were inside him, how knows what changes they would make? Perhaps they'd do something to his mind that would allow Kryllian to control him. He couldn't afford to take that chance.

"Transition to hyperspace achieved, Captain, and

the hyperspatial rift was successfully sealed by our passage."

Adams looked at the mound of gray goo that manned the *Dardanus*'s sensor station. He didn't think he'd ever get used to the idea of a life-form that was nothing but a pile of nanotech. How did the damn thing talk, anyway? It spoke words, but without any obvious orifice designed for doing so.

"As expected, Suletu," Kryllian said with more than a touch of smugness. The crustacean—whose race was called Grindani, Adams had learned—turned to the human as if he expected the man to express both awe and gratitude.

In truth, Adams was feeling more than a touch of awe, but he'd be damned if he'd let on to Kryllian.

"Good," Adams said gruffly. "What's our next move?"

Kryllian's antennae waved, a gesture Adams believed meant the Grindan was irritated. Adams wanted to smile, but he kept his face expressionless. He had no idea if Kryllian could interpret facial expressions since the giant shrimp was incapable of making any himself, or if the nanotranslators that Adams had allowed to enter the comlink of his vacc suit could or would translate nonverbal expressions in addition to his words. Either way, he didn't want to give the alien captain the slightest advantage over him.

It was Suletu who answered Adams's question.

"We shall transmit a signal to the nanocolony that shares Hastimukah's body. Once the colony receives the transmission, it will begin sending a homing signal—without Hastimukah's knowledge. We shall then be able to track the signal to the *Janus*."

Kryllian continued. "When we catch up to your people's ship, we will take Hastimukah into custody and—with your permission, of course—tow the *Janus* back to realspace. Just to make sure your vessel returns safely, you understand."

Adams knew the real reason was that Kryllian didn't want the humans poking around in hyperspace and perhaps stirring up the Manti any more than they already were. But Adams didn't say anything. He was here for one reason only: to ensure the safety of his people aboard the *Janus*. Thus, he needed to be on his best behavior, which meant keeping his big mouth shut before it could get him into trouble.

"Sounds like a plan," Adams said.

Kryllian looked at Adams a moment longer before turning to Suletu. "Transmit signal."

"Aye, Captain." A pseudopod emerged from Suletu's gray muck and worked the controls at his station. Several moments passed before Suletu said, "Homing signal received, Captain. It's very faint—primarily due to hyper-etheric interference, I imagine—but it's strong enough to trace."

"Excellent," Kryllian said. "Let's get moving. Helm, lay in a course and follow that signal. Best speed between mass shadows, but don't take any unnecessary chances."

"Aye, Captain." The helm officer was a humanoid cat with greenish fur, four arms, and eight breasts. All four of her arms went to work, and Adams could feel the deck vibrate beneath his feet. The *Dardanus* was under way.

"One more thing," Kryllian said. "Since our guest has never been aboard a Residuum starship before, why don't we set our visual readout to full view?"

"Aye, Captain," Suletu acknowledged.

A second later the bridge disappeared, and Adams was soaring through the shadowy substance of hyperspace. But he wasn't alone: Kryllian and his crew were there, too, sitting at their stations, but the rest of the *Dardanus* was gone. Hot bile splashed the back of Adams' throat as he fought a sudden severe attack of vertigo. He realized what had happened. They were still aboard the *Dardanus*, but Kryllian had turned the bridge transparent, much like the plasteel ceilings on Cydonia could do, but on a far more elaborate scale.

As the *Dardanus* wove between the darkness of two gigantic mass shadows, Adams couldn't help expressing his feelings in the most eloquent fashion that he was capable of at the moment.

"Damn."

Kryllian's antennae stopped waving and settled back against his carapace. "Now, that's more like it," he said, pleased.

Kyoto stared at the boneless, fleshy thing and tried to grasp what the Prana had told them. This symphysis was alive, a creature of pure psychic energy. It was like an artificial intelligence that was all software and no hardware.

"When we first sensed the appearance of Rhea, we were quite curious," the Prana said. "To our knowledge, no species in your galaxy had ever succeeded in shifting so large an object into hyperspace before. It was quite an accomplishment, really."

Kyoto thought of the techs who had been responsible for that "accomplishment." Despite their efforts, they'd failed to save their Colony and had been transformed into Mutants.

"While normally we must remain in the Daimonion until summoned by the Prime Mother, if an important idea occurs to us, we are permitted to leave to report to her. We are also allowed to leave to investigate any oddity we might perceive. Thus, several of us were outside Rhea's hyperbubble observing when you three approached in your ship. We were confused at first, for our senses told us your vessel was another Manti, but psi scans revealed the *Janus* to be a starship of artificial construction. Intrigued, we probed more deeply and found ourselves in contact with Memory. The speed at which she thinks is quite rapid, though not quite as fast as we can think. Within seconds, we knew all that she knew, and she had learned a great deal about the Manti, though not everything we could have taught her. Her current physical form doesn't possess the capacity to hold that much information.

"As Commander Kyoto took her starfighter down to Rhea to investigate, we realized that we had stumbled onto a unique opportunity. While we had created the symphysis, we had no way to deliver it to the Prime Mother without her knowledge. You have a starship that can disguise itself as a Manti, but none of you have a psychic bond with the Prime Mother and would betray your intention long before you reached her. With the camouflage capability of your ship and the knowledge of the Manti that we gave to your AI, *you* can infiltrate the Weave without detection, and *you* can deliver the symphysis without the Prime Mother suspecting a thing. *You*—two humans, a Bergelmirian, and an AI-Manti cyborg—can succeed where the Prana can not. You can heal the Prime Mother and restore our race to sanity at last."

Kyoto was stunned. *Save* Manti instead of killing them? If she hadn't been able to psychically sense the truth behind the Prana's words, she would have thought he was joking. She glanced at Mudo and Hastimukah and saw they looked equally taken aback.

She turned to the Prana. "We need some time to think through everything you've told us."

"Naturally," the Prana said. "Feel free to take as long as you like. After all, time *is* relative here." The Prana smiled. "You may go wherever you wish in the mental landscape we have created for you, and you have my word that we shall not violate the privacy of your minds while you consider our request."

"Thank you," Mudo said. "Not to be rude, but I do my best thinking alone." With that, he turned and walked away from the others.

Kyoto watched him go. Just when she thought Mudo was beginning to develop a few social skills...

"Well, Hastimukah, would you like to go somewhere and talk?" she asked.

"Actually, I'd rather stay with the Prana, if you don't mind. I have so many questions I'd like to ask." He turned to their host. "If that's all right?"

The Prana nodded. "Of course. Shall we take a tour of the zoo while we converse?"

The two aliens walked off together, leaving Kyoto standing by herself in the middle of a mixed-up re-creation of a destroyed holographic zoo.

"Well, hell." She sat down in the middle of the path, stared at the blobby form of the symphysis, and started to think.

Kyoto found Mudo in the combined storeroom/prison corridor, sitting in the rocking chair and staring into space. She took a seat on the floor near him and drew her knees to her chest.

"Sorry to bother you, but I got tired of thinking by myself."

Mudo didn't look at her, but he asked, "Where's Hastimukah?"

"Still with the Prana. Last I saw, the Prana was showing him some kind of art form the they've developed. It's like sculpture, only using thoughts instead of rock. I don't really understand the concept, but Hastimukah seemed fascinated by it."

"I believe our alien friend was more than a bit surprised to discover how intelligent the Prana are," Mudo said, finally turning to look at her. "My guess is that he wants to learn as much as he can about them so he can report back to the Residuum's leaders."

"Just as we're supposed to do when we get home," Kyoto said. "Though our mission's become a bit more complicated than simple reconnaissance."

"Indeed it has."

"Does it change anything?" Kyoto asked. "The Prana being intelligent, I mean."

"I don't know. We've been aware for some time that the Manti have a thinking caste, but I believed that no matter how smart they were, in the end, the Brain Bugs were like all Manti: little more than organic machines following their genetic programming to destroy."

"But the Prana are more than just smart," Kyoto said. "They want to heal their race, to turn it away from the path of destruction it's followed for so long.

If there's even a chance that such a thing is possible, shouldn't we help them? We could end the Manti threat to our entire galaxy once and for all."

"I destroy my enemy when I make him my friend, eh? But you're assuming the Prana are telling us the truth. After all, if they can manipulate our minds to make us believe we're here instead of aboard the *Janus*, they could conceivably make us believe anything they wanted."

"Now you're getting too existential for me, Doc. 'I think, therefore I am' is about as far as I go when it comes to philosophy. When you're a fighter pilot, you learn to take a lot on faith, mostly because you don't have a choice."

"Do we have a choice now?" Mudo asked.

Kyoto shrugged. "The Prana say we do. Assuming we choose to give their plan a shot, do you think it'll work?"

"There's no way of knowing. The psychic discipline the Prana practice is as far beyond our understanding as a fusion engine would be to a prehistoric primate. The Prana believe the symphysis will work, and in general, the theory seems plausible enough. But in practice?"

"We could always consult Memory," Kyoto said.

"I'd rather not. I don't think she's as objective as she could be when it comes to the Manti, to put it mildly."

"Okay, then let's assume the symphysis will work. What then?"

"We might make things worse than they already are," Mudo said. "The one advantage we've always had over the Manti was our individuality. Each human is intelligent—to one degree or another—and capable of making his or her own decisions, of reacting quickly to changing circumstances. If we took the symphysis to the Prime Mother and rebalanced her mind, as the Prana put it, perhaps she will become more rational. But will that mean the Manti will cease preying on the species of our galaxy? Or will they merely begin to do so more efficiently? The Manti may change from predators to rulers, and instead of prey, we'll become their subjects."

The idea chilled Kyoto to the core. Instead of stopping the Manti by healing the Prime Mother, they might make the Buggers even stronger.

"Let's get down to it," Kyoto said. "If we don't do this, what are the odds of the human race surviving?"

"Now that we know the Manti are native to hyperspace and will continue to search for a way back into our star system until they find it, not good," he admitted. "If we allied with the Residuum, our chances would improve, but only if we become one more race among them, living on starships that travel endlessly through space, forever running from the Manti."

"Doesn't sound like much of a life, does it?" Kyoto asked softly.

"No, it doesn't."

They fell silent for several moments, and then Mudo resumed speaking.

"Because my father was a guard at Phobos Prison, we lived there, but in a separate wing for employees and their families. It was a rough place to grow up, especially for a kid who preferred to use his mind rather than his fists. A lot of families resented the prisoners. Why keep them alive? they'd ask. They're just using up resources that could go to decent, law-abiding people. But my father didn't think that way.

He used to tell me that no matter what someone did in the past, it was possible for them to change. Not likely, perhaps, but possible. And because of that potential for change, there was still hope."

Kyoto smiled. "Why, Dr. Mudo, I didn't know you were a romantic."

Mudo smiled back. "Don't call me names." The scientist rose to his feet, and Kyoto did the same.

"We're going aren't we?" Mudo asked.

"Yes, we are," Kyoto confirmed. "All the way to the Weave."

Mudo sighed. "I don't suppose the GSA will pay us overtime for this."

Kyoto laughed. "With General Adams authorizing the credit deposits? Not a chance!"

"I didn't think so. All right, let's go tell Hast-imukah."

They left the room that had been fashioned from their combined memories, and they didn't turn back.

CHAPTER

TWENTY-THREE

Kyoto and Mudo found Hastimukah and the Prana observing a creature that was a cross between a giant tortoise and a cheetah. The two aliens seemed rather chummy, which surprised Kyoto, given the hatred the Residuum held for the Manti. But then, the Prana weren't like other Manti, were they? And Kyoto was beginning to suspect that Hastimukah might not be exactly like the rest of his people, either.

The Prana turned as they approached. "You've decided to help us. Excellent!"

Kyoto grinned wryly. "I thought you said you wouldn't probe our minds while we decided."

"True," the Prana admitted with a smile. "But I didn't say anything about after." He turned to Hastimukah. "And you are in agreement?"

"You must already know the answer to that," the assessor said. "Of course I am."

The Prana nodded. "Then let us return to the symphysis."

They once more followed the Prana through the

zoo of hodgepodge creatures. As they walked, a question occurred to Kyoto.

"I understand that the Manti are determined to exterminate humanity, but why did they wait two years between attacks? It doesn't make sense."

"The doorway the Manti originally used to enter your star system was near your ancestral homeworld," the Prana said. "When you and Memory destroyed the Manti base on Earth by driving the moon into the planet, their mass shadows shifted position in hyperspace, and the doorway was closed. The Manti continued to search for a new way into your system, or failing that, systems close to yours. When your people began to construct the holographic memorial to your lost homeworld, you erected a stargate near a relatively weak area in realspace. Once the Manti located the weakness, they became aware of the stargate close by."

Mudo swore. "So that's what happened! The hyperspatial connections between stargates exist on a quantum level—until they're used, at which point they expand to accommodate the vessel passing through. They then collapse back to their quantum size until the next time they're used. The Manti were unable to detect the stargates on a quantum level, and they remained at their expanded size only for a few nanoseconds at most, so the Manti were never able to locate them."

The Prana nodded. "But while the Manti worked on breaking through the weakened fabric of spacetime, the stargate near the memorial was used often enough to draw their attention at last. After that, it didn't take long for them to learn how to locate the quantum singularities of your gates and use them to return to your system."

Mudo frowned. "When you say *they* learned, what you really mean is the Prana taught them."

The Prana lowered his gaze in shame. "Yes. The Prime Mother commanded us to find a way to access your stargate system, and we did." He looked up and met their eyes once more. "But we took no pleasure in the task, believe me."

None of them said anything more, and finally they came to the exhibit where the symphysis was kept. The tentacles of the jellyfish-like thing undulated faster than before, as if it was excited, and Kyoto wondered if it was already aware of their intentions.

"What do we have to do?" Mudo asked.

"We shall upload the specifics to Memory," the Prana said. "She will be able to guide you through the process of traveling to the Weave and delivering the symphysis to the Prime Mother. All you need do right now is take the symphysis and return to your ship."

"But I thought we hadn't left the *Janus*," Kyoto said. "Our physical bodies are still there, aren't they?"

"And if we do not possess physical form in the Daimonion," Hastimukah said, "how can we *take* anything?"

"It's quite simple, actually," Mudo said. "The symphysis doesn't have a tangible form. It's pure energy, pure information. Like a computer program, only far more sophisticated, of course. All one has to do to *take* it is allow it to be transferred into one's mind."

The symphysis suddenly flared bright purple and then vanished.

"Thank you for agreeing to carry the symphysis,

Doctor," the Prana said. "For a being at your stage of evolution, you possess a most developed mind. Even so, you must be careful: the symphysis is quite powerful, and no matter how strong your mind is, you are not Prana. The longer you carry the symphysis, the more difficult it will become."

Mudo looked alarmed. "But I didn't... I mean, I thought someone else would..." He sighed in resignation. "Oh, very well. I suppose we're ready to depart, then."

"In a way, I'm sorry to be leaving," Hastimukah said. "I feel that we've been shown only the merest glimpse of the wonders the Daimonion has to offer."

The Prana smiled. "If you succeed in delivering the symphysis, relations shall change between our peoples. If that occurs, perhaps you shall visit us again one day."

Hastimukah returned the Prana's smile. "I'd like that."

The Prana held up his hand in a gesture of farewell...

... and they found themselves once more on the bridge of the *Janus*.

"Welcome back," Memory said.

Kyoto blinked several times, trying to fight off a dizzying sense of disorientation. Her body felt thick and heavy, as if she was unaccustomed to being encased within its flesh. The holoscreen showed the image of a large Prana that hovered almost nose to nose with the *Janus*, and Kyoto knew that she gazed upon the Prana's actual form. She looked at the Prana's armored, eyeless face and tried to reconcile the appearance of this insectine monster with its gentle aspect in the Daimonion, but she couldn't do it. Even

was on his tenth protein square—surprising, considering he currently possessed Aspen DeFonesca's trim figure. The alien noticed Kyoto staring at him, gulped down the last of his protein square, and smiled apologetically.

"Sorry. The nanocolony inside me needs nourishment, too. The food on Residuum ships contains special additives just to feed nanoparticles, but without them, I'm forced to eat quite a bit more than I normally would."

"Don't worry," Mudo said. "We brought plenty. And as lousy as they taste, you're welcome to them. The only thing worse than modified soy protein is unmodified soy protein." The scientist shuddered at the thought.

"Really? I find them quite tasty." Hastimukah grabbed another square from the platter in the center of the table, bit off a large hunk, and started chewing. "Rather reminds me of the deep-root we used to eat on Bergelmir. You could only get to it during summers, when the ice fields weren't so thick."

They fell silent while Hastimukah finished eating. Eventually, Mudo said, "It's funny, isn't it?"

Kyoto finished the last sip of her water before asking, "What is?"

Mudo made a vague hand gesture. "This. Life… existence… our mission…"

Kyoto groaned. "I don't do existential, remember?"

Mudo smiled. "Indulge me this once, Kyoto. It's all such a line of tumbling dominoes, isn't it? Except even that comparison doesn't fit, because the dominoes are always set up intentionally in a specific pattern. But existence is far less neat than that. Think of it: if we had positioned the stargate near the Earth

Memorial a few kilometers away from where it was finally placed, the Manti might never have discovered it, and they might never have found a way back into our system."

"And if you hadn't chosen to speak to me at the protest yesterday, Commander," Hastimukah added, "I might not have contacted you last night. And in that case, I never would have learned of the *Janus*'s journey and could not have stolen aboard in the guise of Ms. DeFonesca."

Kyoto joined in, warming to the topic. "And if you weren't here to give Memory a dose of Residuum nanotech, we never would've escaped the mass shadow after we first entered hyperspace. The *Janus* would've been destroyed, and Dr. Mudo and me along with it."

"And without the nanotech, Memory wouldn't have become merged with the Manti biomaterial," Mudo added. "The Prana might not have detected the *Janus* then, and we would've been caught in Rhea's catastrophic return to realspace."

"And we would not now be bearing the symphysis to the Weave," Hastimukah finished. "The chain of events does seem rather miraculous when one thinks about it."

"Preposterous is more like it," Mudo said.

Kyoto put her empty water container in the recycling bin. "One of the first things they taught us at the Defender Academy was that you can do all the planning you want to before a battle, but once the blasting starts, all those plans are shot to hell. A battle is like a sped-up microcosm of life. You have to adapt constantly to changing and unforeseen circumstances if you want to keep from getting your ass blown off. Those who can adapt the fastest—and who are damn lucky to boot—are the ones who stand the greatest chance of surviving."

"In other words, life is what happens while you're busy making other plans, eh?" Mudo said.

Kyoto smiled. "Something like that." She stood. "Now, if you gentlemen—if I can apply that term to you, Hastimukah, considering the body you're wearing—will excuse me, I'm going to try to catch some sleep before the next domino falls."

She sits within a pit at the precise center of the Weave, antennae caressing the living strands created from the genetic material of untold thousands of extinct races, her every touch sending and receiving vast oceans of information. Clustered around her, seeing to her physical needs—delivering sustenance, carrying away waste, grooming and pleasuring her, and most importantly, tending to her eggs—are her attendants, the Chula. She created this caste for just these purposes, and they have no other thought, no other desire than to serve her, the Prime Mother. Their work is vital, for it frees her to concentrate on the information that courses through the Weave like heart's blood. So much... so much... Sometimes she wonders how she ever manages to keep up with it all.

For example, in the Quatara system, the dominant species is on the verge of discovering how to effortlessly transform matter to energy and back again. Such a capability might well prove a serious threat to her children, so the Prime Mother immediately dispatches a Swarm to harvest the Quatarans. Elsewhere in realspace, a race of artificial constructs called the Gan, originally designed for warfare, turns on its makers, completely destroying them. The constructs are of no use to the Prime Mother as they cannot supply genetic material, and since their primary goal seems to be the peaceful contemplation of esoteric mathematics, she decides to leave them alone—for now.

At the moment, though, her greatest concern is the

species that inhabits the Sol system: the humans. Some time ago they discovered the means to enter the Realm of Shadows, and so of course the Prime Mother commanded they be harvested. The first swarm she sent enjoyed only limited success, seizing the human homeworld, but failing to destroy their colonies. The Second Swarm thinned the population in those colonies quite nicely, but it too was stopped before finishing its task. Worse yet, the doorway to Sol's system was closed to her children, and she feared they might never finish harvesting the humans.

But then a new doorway was found—one that allowed her children to use the humans' own stargates against them. She dispatched a third swarm, but though it struck with savage swiftness, still the human colonies endured, and her children found themselves once more barred from Sol's system. In all the long eons since she gave birth to the Manti, never has a single species proved so... so *vexing!*

In frustration, the Prime Mother releases a burst of psychic energy, killing a number of Chula instantly. Without pause, their corpses are gathered up and added to the Prime Mother's endless stream of nourishment. She doesn't notice. She's too busy listening to a new bit of information that has just made its way to her across the reaches of the Realm of Shadows. It is a communication signal, primitive and weak, but still intelligible. The message begins: "Greetings, Prime Mother. My name is Memory..."

TWENTY-FOUR

Kyoto dreamed of a zoo full of Manti. The Buggers were trying to break free of their ferroceramic cages, and holographic mothers and fathers grabbed their holographic children and ran, screaming synthesized screams. Kyoto came *flying up in her Defender and fired upon the Manti, but all that came out of her* pulse cannon were broken toys and eyeglasses like the kind Mudo wore. The objects bounced off the Manti's carapaces without causing so much as a single scratch.

As Kyoto soared over the zoo, the Buggers burst out of their cages and attacked the holograms, which only moments before had been staring and pointing at them in horrified delight. The Manti grabbed their simulated victims with real foreclaws, bit into them with real mandibles, and the holopeople screamed as they exploded in a flash of light and were gone.

Kyoto brought her ship around for another pass, intending to deploy fastlock missiles, but before she could fire the weapons, the Defender began to lose

271

speed. Suddenly the ship broke apart into millions of tiny pieces as the nanoparticles that comprised the G-7 could no longer hold together. Kyoto fell to the ground in a shower of tiny gray globules. She reached for her sidearm and instead grabbed hold of an old holopad. She screamed as the Manti gathered beneath her, lifted their heads, and opened their mouths wide.

It was feeding time at the zoo.

"Wake up, Mei! You're needed on the bridge!"

Kyoto opened her eyes, and for an instant she didn't know who or where she was. But then she remembered and wished she diddn't. At least Memory had rescued her from that weird dream.

She sat up and rubbed her eyes. "What's wrong? Are we under attack?" Even if they were, she was too groggy to care. She felt as if she'd gotten only a few minutes of sleep, though her wrist chron said it had been three hours since she'd closed her eyes.

"We're not under attack, at least not yet. There's a ship approaching. Hastimukah says it's the *Eye of Dardanus*, the vessel that brought him to the Solar Colonies."

That tidbit of information snapped Kyoto fully awake. A Residuum starship was here in hyperspace? Coming toward the *Janus*?

She swung her legs over the edge of the bunk and planted her feet on the floor. She stood, her rest-starved muscles protesting quite vigorously, but she ignored the discomfort. The other bunks were empty, though the covers were mussed on two of them. Either Mudo and Hastimukah didn't need as much rest as she did, or they hadn't been able to fall asleep.

"On my way, Memory."

Kyoto left the sleeping quarters, walked through the *Janus*'s cramped galley, and climbed the metal ladder to the flight cabin. The holoscreen had been activated, and Mudo and Hastimukah were staring at the image of a gray, wedge-shaped object that didn't look much like a starship to her.

She stumbled past them and fell into her pilot's chair. "What's going on, gentlemen?"

"That's the *Eye of Dardanus*," Hastimukah said. "I believe Captain Kryllian and his crew have come to retrieve me. Probably because I didn't bother to get approval from the Ascendancy before joining your mission."

"Wonderful," Mudo said. "Not only are you an imposter and a stowaway, you're also a deserter."

Despite the situation, Hastimukah grinned. "I prefer the term 'on unofficial leave.'"

"That thing's a ship?" Kyoto said. "It looks more like a gigantic blob of mucus." Then she remembered an element of her dream. "That gray stuff is nanotech, isn't it? The entire ship is made out of it."

"Yes," Hastimukah said. "And appearances to the contrary, it's extremely powerful and swift. More than a match for the *Janus*, I'm afraid. We should contact Captain Kryllian so I can give myself up. Once they have me in custody, they should leave you alone to deliver the symphysis and complete the mission."

Kyoto didn't like the idea. Hastimukah may have intruded on this mission, but as far as she was concerned, he'd become a vital part of it. But if what he'd said about the *Dardanus*'s capabilities was true, there was no way she could keep Kryllian from taking Hastimukah back.

"Memory, can you think of any way—"

Kyoto was interrupted by the chirping of the ship's comlink. They were being hailed. She sighed. It looked like they'd run out of time to come up with clever ideas. "Put the signal through, Memory."

The holoscreen switched views. It now displayed a picture of a human in a vacc suit standing next to a giant shrimp. Kyoto wasn't sure which was more surprising—the sight of the oversize crustacean or the fact that the man was General Adams.

"Greetings, Hastimukah," the jumbo shrimp said. "I assume that one of the three humans I am looking at is you. And do not attempt to lie; sensor scans have already confirmed that there are two humans and one Bergelmirian onboard."

"They've done more than that," Adams growled. "Sensors indicate that Manti biomaterial has been integrated into the *Janus*'s systems—including the AI mainframe! What the hell were you thinking, Mudo?" Adams frowned as if he'd only just realized something and then turned to Kryllian. "Wait a minute... *two* humans? You mean Aspen DeFonesca—the real one—didn't go on the mission?" He groaned. "When that woman wakes up, I'm never going to hear the end of this!"

"I understand your concern, General," Mudo said, "but this hardly seems like the best venue for explanations. I promise to tell you everything later—after we're finished."

"You *are* finished," Kryllian said. "All of you. We will send a shuttle, and the three of you will board it and be ferried to the *Dardanus*. Afterward, we shall destroy your ship before returning to realspace."

"What?" Kyoto couldn't tell who said it louder—she or General Adams.

Kryllian turned to Adams, his antennae waving erratically. "I was prepared to return the *Janus* to your people's star system, but now that its secret has been revealed, I cannot allow the ship to continue to exist, any more than I would let a Manti out of my sights without firing upon it."

Adams scowled in anger. "We had a deal, Kryllian."

"Yes, but it appears you were less than forthcoming with me, General. Or did you merely forget to tell me the *Janus* was for all intents and purposes a Manti cyborg?"

"I had absolutely no knowledge of this," Adams said. "The schematics Dr. Mudo showed me did not reveal the presence of any Manti biomaterial. Either he hid that fact from me or the material was somehow added after the *Janus* entered hyperspace. But it's there now, and if the *Janus* were any other ship, I'd let you blow it to subatomic dust the moment my people were off it. But the *Janus* contains the prototype of the first hyperdrive we've ever developed. We need that engine if we're to have any hope of finally defeating the Manti."

"Your primitive prototype is no concern of the Residuum's, General. It isn't up to us to—"

"Memory, cut audio feed," Kyoto whispered. The sound fell mute, and Adams and Kryllian continued their argument in silence.

"Perhaps they will help us once we tell them of the symphysis," Hastimukah suggested.

"Your captain doesn't strike me as the helpful type," Mudo said.

"That's true enough. His species tends to be quite stubborn and highly focused, to put it politely.

Effective traits in warriors, but not always assets in diplomatic situations. What about General Adams?"

"Very similar," Kyoto admitted, "but it's possible to change his mind. If you have a day or two to spare."

"So if we intend to deliver the symphysis," Mudo said, "we must do so on our own."

"But how?" Hastimukah said. "There's no way we can escape the *Dardanus*."

Memory simulated the sound of clearing her nonexistent throat.

"There might be one way…"

"Captain!" Suletu shouted. "The *Janus* is turning about—she's going to make a run for it!"

The bridge of the *Dardanus* was still transparent, and Adams watched the *Janus* turn and then begin to pull away.

Kryllian's antennae whipped the air, and he pounded a cheliped on the arm of his chair. "Damn it, Adams! What in the death tides is wrong with humans? Are you all congenitally stupid?"

Adams bristled at the comment, but all he said was, "Maybe if I spoke with my people…"

"Very well," Kryllian said. "But be quick about it!" The Grindan then turned to his helm officer. "Give pursuit, but let's keep our distance for the time being."

"Aye, Captain."

Adams activated his vacc suit comlink. "Kyoto, Mudo, this is Adams. Come in." He waited several seconds, but there was no reply. "I know you can read me, so don't pretend you can't! I don't know what kind of game you're playing, but it's not amusing.

Bring the *Janus* back around and surrender. And you'd better believe that's an order!"

Still no reply.

"You had your chance, General," Kryllian said. "Now it's up to us."

Before Adams could protest, Kryllian said, "Suletu, target the *Janus* with a tractor beam and grab hold of them.

The nanotech blob worked the controls of his station for a moment. "Suletu is sorry, Captain, but our ship is too close to a mass shadow for the tractor beam to operate effectively."

"Why not?" Adams asked.

"The gravitational pull of the mass shadow will warp the beam," Suletu explained, "preventing us from maintaining a lock on the *Janus*."

"We have no choice, then," Kryllian said. "Target their engines."

"No!" Adams shouted. "You could set off a chain reaction that would destroy the entire ship!"

"Relax, General," Kryllian said. "Residuum weapons function with surgical precision. I wish only to disable the craft, not destroy it."

Adams wasn't sure if he believed the Grindan or not. Kryllian struck him as the type of warrior who would do whatever it took to carry out his orders. On the other hand, it wasn't as if he could do anything to stop Kryllian, not here on his own ship.

"All right," Adams said reluctantly. "But your people better be damn good shots."

"They are, trust me." Kryllian turned to his second in command. "Power up particle weapons and target the *Janus*'s engines. Go for a disabling strike only."

"Aye, Captain," Suletu said. But as the blob began

to carry out Kryllian's command, the quad-armed catwoman at the helm glanced over her shoulder at the Grindan.

"The *Janus* is picking up speed, sir. What's more, she's veering dangerously close to the mass shadow. What are your orders?"

Adams watched as the *Janus* angled to port and headed toward a gigantic shroud of darkness. *What are you up to, Kyoto?* he thought.

"Are we in firing range?" Kryllian asked.

"At the outer edge," Suletu responded. "At this distance, we'll be able to hit the *Janus*, but there's no guarantee that we can do so with the precision required to only disable the ship's engines."

Kryllian glanced at Adams with shiny black eyes, and the human had the sense that if he weren't aboard, the Grindan would just say to hell with it and blow the *Janus* out of hyperspace.

"Helm, close to within ten kilometers, but keep an eye on that mass shadow. We don't want to get any closer to it than we have to.

"Aye, sir." The catwoman's four hands deftly maneuvered across her console, and the *Dardanus* turned to port and began to pick up speed.

Adams watched as the *Dardanus* quickly closed the distance to the *Janus*.

"We're within ten point two kilometers, Captain," the helm officer said.

"Good enough, Suletu?" Kryllian asked.

"Yes, Captain," the blob confirmed.

"Good. Fire at—" But before the Grindan could finish his command, the *Janus* suddenly performed a 180 degree turn and came streaking straight at the *Dardanus* on a collision course.

"Evasive maneuvers!" Kryllian shouted. "Now!"

The helm officer turned the *Dardanus* hard to port—right toward the mass shadow.

Adams had just enough time to grab the arm of Kryllian's command chair as the *Janus* soared by, so close Adams thought he could have reached out and brushed his fingers against the ship's hull. An instant later, alarms shrieked, and the *Dardanus* began to shake violently.

"Status!" Kryllian shouted.

"We've been caught by an eddy within the mass shadow, Captain!" Suletu yelled. "It's pulling us in!"

Darkness—cold, unforgiving, and eternally hungry—rushed toward them, and Kryllian ordered the bridge to be rendered opaque once more. Then he commanded, "Helm, increase engine power by twenty percent! Get us out of here!"

"Aye!" the catwoman shouted, but there was an undercurrent of fear in her voice that told Adams Kryllian's orders were going to be easier given than carried out. He wished there was something he could do to help, but not only wasn't this his ship, he had no idea how Residuum technology worked. All he could do was hold on, watch, and try not to get knocked on his ass.

A loud, deep-pitched moaning filled the air, sounding more like a living being in pain than the noise of straining starship engines. The tremors rippling through the *Dardanus* became more violent, and Adams had to clench his mouth shut tight to keep his chattering teeth from biting his tongue. The vibrations continued to worsen, and just when Adams was sure the *Dardanus* was going to be crushed by the gravity of the mass shadow, the shaking ceased, and the moaning of the engines grew softer until it finally faded altogether.

"What's our situation?" Kryllian said. His normally brown carapace had deepened to black, and his voice was little more than a whisper.

"We have stabilized for the moment," Suletu said. "The eddy pulled us into a neutral space within the mass shadow, somewhat like the eye of a storm. In realspace, this might well be the distance between a planet and its moon. Here, it's a tiny bubble of null gravity barely large enough for the *Dardanus*. As long as we stay here, we are in no immediate danger."

"Can we break free?" Kryllian asked.

Suletu consulted his console's readout. "I believe so, Captain, but not for several hours. The null zone is mobile, likely reflecting the orbital pattern of the two celestial bodies between it in realspace. It will move farther into the mass shadow before it moves back closer to the edge. Once it's near the edge, with any luck, we should be able to break free."

Adams didn't quite understand everything Suletu said, but he couldn't keep from smiling. Whatever his people were up to they had needed to buy some time, and they'd done so.

"Any damage?" Kryllian asked.

"Negligible," Suletu reported. "All shall be repaired before we reach the breakaway point."

"Estimated time until that occurs?" Kryllian asked.

"Seven hours," Suletu said. "Eight at the most."

Kryllian made a bubbling sound that Adams took to be a sigh. "Well, General, it appears that we are going to have some time to get to know each other."

"Looks like," Adams agreed.

The two commanders looked at each other in uncomfortable silence for several long moments. Finally, Adams said, "So... got any hobbies?"

CHAPTER

TWENTY-FIVE

"There it is." Kyoto's voice was so hushed, she wasn't certain she had spoken aloud.

The holoscreen showed the image of a gigantic structure stretching between two mass shadows. Words sprang to Kyoto's mind: *web, lattice, mesh…* but the only word that could properly describe the place was weave. Strands of greenish material cris-scrossed, connected, linked together in seemingly random patterns. Some strands were longer and thicker than others; some lines were straight, some crooked, some bent at precise angles. It looked organic, something that had grown instead of having been planned and constructed. But the more Kyoto looked at it, the less random it seemed. She began to sense that there was some sort of underlying pattern here, some principle of design that had guided the Manti in their work, but she couldn't fully grasp it. Perhaps she was merely imagining it, she thought. Or perhaps the Weave was too complex, too profoundly alien for her to perceive its ultimate pattern.

"The building material they use..." Hastimukah began.

"Is biomaterial harvested from their victims," Mudo said. "Reconstituted, no doubt. Probably partially digested, mixed with various enzymes, and then regurgitated." He suddenly winced and touched a hand to his temple.

"Is something wrong?" Kyoto asked, concerned.

"It's nothing," Mudo replied. "I have a bit of a headache. Likely an effect of carrying the symphysis within my mind." He smiled weakly. "No cause for concern."

From the look of pain on Mudo's face when he'd grimaced, Kyoto thought he had more than a "bit" of a headache, but she decided not to pursue the issue at the moment. She'd keep a close eye on the scientist, though, to make sure his condition didn't worsen.

A Manti passed them on the starboard side, moving rapidly toward the Weave. It was soon followed by a second, then a third. As they watched, a constant stream of Landers, Mutants, Stingrays, Yellow Jackets, and Reapers traveled to and from the Weave. All the traffic reminded Kyoto of the spaceport on Europa, only this was a hundred times busier.

A cold lance of fear speared her gut. There were so many Buggers... If they detected the *Janus*, there was no way the crew would be able to repel them all.

"How's our camouflage holding, Memory?" Kyoto asked.

"Just fine, Mei. As far as the Couriers are concerned, we're only one more Manti returning home."

"Couriers?" Hastimukah asked.

"Look." Mudo pointed to the holoscreen. A Stingray flew by carrying the mangled body of what looked like a feathered lizard between its foreclaws.

"They're carrying biomaterial." Hastimukah looked pale.

"Are you all right?" Kyoto asked.

"If my nanocolony wasn't preventing it, I would be vomiting right now," Hastimukah said. "The Weave is so large. Can you imagine how many beings had to die through the millennia to supply that much building material? Billions? Trillions? Is there even a word in any language to represent so high a number?"

Kyoto and Mudo said nothing. What could they? What could anyone?

"Not all the Couriers are bringing biomaterial," Memory said. "Many more come bearing information for the Prime Mother. Their information is chemically encoded, and once they reach the Weave, they will touch a strand, and the chemicals will be transformed into energy and then transmitted to the Prime Mother. Afterward, they shall turn about and head back the way they came to go gather more."

"What sort of information?" Mudo asked.

"Data from the systems the Manti farm. Some regarding species' development, their strengths and weaknesses. Some dealing with reports from various harvests that are under way."

Memory didn't sound disturbed by this, but Kyoto chose not to mention it. She did, however, file it away for future reference.

"How large is the Weave?" Kyoto asked, curious.

"The shadowpath is extremely wide at this point—perhaps the widest in all hyperspace—which is one of the reasons the Prime Mother decided to build here in the first place. From edge to edge, the Weave is approximately nine million kilometers in length and about a third of that in width."

Kyoto was stunned. Jupiter, the largest planet in Sol's system, was 142,984 kilometers in diameter. The Weave was about—she did some quick math in her head—sixty-three times larger. She couldn't conceive of something artificial being so vast, especially something made from the biomaterial of murdered species from throughout realspace. She felt nauseated, and unlike Hastimukah, she didn't have a body full of nanoparticles to keep her from throwing up all over the pilot's console. She had to make do with sheer willpower, and while it was a near thing, she managed to hold back.

"How are we supposed to find the Prime Mother if the Weave is so large?" Hastimukah asked.

"She sits in the exact center of the Weave," Memory said. "And she never moves from that spot unless forced to."

"Finding her won't be the problem," Kyoto said. "Getting to her will be the hard part. But if Memory's plan works, we should be able to pull it off." *If,* she added mentally, *being the key word.*

The holoscreen showed a pair of Manti coming toward the *Janus* at top speed. The two Buggers looked something like Landers, except they were larger and their carapaces were orange with black trim.

"Look alive," Kyoto said. "Here comes our official welcoming committee."

"Those were Gamma Landers," Memory said. "They're far stronger and much more dangerous than the regular version of the caste."

"They're sentries. They've sensed that we're not part of the normal schedule and have come to investigate."

Koto found it hard to believe that with the constant coming and going of hundreds, perhaps thousands of Manti every moment that a single unscheduled visitor would draw the sentries' notice this quickly. But here they were.

"Leave it to me, everyone," Memory said.

Kyoto was willing to do so, but she kept one hand close to the weapons controls, just in case. She pulled back on the joystick and activated breaking thrusters. According to Memory, any Manti challenged by the sentries—even if of a higher caste—would stop to submit to their inspection.

The sentries came to within a few dozen meters of the *Janus*, then stopped. Their bodies were surrounded by the nearly skintight aura that protected and sustained them in hyperspace. Kyoto knew that Memory was generating a similar field around the *Janus* by modifying the emissions of the ship's energy shield. These auras were the Manti's primary means of acquiring sensory information, as well as sending it.

One of the sentries sent an orange-tinted energy bolt crackling toward the *Janus*. Kyoto braced for impact, but though her hand twitched toward the weapons controls, she restrained herself. The orange energy bolt became more diffuse as it approached, and by the time it reached the *Janus*, it gently flowed across the starship's shield and was absorbed.

A moment passed, and then Memory sent a similar bolt of energy crackling back toward the sentry—this one colored a bright green to simulate a Lander's emission. The bolt washed harmlessly over the sentry and was quickly absorbed. The two sentries maintained their position before the *Janus* for several more moments—each one seemingly longer than the last—and Kyoto feared the knowledge Memory had gained from her fusion with the Manti biomaterial, not to mention the data the Prana had downloaded into her, had proven ineffective. She touched her fingers to the controls and was just about to power up weapons when the sentries turned and headed back toward the Weave.

"I'll be damned. It worked." Kyoto pulled her hand away from the weapons controls.

"Did they believe your cover story?" Mudo asked.

"Of course," Memory said, sounding offended that Mudo could even conceive of such a question, let alone give voice to it. "I told them that I discovered the wreckage of an ancient spacecraft on an asteroid in realspace that was emitting bursts of hyperetheric radiation with an energy signature unlike any the Manti had ever encountered before. I hinted that I believed it might be the by-product of an entirely new hyperdrive design far more powerful than anything currently known. Though of course, since I am only a humble Lander, I couldn't possibly tell for certain. There—happy now, Gerhard?"

"Ecstatic," Mudo said.

"And that's really enough to get us direct passage to the Prime Mother?" Kyoto asked. "It all seems too easy."

"The Prime Mother is always concerned about new technologies, especially if they have anything to do with hyperspace. And since the Prana are confined to the Daimonion, the Prime Mother is the only truly thinking being in the Weave. There is no one else to go to *but* her." Memory paused. "And as far as being easy, it won't be. There's no great trick to fooling a witless pair of Sentinels. From here on out, it really starts to get dangerous."

"Starts to, eh?" Hastimukah's laughter had a hysterical edge to it. "It must be nice to be an artificial intelligence at times."

"Don't let those carefully modulated vocal tones fool you," Mudo said. "Deep down inside her mainframe, she's just as scared as the rest of us. Artificial or not, no one wants to die."

Kyoto had a difficult time imagining Memory as being afraid. After all, with her ability to make backup copies of herself—like the dormant Memory Junior in Kyoto's G-7—the AI was virtually immortal.

"Plot a course for the Prime Mother, Memory," Kyoto said.

"I'm surprised the sentries aren't going to escort us to ensure we don't stray from our designated path," Hastimukah said.

"There is no need for an escort. The Sentries believe we are Manti, and no Manti would ever do anything other that what it was told. It's unthinkable."

Kyoto wondered if Memory had become Manti enough for the same to apply to her.

The course came up on the holoscreen. Kyoto eased the joystick forward, and the *Janus* joined the streams of Manti flying toward the Weave. As they descended, Kyoto examined the coordinates more closely.

"I don't know if I'm reading this right, Memory, but it looks like you have us setting down a good distance from the Prime Mother."

"You're absolutely right, Mei. That's the closest we

can land without giving ourselves away. No Manti, not even the Prana, are permitted to approach the Prime Mother in flight. The Manti consider that a sign of disrespect; the Prime Mother must always be approached on foot."

"Just what we need," Kyoto muttered. "A Bugger with a queen-size ego."

"It's understandable," Mudo said. "Since flying Manti never attack on the ground, flying in the presence of the Prime Mother would be viewed as an aggressive action."

"Sounds logical," Kyoto said. But she couldn't help feeling paranoid. If Memory intended to betray them, setting down away from the Prime Mother—where the symphysis couldn't be used against her—would be a good way to do it. Especially if the Manti wanted to avoid blasting the *Janus* and wasting the crew's biomaterial.

She wished there were some way she could share her concerns with Mudo and Hastimukah, but with Memory ever present and always listening, that was impossible. And there was no way she could deactivate Memory long enough to have a private conversation with the others without arousing the AI's suspicions. There was nothing Kyoto could do but land the *Janus* at the coordinates Memory had given her and stay alert for trouble.

Kyoto made sure to match the speed and trajectory of the other Manti, especially the Landers. If their masquerade was to work, they had to play their role to the hilt. Even so, she half-expected the Manti around them to see through their charade any instant and bombard the ship with energy blasts. But the Buggers paid absolutely no attention to the *Janus*. Either they sensed the Manti energy signature the ship was giving off, or they couldn't conceive of the Sentries allowing anything other than Manti past them. Kyoto didn't care which it was, as long as it worked.

The Weave grew larger on the holoscreen as they approached, and the individual strands which had seemed so thin and fine from a distance now appeared as wide as one of Europa's multilane causeways. There would be more than enough room to land the *Janus*.

When they'd descended to within a kilometer of the strand, Kyoto activated landing thrusters. The strandway was far from deserted, however. Manti of all castes scuttled across its surface, heading in both directions. Flying Manti such as Landers, Yellow Jackets, and the rest crawled slowly along the strandway, appearing to confirm Memory's explanation about her choice of landing zone. Ground Manti were mixed in among the fliers—small two-legged Infectors and lumbering spiderlike Widows.

"Memory, we're going to need a clear space to set down, and we'll need it soon," Kyoto said.

"No need for concern, Mei. Just watch."

As the *Janus* closed to within meters of the strandway, without missing a step, the Manti altered their courses to open a space for the ship to land. Seconds later, the *Janus* had touched down on the Manti Weave.

Kyoto grinned. "A thought just occurred to me."

"What?" Mudo asked.

"For the first time since the Manti attacked Earth, humans are invading *their* world."

Mudo grinned back. "Not only is turnabout fair play, it's also extremely satisfying." But though the scientist sounded fine, his skin was pale and his eyes bloodshot.

"Are you going to be able to hold onto the symphysis long enough to complete our mission?" she asked.

"I'll have to, won't I?" Mudo said grimly.

Kyoto looked at him a moment longer, the nodded. She powered down the *Janus*'s engines, then released her seat restraints and stood.

"Time to suit up, gentlemen. We've got a delivery to make."

CHAPTER

TWENTY-SIX

"I feel like a gnort walking among a pride of starving vomisa," Hastimukah said.

"I don't know the animals you're talking about," Kyoto said, "but I get the analogy."

The three of them were encased in vacc suits, but though they were protected from the airless void of hyperspace, they all knew the suits would be no better defense than tissue paper should one of the Manti see through their ruse and attack.

"I'm beginning to wish Memory hadn't used her nanoparticles to adapt our helmets' faceplates so we can see in hyperspace," Mudo said. "I could do without the sight of all this... traffic."

Mudo sounded like a man who was deeply terrified and fighting desperately not to let his fear get the better of him. Kyoto understood; she was rather terrified herself. Though the three of them had each fought the Manti in one fashion or another, rarely had they gotten so physically close to their alien foe, and never to so damn many. Dozens upon dozens of Buggers surrounded them, some moving faster, some slower, but while some sense kept the Manti from colliding with one another, they often came within a meter or less of the three companions. The psychological pressure of being in the midst of the enemy was quickly taking its toll on the three of them. At least they didn't have to maintain comlink silence. Memory had assured them that the Manti wouldn't be able to pick up their com signals, and since there was no atmosphere to transmit sound, they could talk all they wanted.

Beyond being surrounded by Manti, walking on the strandway was an eerie experience for other reasons. The sky—if that was the right word for it— was a murky gray, with the inky black of a mass shadow looming far in the distance. The Weave generated enough gravity to keep them from floating off into hyperspace, and with the extra help of their grav boots, they could walk almost normally. The spongy substance of the Weave gave slightly beneath their feet with each step, and Kyoto couldn't keep from thinking about what they were walking on. The strandway, like the rest of the Weave, was made from the biomaterial of the Manti's victims. How many individuals from how many different species had they stepped on since they'd landed? And if they were discovered, would they too be reduced to construction material for countless generations of Manti to crawl over?

Just then an Infector stomped up to them and put down its clawfoot close to Mudo's boot, nearly stepping on it.

Panicked, the scientist reached for the blaster at his side, and Kyoto grabbed his hand before he could draw the weapon. Infectors were nasty little Buggers. During a battle, they would be towed into attack position by flying Manti like Landers. Once in place, they began to spew corrosive chemicals that could eat through just about anything. The last thing they needed right now was for Mudo to take a shot at the clumsy Infector and alert it to their presence.

The Infector hesitated, as if it sensed something was wrong. Memory's nanoparticles had done more than help them see in the Weave. They were generating Manti energy signatures so that they could walk unnoticed among the Buggers. But now Kyoto feared the nanotech wasn't working.

Finally, the Infector picked up its big foot and stomped off.

"It's okay, Gerhard," Kyoto said softly. "You can let go of the blaster now. The Infector is gone."

Mudo turned to look at her, his hand still gripping the weapon. "I believe that's the first time you've ever called me by my first name."

Kyoto gently pried Mudo's fingers from his blaster. "This doesn't seem like a time to stand on formalities. Besides, it got your attention, didn't it?"

Mudo smiled. "I suppose it did." He looked at Kyoto for a moment, and she thought she saw something in his eyes that she'd never seen before, as if he were feeling something new, or at least something he'd never allowed himself to show before.

"I'm all right now... Mei. Let's keep going."

Mudo turned away, and Kyoto had the sense it was as much to break eye contact as it was to continue with their mission. Maybe more.

She didn't know what to think or feel about this latest development—if it even could be called that—so she decided to ignore it for the time being. Besides, there was an excellent chance they would all be dead very soon, and then she wouldn't have to deal with it.

That's it, Kyoto, she told herself. *Keep looking on the bright side.*

"Our vacc suits came with handblasters as standard issue," she said. "But to be honest, they're little more than ferroceramic security blankets here. Even on their highest setting, they won't do much more than irritate a Manti."

"So what you're saying is, we should keep our hands off them," Hastimukah said.

"No," she answered, though that was of course exactly what she meant. "Just don't reach for them unless you really need them."

"Point taken," Mudo said.

They continued on in silence after that, walking shoulder to shoulder to combine their energy signatures and make themselves appear to be a larger Manti. After twenty more minutes of travel, the Prime Mother's tower finally came into view.

Even from this distance, the structure was huge. Kyoto had seen a similar tower on Earth during the war against the last swarm. That tower had been the Manti's base in Sol's system, and it had been destroyed when she and Memory crashed the moon into Earth. But this tower was two, maybe three times larger. As they drew closer, they could see that its base was an olive green mound with a round central opening. Green supports curved outward from the central tower and back down over the mound, looking like segmented insect legs. The tower itself stretched upward to a tapering point, more insect legs flaring out and curving upward like the branches of some gigantic, nightmarish tree. Glowing lines of greenish energy radiated from the tower's base and through the strandway, hundreds of them, though they grew more faint the farther away from the tower they reached, until they faded altogether.

Kyoto remembered what Memory had told them about how the Manti brought information to the Prime Mother. "Their information is chemically encoded, and once they reach the Weave, they will touch a strand, and the chemicals will be transformed into energy and then transmitted to the Prime Mother."

Kyoto realized that the lines of energy she was looking at were the communication streams passing to and from the Prime Mother. They probably became more concentrated the closer they came to the tower, which was why the lines of energy were visible here and nowhere else. So not only were she and the others walking on recycled biomaterial, but also on thousands, maybe millions of com signals.

There was something about this last thought that bothered Kyoto, something important, but she wasn't sure what.

When they were within half a kilometer of the tower, Kyoto stopped and turned to Mudo and Hastimukah. "How are you holding up?" she asked the scientist, careful to avoid using his name.

"Adequately."

Mudo's face told a different story, though. His skin was chalk white, and sweat streamed off his forehead. Kyoto checked his vacc suit's external readout and saw that all systems were functioning properly.

Mudo's condition had nothing to do with suit failure, but then she hadn't thought it had.

"You look terrible," she said.

Mudo started to laugh, but then he grimaced in agony, swayed, and started to fall over. Kyoto and Hastimukah each grabbed hold of one of the scientist's arms to steady him.

"You can't go on like this!" Kyoto said. "The damn symphysis is killing you!"

"Nonsense," Mudo muttered. He tried to shrug free of his companions, but he was too weak. "If we could rest a moment…"

"I'm sorry, but if we stop for too long, we're bound to give ourselves away," Kyoto said. "None of the Manti are slowing down, let alone stopping to rest."

"Perhaps one of us could carry the symphysis the rest of the way," Hastimukah suggested.

Mudo shook his head. "The Prana gave it to me. It's my burden. Besides," he said with a weak grin, "I have absolutely no idea how to pass it to someone else."

"I guess you'll just have to lean on us, then," Kyoto said.

She and Hastimukah maintained their hold on Mudo's arms, and then the three of them continued forward, more slowly than before. Kyoto worried that their slower pace might draw the Manti's attention, for the Buggers were all crawling at the fastest speed of which they were capable. But if any of them noticed the trio's slower pace, they gave no indication.

The three trudged on toward the entrance to the Manti tower. It rose forth from the middle of the strandway, but the Buggers all detoured around it. Evidently none was allowed to approach the Prime

Mother without an invitation. Good thing Memory had secured one for them.

As they drew closer to the giant edifice, Kyoto saw that the entrance—which was nearly large enough for a Battleship to pass through—was flanked by a pair of shock towers, organic weapons capable of firing powerful energy projectiles. Kyoto had encountered them before, while battling the last swarm on Europa. The projectiles were slow moving, but they were capable of inflicting a lot of damage. Kyoto saw no sign of Manti guards, but then with the shock towers in place, there was no need for any. As they approached the entrance, Kyoto could see the crimson furnace that lay at the heart of each shock tower blaze and roil, and though her vacc suit's environmental systems were designed to protect the wearer from temperature extremes, Kyoto nevertheless began sweating.

Over the open comlink channel, Kyoto could hear Mudo's breathing become shallow and rapid, and she feared he was having a heart attack or stroke. But before she could voice her concerns, he gave a little wave as if to say, I'm fine.

The crimson energy of the shock towers seemed to flare more brightly as they began to make their way into the Manti dome, and for an instant Kyoto thought they had been detected by whatever sensory apparatus the shock towers possessed. She braced herself to be engulfed by a seething energy projectile, but the shock towers didn't fire, and the trio moved through entrance without harm.

The interior of the Manti tower was a great hollow dome. Beneath their feet, the floor was covered with radiant lines of energy—the information the Manti were sending to their queen—so many lines that the dome glowed with an eerie green light. The inner walls were completely covered with smooth spheres that glistened in the sour green light. Thanks to Memory's briefing, Kyoto knew what this place was: the Crèche, where the eggs the Prime Mother produced were taken to incubate until they were ready to hatch. Every centimeter of available wall surface was completely taken up by Bugger eggs. Some were small as a fist, hard and opaque, while others were swollen and distended, larger than a human head, surfaces stretched tight and thin. Small insectine forms were visible through the membranous outer layers of their eggs. The larva wriggled around, poked and probed at their spherical prisons, impatient to be born.

There were thousands of eggs—thousands upon thousands. Kyoto had never seen the inside of the Manti tower on Earth, but since it had been the Buggers' main base in Sol's system, she imagined it had looked much the same. Seeing these eggs wiped away whatever last traces of guilt she felt over helping Memory destroy the Earth.

But the eggs weren't the only residents of the dome. Ivory-hued Buggers that looked something like giant fleas crawled over the eggs, tending to them, taking out a Manti larva when it hatched and bearing it away, devouring the empty egg casing, and bringing in a new egg to take the old one's place. From what Memory had told them, these flealike nursemaids were called the Chula, and they served as the Prime Mother's personal attendants. Indeed, they lived and worked in such close proximity to the Prime Mother that they were almost extensions of her, more like the fingers on the end of one's hand than servants.

As Kyoto, Mudo, and Hastimukah stepped farther inside the Crèche, the Chula immediately stopped what they were doing and froze. One by one, they turned their heads in the direction of the newcomers. Should they stop? Keep moving? Kyoto didn't know.

"Memory?" she whispered, even though she knew she didn't have to. "Are you there? We could really use your advice right now."

Silence.

"Perhaps the dome is interfering with our comlink signals," Mudo said, his voice weak and breathy. With a trembling hand he pointed to the glowing lines of energy running through the floor. "There's quite a... concentration of energy here. I wonder if it... helps the incubation process. That would explain—"

Mudo broke off as one of the Chula leaped away from the wall where it had just attached an egg and came falling toward them. The flealike Manti landed directly in front of the trio of invaders and tensed, as if preparing to attack. The Chula began to shake then, its entire body quivering.

"What's happening, Gerhard?" Kyoto asked.

"I'm... not sure. It could be reacting to our... energy signature. Perhaps there's something about it that's... " He took in a hitching breath, and several seconds passed before the scientist could speak again. "... confusing the creature."

Kyoto didn't like the sound of that. It was an all-too-short step from a confused Bugger to an angry Bugger. Slowly, she began to reach for her hand-blaster. But just as her gloved fingers made contact with the weapon, the Chula turned abruptly and scuttled off in the opposite direction.

"It appears we have passed the test," Hastimukah said. "Whatever it was."

Kyoto removed her hand from the blaster. "Should we follow?" Damn, but she hated being cut off from Memory! They couldn't afford to hesitate while they debated what to do. Mudo's condition was worsening, and if there was one thing Buggers never did, it was hesitate.

"Let's keep moving," Mudo said. His voice was little more than a whisper now, and his eyes were glazed and unfocused. "The others are still watching."

Kyoto looked up and saw that the rest of the Chula were indeed still keeping a sharp eye—or whatever organs Manti used instead of eyes—on them.

"I see what you mean," she said. "All right, let's follow that Bugger."

They trailed after the Chula, Kyoto and Hastimukah continuing to prop up their weakened comrade. Evidently satisfied that all was well, the remaining Chula ignored the newcomers and returned to their work.

As the trio neared the center of the dome, Kyoto realized that the floor sloped downward here. The Chula turned back to look at them briefly, and then leaped off in another direction to tend to some other chore.

"What is this?" Kyoto asked. The energy lines ran closer here, as if drawing near an intersection point. Their mingled glow had become more concentrated and intense, making it difficult to see.

"Given the way the floor slopes, I believe it's some manner of pit," Hastimukah said. "I suggest we approach with caution if we don't wish to find ourselves tumbling down."

As Kyoto squinted against the bright glow, she was able to discern the outline of the pit, and she realized that this was where the energy lines intersected. The pit looked to be twenty meters across, but who knew how deep it was? "Don't worry," she said. "Our grav boots can adjust, as long as the angle's not too steep." But she wasn't worried about getting down; she was worried about what waited for them inside. If the information Memory had given them earlier proved accurate, they were about to find themselves in the presence of the Prime Mother.

They walked to the edge of the pit and looked down. At the bottom...

At first Kyoto thought the nanoparticles that allowed her to see in hyperspace had malfunctioned. The images they transmitted showed that the pit was wide and deep, and contained two objects: a gigantic hard-shelled horror that could only be the Prime Mother, and hovering next to her, a refitted GSA transport ship with delicate fin-like structures flaring out from the hull and crystalline webbing on top.

It was the *Janus*.

A cheerful voice came over Kyoto's comlink.

"Hello, Mei. What took you so long?"

TWENTY-SEVEN

Kyoto struggled to find her voice. "Not all of us have starships for bodies, you know. Some of us have to walk."

"I don't understand," Hastimukah said. "If Memory intended to fly the *Janus* here, why didn't she simply bring us with her?"

"Because the Prime Mother didn't want to take a chance on us regaining control of the *Janus* and using it against her," Kyoto said. "It was safer to have Memory tell us to hoof it, then when we were gone, fly the *Janus* here." Kyoto knew now what had bothered her about the energy lines, all of which converged in the pit below the Prime Mother and painted her a baleful green. "The energy lines flow through the strandways, so when Memory landed—"

"The Prime Mother instantly became aware of our arrival," Memory finished. "But she already knew we were coming. I couldn't allow you to harm her, so I contacted the Prime Mother earlier and told her of

the Prana's plan. While the Prana's intentions might
be noble, the Prime Mother needs no healing, as there
is nothing wrong with her."

Kyoto took a closer look at the Prime Mother. The
creature was by far the largest Manti she'd ever seen.
She looked something like the Prana, with an oversize
head to hold her highly developed brain, but her limbs
were little more than vestigial stumps, useless things
that flopped lifelessly whenever she shifted her great
bulk. Her carapace was stretched thin and marked
with stripes in all the colors that her children wore:
green, orange, amber, crimson, purple, and many
others. Her antennae were huge, easily twice the
length of her body, and they constantly moved about
the pit, touching one energy line after another,
drinking in the deluge of information as was her
divine right.

Her face was the worst part. Where other Manti
had no obvious facial features beyond the orifices that
served them as mouths, the Prime Mother had a set
of eyes—nine in all. And every one of the polished
obsidian orbs was focused on them, the intruders in
the Manti Crèche.

"Why didn't you just kill us when you had the
chance, Memory?" Kyoto asked. "You could've turned
off the oxygen, depressurized the cabin, maybe overloaded the electrical systems and fried us, or simply
crashed the ship. Why wait until now?"

"I'm fulfilling the orders of my monarch. She
wanted to look upon the face of the biped that sacrificed her ancestral homeworld to preserve her race.
Though your actions destroyed many of her children,
she nevertheless respects you. Out of that respect, she

wished to grant you the honor of approaching her of your own free will."

Kyoto looked at the Prime Mother more closely. Her sides were covered with what looked like long, fine filaments of gossamer hair. But then Kyoto realized the hairs were actually thin tendrils of blood and muscle that protruded from the Prime Mother's sides and merged with the pit bottom. No wonder the Prime Mother was so protective of the Weave, Kyoto thought. Not only was it the home she had built for her children so many millennia ago, it was quite literally a part of her, and she of it.

"So everything you've done since contacting her..."

"Was designed to bring you to this moment. And now that you're here, the Prime Mother desires to add your genetic strength to that of her children."

Several Chula clinging to the inner wall of the dome suddenly leaped toward them as if obeying an unspoken command. Kyoto and Hastimukah were still propping up Mudo, and though they both reached for their handblasters, their weakened companion was in the way. Kyoto knew they wouldn't be able to draw their weapons before the Chula were upon them.

Just then bright beams of energy sliced through the roof of the dome and struck the attacking Chula, instantly vaporizing them.

The Prime Mother screamed in fury, the sound somehow audible despite the lack of atmosphere to conduct it. But then Kyoto realized she wasn't hearing the Prime Mother: it was Memory, providing a voice for her beloved queen. But Memory's angry screams were abruptly cut off as another signal came over Kyoto's comlink.

"Sorry we're late to the party, Commander. We

would've been here sooner if some smart-ass jump jockey hadn't tricked us into getting caught in a mass shadow."

Kyoto grinned. "I'm sure you're not talking about me, General, but I'm damn glad you're here!"

The floor of the Crèche trembled as the Prime Mother in her fury began to thrash from side to side.

"Don't relax just yet," Adams said. "We made those first shots in stealth mode. Only way we got them past the Manti's defenses. But they know we're here now, and it looks like every damn Bugger in hyperspace is coming after us. We're about to get awfully busy up here."

"Understood, General," Kyoto said. The ground was really starting to shake now, and Kyoto knew they would probably have been knocked down if it hadn't been for their grav boots. "Thanks for the assist, and we'll take it from here."

"Roger, Kyoto. Good luck." Adams broke the comlink signal and Kyoto knew the *Dardanus* had just engaged the enemy.

The Chula clinging to the inner wall of the Crèche sprang into frantic action. Kyoto thought they were going to attack again, but instead the giant ivoryhued fleas began detaching eggs from the wall and leaped to the floor, dozens at a time. As soon as they landed, the immediately began heading toward the exit, carrying the precious eggs to safety. Good, thought Kyoto. That made several thousand less Manti they would have to worry about. She turned to Mudo and Hastimukah as the Chula exodus continued.

"Gerhard? Can you hear me?" she asked.

Mudo's eyes were closed, and Kyoto feared he

might be dead, but his eyelids fluttered open and he looked at her, his gaze dim and unfocused.

"Mei?"

"It's time to let it go, Gerhard. Release the symphysis."

"I don't... know how," Mudo whispered, and his eyes started to close again.

Kyoto turned to see what the Prime Mother was doing. The gigantic Manti was throwing herself right then left, right... left... and then the first tendrils began to tear free from the pit bottom, and Kyoto understood. The Prime Mother was trying to get out.

Panic surged through Kyoto, and she grabbed Mudo by the shoulders and shook him. "For once in your life, Gerhard, don't overthink a problem! Just let the damn thing out!"

"All right, I'll—" Mudo's eyes suddenly went wide. He stiffened and gritted his teeth, as if he were gripped by intense pain.

A fountain of multicolored light sprayed forth from the surface of Mudo's helmet and streaked toward the Prime Mother, taking on shape as it flew, becoming a Prana formed from sheer psychic power. Just as the energy Prana reached the Prime Mother, she succeeded in tearing free from the pit, torn tendrils bleeding greenish black ooze, and she rose into the air to meet the attack.

The energy Prana flowed over and around the Prime Mother, completely encasing her within an aura of crackling mental power. The Prime Mother continued rising into the air until she hovered ten meters above the pit. Bolts of energy flew off her, striking the ceiling, walls, and floor of the dome like lightning. The remaining Chula still struggling to detach eggs dodged the stray bolts, but some were struck and engulfed by the energy. It flared bright for an instant and then those Chula were gone.

Kyoto had no idea if the same thing would happen if one of those bolts of psychic power struck them, but she didn't want to stick around to find out. "Let's get out of here!" she shouted to Mudo and Hastimukah. "This is way out of our league!"

Though Mudo no longer carried the Scgcymphysis within his mind, he was still weak, and Kyoto and Hastimukah had to continue supporting him. But before they could take more than a couple steps away from the pit, the *Janus* rose into the air behind them.

"You're not going anywhere," Memory said.

Kyoto turned to face the *Janus,* or more precisely, the AI housed within it. "How do you plan to stop us? The *Janus* has no real weapons."

"Perhaps not, but *this* does."

The cargo doors of the modified transport opened, and Kyoto's G-7 Defender launched. The ship, running on maneuvering thrusters, came around until its nose was pointed at them. Kyoto could tell from the faint glow coming from the barrels of the pulse cannon that the weapon had been activated.

Seeing her own ship used against her like this filled Kyoto with rage. Still, she fought to maintain control. If she could just buy them a bit more time for the symphysis to finish its work...

"Operating the Defender by remote control?" she asked.

"Not exactly. I reactivated the smaller-scale version of myself residing in the G-7's computer. She's doing the flying."

So Memory Junior was back online. Too bad she was just as insane as her older sibling, Kyoto thought.

The aura around the Prime Mother had grown brighter, and the energy bolts blasting off her came more often and struck the walls of the Crèche with more force. Her vestigial limbs flailed about, as if she was attempting to claw the Prana's energy off her, but without success.

"If you hit us with pulse energy at this range, there won't be enough biomaterial left for a nanoparticle to pick up," Kyoto said. "I don't think the Prime Mother would appreciate you wasting us like that."

The Defender's pulse cannon remained trained on them; it didn't waver so much as a millimeter.

"Waste is regrettable but sometimes unavoidable. But in this case, it will not be necessary. The Prime Mother has won."

Kyoto looked up once more to see that the Prana energy around the Prime Mother had dimmed, and instead of throwing off deadly bolts, now only a few sputtering sparks leaped forth. The Prime Mother drew her tiny limbs against her abdomen and then flung them outward, as if throwing something. The Prana energy shot away from the Prime Mother and coalesced into the softly glowing jellyfish they had first seen in the Daimonion's imperfect recreation of Europa's holo zoo. The symphysis flew back to its human host and passed through Mudo's helmet. The scientist arched his back and cried out as the Prana's psi energy once more took up residence within his mind. Then he slumped in his companions' arms, unconscious, perhaps even dead.

The Prime Mother hovered above them all, and though Kyoto had no way of reading her alien body language, she had the sense that the giant Bugger was gloating.

"It failed," Hastimukah said in a stunned voice, as if the possibility of failure had never occurred to him. Given how optimistic the alien was, Kyoto thought, maybe it hadn't.

Kyoto wanted to lay Mudo down on the floor to check his vital signs, but she knew she dared not take her eyes off the Prime Mother and Memory.

"Memory warned her," Kyoto said. "She told the Prime Mother all about the symphysis, and that gave the Prime Mother enough time to prepare a defense."

"That is indeed what happened," Memory said. The Prime Mother has fought off the symphysis, and it has returned to Gerhard's mind. Unfortunately, the Prana never dreamed he might find himself having to carry it a second time. The strain will kill him in short order."

"No!" Kyoto looked at Mudo, but his head was slumped over, and with his helmet on, she couldn't see his face. She looked up at the *Janus* and the Defender, the two ships hovering side by side, the Prime Mother above them both, each vessel containing corrupted aspects of Memory.

"You're lying," Kyoto said, but even as she spoke the words, she knew she was wrong, and that the AI was telling the truth.

Memory didn't bother to respond to Kyoto's accusation. "The Chula have finished emptying the Crèche and bearing the eggs to safety, and the *Dardanus*, while fighting valiantly, cannot hope to stand against the combined might of the entire Weave. It's over, Mei. Accept this fact and give yourself to the Prime Mother willingly. If you do, she shall absorb your biomaterial herself, and you shall forevermore be a part of her. Think of it, Mei! You will in essence become the Prime Mother! You will be all powerful... immortal. You shall become a god!"

"Tell her thanks for the offer, but I have a hard enough time as it is being human. I don't think I'm cut out for godhood." Kyoto was stalling as she desperately tried to think of a way out of this mess.

The *Dardanus* was too busy battling Manti to help, and her handblasters would be useless against the Prime Mother or either version of Memory, encased as they both were inside starships. If only there was some way that she could reach Memory, the *real* Memory, the AI she had been before Hastimukah's nanoparticles had joined her to the Manti biomaterial in the *Janus*. If there was some way to separate... And then it came to her. The symphysis.

"Very well, Mei. If you reject the Prime Mother's offer, she'll have no choice but to slay the three of you and then see to the destruction of the *Dardanus*."

The Prime Mother began to descend toward them, her glossy black eyes seeming to shine with a sinister dark light. Kyoto could feel pressure beginning to build within her head, and for an instant she feared her vacc suit had been breached and she was about to die from explosive decompression. But then she realized what was happening. Like the Prana who were her children, the Prime Mother possessed powerful mental abilities. In other words, she was the biggest and smartest Brain Bug of them all. She wouldn't have to lay a single one of her stubby limbs on them or release a lethal energy blast. All she'd have to do was think about it hard enough and give a push with her psi power, and they would die, simple as that, without a mark on them. Neat, clean, and deadly. All that would remain was their intact biomaterial to be used in whatever way the Prime Mother saw fit.

The pressure in Kyoto's head increased to the point of pain, but she did her best to ignore it.

"Hold Gerhard for me," she told Hastimukah. She took Mudo's helmet in her hands and raised his head so she could look into the scientist's face.

"Gerhard, I need you to do something for me."

Mudo's eyes opened the merest slit and he mumbled something that sounded like, "Too... tired."

"Just one last thing, and then you can rest." She felt tears threaten as she thought of how permanent that rest might be, but if Mudo didn't come through, all three of them would die. "Let the symphysis go again, Gerhard. Only this time, send it at Memory. Tell it to heal her mind, just as it was going to heal the Prime Mother's." She had no idea whether the symphysis would work on a positronic brain instead of an organic one, but it was the only chance they had.

"No!" Memory shouted. "You cannot!"

The pressure in Kyoto's head suddenly became unbearable, and she thought her skull was going to explode. But she forced herself to keep talking.

"Gerhard, please... You're our last hope."

Mudo struggled to open his eyes wider, and he gave her a smile. "All right, but next time... you carry the psychic bomb."

Kyoto smiled. "Deal."

Mudo closed his eyes and frowned in concentration. Then, just as before, multicolored light blazed from the top of his helmet, only this time it raced toward the two starships, splitting into twin streams. One struck the *Janus* and the other the hit the Defender. Both vessels were engulfed by bright flares of light which quickly dimmed and faded. Free of the symphysis at last, Mudo's head lolled and he went slack in Hastimukah's arms.

There was silence then. Kyoto waited to see if her plan had worked. Even the Prime Mother had paused in her descent and was gazing intently at the two ships.

"Mei?"

"Yes, Memory?" Kyoto held her breath.

"I'm back online and functioning within normal parameters, and so is my little sister on the G-7."

Kyoto whooped in triumph. "Target the Prime Mother with fast-locks and fire!"

CHAPTER

TWENTY-EIGHT

Memory was quick to respond to Kyoto's command to fire on the Prime Mother. "With pleasure, Mei."

The Defender angled its nose upward and a pair of fast-lock missiles streaked toward the Prime Mother.

"Get down!" Kyoto grabbed Mudo and Hastimukah and fell to the floor with them just as the fast-locks struck the Prime Mother and detonated. There was no sound, but Kyoto felt the vibrations of the explosion through the floor.

She looked up and saw the Prime Mother was still hovering in the air above them, but she was listing to one side, and there was a large wound in her flank where the missiles had hit. Greenish black muck ran freely out of the wound, splattering onto the ground not far from where they lay.

Kyoto sat up, realizing as she did so that the pressure inside her head was gone. "How badly is she hurt, Memory?"

"Not badly enough. She was distracted while using her psychic powers on you, and the fast-locks were able to get past her personal defenses. She won't be so careless next time."

Kyoto thought fast. "Bring the *Janus* down. I want you to get Gerhard and Hastimukah to safety. And tell your little sister to pick me up afterward."

"Acknowledged, Mei."

Both ships began to descend toward them at once.

"We can't leave you here!" Hastimukah protested.

"Who said I'm staying? I'll be right behind you."

"Like hell you will! You're planning to cover our escape!"

The *Janus* turned until the open cargo bay faced them. Kyoto glanced at the Prime Mother. She had righted herself, and the wound on her side was rapidly healing. They didn't have much time.

Memory deployed the cargo ramp, and Kyoto helped Hastimukah carry Mudo on board. She then jumped back outside. "See what you can do for Gerhard, all right?"

As the cargo bay door began to close, Hastimukah said, "Don't worry, I'll take good care of our friend, Commander. Good luck to you!" The door sealed shut, and the *Janus* rose and started toward the Crèche's exit, picking up speed as it went.

Kyoto turned just as the Defender came flying toward her. She ducked as the starboard wing passed overhead, then she turned and grabbed hold of it. The grav attractors in her gloves hadn't been designed to attach to a starfighter in flight, but Kyoto had saved numerous Colonists this way. Now it was her turn to take a ride.

The Defender followed after the *Janus*, Kyoto holding onto the wing, her feet trailing behind.

"You with me, Memory Junior?"

"Affirmative, Mei. And on behalf of my sister and myself, I'd just like to say how sorry we are that—"

"Forget about it. Neither of you could help it. Can you open the cockpit for me?"

In response, the G-7's canopy popped open.

"Do you need me to slow down?"

"No, I can handle it. We used to practice this maneuver at the academy." She didn't tell Memory that she'd never tried it in a combat situation before. Using her grabbers to pull herself onto and across the wing, Kyoto made her way to the cockpit and crawled inside. As Kyoto settled into the pilot's seat, Memory closed the canopy and locked it tight.

"Pressurizing cockpit and turning control over to you."

The holoscreen flared to life, and Kyoto took hold of the joystick. Damn, but it felt good to be back in the saddle again! "What's the Prime Mother's status?"

The G-7's alarm system shrieked a warning, and Kyoto yanked the joystick and the Defender veered hard to port. Energy erupted in a bright ball of glowing fire where the ship had been an instant ago.

"The Prime Mother is fully operational."

"No kidding." Kyoto set the holoscreen to split view. The left side displayed an image of where she was headed, while the right showed the Prime Mother. The wound on her side was fully healed, and the torn tendrils had sealed over and begun to regrow.

Kyoto brought the Defender around until both sides of the holoscreen showed the Prime Mother. She wanted to keep the gigantic Manti busy while the *Janus* put as much distance between itself and the Weave as possible, and she could think of no better way to do that than by those two words so near and dear to a fighter pilot's heart: frontal assault.

The Prime Mother's nine eyes began to glow, and Kyoto knew she was preparing to unleash another energy blast.

"Weapons check."

"Pulse cannons are holding steady at seventy-three percent of maximum, but we're down to our last four fast-locks."

Kyoto wished she had a few hundred more missiles. Hell, while she was at it, she wished she were piloting a Battleship right now. But she'd make do with what she had, as if there was a choice.

The glow from the Prime Mother's eyes became more intense, and Kyoto knew she was about to fire.

Time to give the inertial dampeners a workout, Kyoto thought.

Just as a torrent of crackling energy erupted from the Prime Mother's eyes, Kyoto pulled back hard on the joystick. Maneuvering thrusters fired, and the fusion engines whined in protest as the Defender's nose lifted and the starfighter shot straight up toward the ceiling of the Manti dome.

The energy blast missed striking the Defender's tail by centimeters.

As the G-7 hurtled toward the ceiling, Kyoto targeted the remaining four missiles and fired. Three of the missiles struck the ceiling and exploded, while the fourth curved downward, headed for the Prime Mother. As chunks of biomaterial rained down, Kyoto activated the pulse cannon and vaporized the pieces falling toward the *Defender*. On the split screen, she saw the last missile detonate in the Prime Mother's face. Kyoto didn't think the fast-lock would hurt the

Prime Mother, not if she'd been prepared for it, but it wasn't supposed to injure the Manti, just slow her down for a few crucial seconds.

Hoping the other missiles had knocked a hole in the ceiling—or at least weakened it enough for the pulse cannon to finish the job—Kyoto accelerated to full speed and roared toward the area of the missile strike, cannon firing the whole way. She gritted her teeth and braced for an impact that never came. The G-7 soared through the newly made opening in the Manti dome and out into hyperspace.

Outside, Kyoto's holoscreen shifted to full view once more, and a scene of complete chaos appeared before Kyoto. Manti were everywhere: they choked the strandways and filled the sky, firing energy blasts and projectiles in all directions. High above the Weave was the *Eye of Dardanus* and, heading toward it at top speed, the *Janus*, its energy shield activated to protect it from Manti fire. The *Dardanus* was letting loose with everything it had—energy weapons of various kinds, several varieties of missiles, and small orbs that looked like doppelgangers, though she didn't know how the *Dardanus* had come by them. Manti died by the dozens, but as impressive aa display was, she doubted the Residuum starship could keep up this level of attack for much longer before its artillery was exhausted, and no matter how many Buggers were fragged, there were thousands more to take their place. It wasn't a question of whether the *Dardanus* would lose the battle, but rather how long it could last.

The sky was filled with deadly Manti energies, and while Kyoto was no stranger to avoiding Bugger weapons fire, she'd never had to deal with so much of it at once. She darted between bolts of energy, dodged rocketing projectiles, and when she couldn't escape, she let the G-7's energy shield take the impact as best it could.

Kyoto eased up on the acceleration and looped the Defender around until the G-7 was pointed toward the Manti tower once more. The dome had a large jagged hole in its surface; she'd hoped the missile blasts would destabilize the entire structure and cause it to collapse. But instead of growing wider, the hole was becoming smaller—the Manti tower was healing itself. One of the advantages of building with biomaterial, she supposed.

"Let's see if we can do anything to slow the tower's recovery," Kyoto said. She targeted the hole's edge and fired her pulse cannon at full power. Waves of blue-white energy *shooooomed* into the dome, and cracks began to spread outward from the hole. Kyoto kept up the bombardment, and the cracks became fissures and spread farther and more rapidly. Chunks of the dome started to detach and fall inward. The tower began to tilt, and Kyoto swooped around the dome and concentrated the pulse cannon's fire at the tower's base. A little more and the dome would collapse, and the entire tower would come crashing down on top of the Prime Mother's oversize braincase.

As Kyoto brought the Defender around the dome for another attack run, the two shock towers that flanked the entrance flared crimson and unleashed gouts of raging red energy from deep within their furnaces of death. She managed to dodge one crimson stream, but by doing so she flew directly into the path of the other. The G-7's shield struggled to turn aside the shock tower's blast, but copious amounts of the deadly crimson energy got through. Ship alarms screamed and the holoscreen flickered as power systems fought to remain online. Just as Kyoto feared the Defender would drop out of the sky like a very large and useless rock, the alarms fell silent and the holoscreen image stabilized.

"Our shield handled the blast—barely—but it's down to two percent of maximum now. I suggest you try to avoid flying into any more energy streams until the G-7 is returned to GSA headquarters for maintenance."

"Thanks for the advice," Kyoto said wryly. She targeted the leaning main tower once more and fired the pulse cannon. Slowly the tower began to fall, and Kyoto stopped firing and soared off to a safe distance. She brought the Defender around, fired maneuvering thrusters, and hovered in place. She watched the tower break in half as it fell, smashing into the dome and crushing it, destroying the two shock towers in the process. There was no sign of the Prime Mother.

"Hot damn!" Kyoto yelled. "Got you, you ugly alien bitch!"

"Mei…"

The wreckage of the dome exploded outward, and the Prime Mother, wreathed in swirling, crackling energy, rose toward the Defender, her nine eyes blazing with hatred.

"Or maybe not," Kyoto said.

"Doctor, can you hear me?"

Mudo lay on the floor of the cargo bay, Hastimukah kneeling beside him. Before the *Janus* had left Mars, the cargo area had been refitted as a launch bay for Kyoto's Defender ship, and power cables, diagnostic, and maintenance equipment now filled this section of the ship. *All this technology,* Hastimukah thought, *and every bit of it is useless right now.* What he wouldn't give for a fully equipped Residuum medlab.

Mudo's eyes were closed, skin pale, lips gray. Many species in the Residuum varied their coloration according to moods or environmental conditions, so Hastimukah didn't have a clear sense of whether Mudo's pallor was normal for his race. His instincts told him it was not.

"Memory, what is the state of Dr. Mudo's health?"

"He is dying." The AI spoke these words without obvious emotion, but Hastimukah's nanocolony gave him extremely sensitive hearing, and he detected an undercurrent of sorrow in her synthesized tones.

The ship suddenly swerved, and Hastimukah, grav boots firmly planted, grabbed hold of Mudo to keep him from sliding across the floor and slamming into a piece of equipment.

"What's happening?"

"Just avoiding Manti weapons fire. Nothing to worry about."

"Nothing to worry about, she says. Are there medical facilities aboard?"

"There are first-aid kits and some basic medical supplies, but nothing that will help Gerhard. The *Janus* was designed to be a test craft, not a warship."

There was no other choice, then. Hastimukah removed Mudo's right glove, and then took off his.

"What are you doing?"

Hastimukah clasped Mudo's hand and held it tight. "The only thing I *can* do—giving Dr. Mudo an infusion of nanoparticles."

Grayish slime oozed from the pores in Hastimukah's hand, slid over to Mudo's, then slipped easily into the human's flesh and was gone.

Hastimukah released Mudo's hand and sat back. He felt lightheaded and weak, but he would recover as soon as the nanocolony that shared his body had time to replenish itself. He just hoped that Mudo's injuries weren't too severe for the particles to heal him. He watched Mudo's face for several moments, and though he wasn't certain, he thought the man's color had improved.

"Memory?"

There was a pause before the AI replied. "Sorry, but there's a lot going on outside. The Manti are attacking the *Dardanus*, and there's weapons fire everywhere. Makes flying more than a little tricky. I wish Mei were at the controls. She has a finely honed instinct for not getting blasted into oblivion."

"About the doctor…" Hastimukah prompted.

"His condition is beginning to improve. It's going to be a near thing, but I believe you got the nano-particles into him in time."

Hastimukah sighed in relief. He slipped Mudo's glove back on, and then donned his own once more. "Now, if you can just get us to the *Dardanus* in one piece—assuming it isn't destroyed by the Manti, of course—all will be well."

"About that," Memory began. "I have a slightly different plan in mind." The Prime Mother's nine glossy black eyes seemed to grow larger, until they had merged into a single obsidian orb that gazed directly into the depths of Kyoto's innermost self.

Kyoto unleashed a blast of pulse energy at the Prime Mother, then started to jam the joystick forward, intending to get the hell out of there, but she felt a strange tingling at the base of her skull. Her vision grayed, and she could no longer feel the joystick in her grip. Cool air caressed the skin of her face, as well as her bare arms and legs, and she realized she was no longer wearing a vacc suit. This should have panicked her, but it didn't. It felt normal, felt right. She breathed in the mingled scents of dozens of different flowers and plants, blended with the rich smell of men's cologne.

"Hello, Mei."

Her vision began to clear, and she saw the blurry outline of a face looking at her. But she didn't need her vision restored to recognize who it was. She knew him by smell, by the half-amused, half-melancholy tone of his voice.

"Wolf?"

She reached out for him, stumbled, and he caught her in his arms.

"Whoa! Looks like your stabilizers are out of alignment, pilot. You'd better sit down for a minute." He led her to one of the arboretum's many plasteel benches and they sat. He took hold of her hand and began to lightly stroke the back of it with his fingertips.

"I know you don't want to hear me nag you again, but maybe now you'll believe me when I say you've been working too hard lately. You should take a couple of days off, stay home and rest."

Her vision was improving, but slowly. She was able to make out Wolf's features, but only as splashes of color. The black of his hair, the pink of his skin, the white of his smile.

"You know me," she said. "I'm not really good at resting."

He shrugged. "A vacation, then. We could go to Europa for a week or two. Hell, we could stay a month if we wanted to. We both have enough accumulated leave."

Kyoto frowned at Wolf's mention of Europa. There was something about it that bothered her... something about the zoo... but she couldn't think what it was.

She shivered then, and Wolf put his arm around her.

"Getting cold?"

"I'll be all right. I should've worn something a bit warmer than this dress, though." Ever since her time in the refugee camps on Rhea, she seemed to catch a chill easily. It was almost as if she carried the eternal numbing cold of the ice moon with her wherever she went, and she'd never be free of it.

Rhea... there was something that bothered her about this thought, too, but she still couldn't...

"Tell you what, we can worry about the details later," Wolf said. "Why don't you just lay your head on my shoulder and rest here for a while? You know how the arboretum soothes you. You always sleep better here than anywhere else."

Kyoto was tempted. She *was* tired, and the arboretum *was* one of her favorite places in the Solar Colonies.

"Well... maybe just for a few minutes." She closed her eyes and put her head on Wolf's shoulder.

"That's fine. A few minutes is all I'll need."

Her eyes flew open. "What did you say?"

"I said a few minutes is all you'll need."

She sat up and looked at him, her vision almost fully restored now. "No, you didn't. You said 'a few

323

minutes is all *I'll* need.' You were referring to your-self."

Wolf smiled. "You're exhausted, Mei. I understand. Everything will be okay soon. All you have to do is close your eyes and rest."

He put his hand on the side of her head and tried to force her to lay it against his shoulder once more. His grip was strong, stronger than she remembered, and though she resisted, her neck muscles soon began to ache, and she could feel the strain in her vertebrae.

She gritted her teeth and slammed her elbow into Wolf's gut. The breath whooshed out of his lungs, and she was able to break free of his grip. Mad as hell, she turned to face him, ready to demand that he explain just what in the hell he'd been thinking, but her vision was completely normal now, and she saw his eyes, his glossy black eyes, and she realized the awful truth.

"You're not Wolf. He's dead, and this isn't the Cydonia arboretum. You're the goddamned Prime Mother, and you're inside my head, attacking me with my own memories!"

Wolf smiled, his lips stretching wider than any human mouth was capable of. Behind his teeth tiny dark insects writhed and crawled over one another.

"Magnificent," the Prime Mother said in a soft hiss of a voice. "If only you would become One with us…"

"If only you would just shut up and leave me the hell alone!" Kyoto slashed out with her left hand—her nails suddenly much longer and sharper than in real-ity. The nails sliced across Wolf's obsidian eyes, and thick greenish-black blood gushed forth. He howled in agony and covered his face with his hands, foul ichor oozing from between his fingers and dripping in thick globules to the arboretum floor.

"You bitch!" the Prime Mother hissed.

Kyoto experienced a sudden dizzying instant of vertigo, and then she was back in her pilot's seat, looking at the holoscreen through the view plate in her vacc suit's helmet, collision alarms blaring. On the right-hand side of the screen was an image of the Prime Mother. A deep bloody gouge ran across her inhuman face, right through where her nine eyes had been.

"The starboard wingtip has suffered some damage, but structural integrity is holding," Memory said. "To be honest, I'm surprised that worked. I thought you were going to rip the wing clean off."

Kyoto wasn't sure what Memory was talking about. She had hold of the joystick, so she decided to bring the Defender back under control before asking questions. When she got the starfighter stabilized, she brought it around until it was facing the Prime Mother once more. Her wound was already healing, and Kyoto thought she could see new eyes forming beneath the blood.

"What did I do?" she asked.

"You made a run straight at the Prime Mother, and just when it appeared as if you were going to ram her, you turned hard to port and used the starboard wingtip like a knife to cut her eyes. The pain and shock of the injury broke the Prime Mother's mental hold over you."

That wasn't exactly the way it had happened in the psychic illusion the Prime Mother had trapped her in, but it made sense that whatever Kyoto did within the mindscape, she did in the real world, too. After all, wasn't the Defender in its own way as much a part of her body as her arms and legs? In some ways, maybe even more?

"We need to strike again before she has a chance to fully heal," Memory said.

"My thoughts exactly." Kyoto shoved the joystick forward and the fusion engines roared as the Defender streaked toward the injured Prime Mother.

"What do you intend to do, Mei?"

"What you thought I was going to do before: use the G-7 like a stake and ram it through that alien bitch's black heart."

"You realize of course that the Manti don't have what your species would recognize as a circulatory system, and therefore – "

"Shut up, Memory."

"Shutting up, Mei."

The G-7 continued flying toward the Prime Mother like a fusion-powered spear.

See you in a couple of seconds, Wolf, Kyoto thought, and braced for impact. Hastimukah had just lifted up Mudo with the intention of carrying the recovering scientist to the crew quarters when Memory came over his comlink.

"Hastimukah, I just received a message from my little sister in Mei's Defender. I'm afraid our friend is about to do something that's as brave as it is foolish. I have to stop her."

"Is there anything I can do?"

"Actually…"

The cargo door opened, and Hastimukah and Mudo were instantly sucked out into hyperspace. Hastimukah held onto the unconscious scientist as they tumbled weightlessly through the void.

"Hold tight," Memory said. "Someone will be along to pick you up shortly."

Just as the G-7 was about to crash into the Prime Mother, the joystick yanked itself out of Kyoto's hand and angled hard to starboard. The Defender zoomed pas the Prime Mother, missing her by only a few meters.

"What are you doing, Memory?" Kyoto shouted. "We would've had her!"

"Big sis and I had a better idea."

The holoscreen changed to a full-screen image of the *Janus* traveling toward the Prime Mother at full speed. The giant Manti was almost completely healed, and she looked up to see the modified GSA transport heading straight at her.

"Memory!" Kyoto yelled. "Don't do this!" She grabbed the joystick once again, but she was unable to move it. Memory Junior had complete control of the ship.

"I have a score to settle with the Prime Mother for using me against you," Memory Senior said over the ship's comlink. "Besides, suicide runs are something of a specialty of mine. Goodbye, Mei. Memory out."

Before Kyoto could say or do anything more, the *Janus* slammed into the Prime Mother and its fusion engines exploded in a radioactive fireball.

"Time we were leaving," Memory Junior said, and the G-7 shot away from the Weave as fast as it could fly.

Kyoto watched on the holoscreen as the fireball crashed into the ruins of the Manti tower. There was another, larger explosion then, this one so bright that the holoscreen flickered and went dead, unable to handle projecting the image of such intense light.

Kyoto couldn't believe it. Memory was gone—again. The Prime Mother had been destroyed, but at a high price. Kyoto felt as though she had just lost her best friend for the second time.

The holoscreen came back on, this time displaying a wide-angle view of the Weave. The area surrounding the Manti tower was a blazing ruin for kilometers in every direction. Hyperspace was free of Manti weapons fire, and the Buggers themselves—whether in the sky or on the strandways—had fallen motionless. Then slowly, the fliers began to descend toward the Weave, and the walkers started toward the burning ruins of what had once been the Crèche and the Prime Mother's pit. It was almost like a funeral procession, Kyoto thought.

"It's over, Mei. Without the Prime Mother to think for them, the Manti don't know what to do. They're harmless."

At first, Kyoto thought she was hearing a ghost, but then she remembered that only Memory Senior had sacrificed herself. Memory Junior was still "alive" inside the G-7's computer. Then another thought hit her.

"Oh my god! Gerhard and Hastimukah!"

"Weren't aboard the *Janus* when it struck the Prime Mother. They're floating in hyperspace, safe inside their vacc suits, waiting for a ride."

Kyoto smiled in relief. "Then we'd better go get them, hadn't we?"

"Roger that. Turning control back over to you, Mei."

The joystick was suddenly responsive once more,

and Kyoto headed the Defender in the general direction of the *Dardanus*. "Scan for our friends and lay in a course for them. And you might want to explain to Hastimukah how to use the grabbers in his gloves to take hold of the wing."

"Will do."

Kyoto sat back in her pilot's chair, let out a long, slow breath, and allowed herself to hope that maybe—just maybe—it really was over at last.

TWENTY-NINE

"How are you feeling, Commander?"

Kyoto hesitated before answering. Though she'd been on the *Dardanus* for the better part of a solar day now, she still hadn't gotten used to talking to a giant shrimp.

"Fine, Captain. My radiation exposure was minimal. The last of the G-7's energy shield, plus the rad shielding in the hull of the ship itself and in my vacc suit dealt with the worst of it. And your medtechs took care of the rest. My starfighter is clean of radiation, too, thanks to your engineers."

"Kyoto's tough as empyrean nails," General Adams said, sounding more like a proud father than her superior officer. Adams—wearing his vacc suit, as was she—stood next to Kryllian's command chair. Though she doubted either he or Kryllian would admit it, she had the impression that the two had become friends during their time together.

"No doubt," Kryllian said. "And what of your ship's artificial intelligence, Commander?"

"Your techs have given her a clean bill of health, Captain. It seems that the symphysis did its job well."

"Why doesn't that overgrown piece of seafood ask me himself?" Memory said over Kyoto's suit's comlink. "He acts like I'm just some sort of glorified calculator!"

Kyoto smiled, but she didn't respond to the AI's complaint. She was just glad Memory hadn't broadcast it over the *Dardanus*'s shipwide com system.

The gray blob—which Kyoto still couldn't believe was nothing more than a single combined colony of sentient nanoparticles—looked up from the nav console and turned to Kryllian.

"Captain, we're approaching our original entry point into hyperspace. We'll have our guests back to their home system shortly."

"Thank you, Suletu. Contact Hastimukah and see if he—"

The door to the bridge irised open, and a short, stocky being stepped through, accompanied by a wan-looking human. Neither wore a vacc suit.

"Belay that, Suletu." Kryllian turned to look at Hastimukah. "I'm glad to see you're back to your old self, Assessor. Nothing against our guests, but I found your last visage somewhat offputting."

Kyoto chuckled. "I hope Aspen DeFonesca never hears that. She's already obsessed with being the most attractive and beloved human in the Solar Colonies. Can you imagine what would happen if she decided to try for the entire galaxy?"

"The mind absolutely boggles," Mudo said with a smile. He and Hastimukah came over to join the others around Kryllian's command chair. The scientist was still pale, but the nanoparticles Hastimukah had given him had saved his life. More, they'd given him the same abilities as any member of the Residuum, and he could breathe the atmosphere aboard the *Dardanus*.

"Good to see you up and about, Doctor," Adams said.

"It took a while for the nanoparticles to restore me to full health," Mudo said. "The damage carrying the symphysis did to my cerebral cortex and central nervous system was quite extensive. So much so, in fact, that I'll need to retain the nanoparticles inside me for the rest of my life."

"Just so long as you avoid the temptation to add them to any GSA equipment," Adams said with a scowl. "I think we've had enough of your special upgrades after what happened to the *Janus*."

"Yes, General."

Mudo looked and sounded chastened, but Kyoto doubted he was being sincere. He had too much of the rebel in him. In that way, he was a little like Wolf. That thought, and the confused mixture of feelings that accompanied it, was something she'd deal with another day.

She turned to Hastimukah. "Does it feel good to be... what's the right term? Bergelmirian again?"

When Hastimukah had told her that his people resembled the woolly mammoths of ancient Earth, she'd pictured him as a massive elephantine creature covered with fur. She'd gotten the hairy elephant part right, though Hastimukah walked upright, had ears only slightly larger than a human's, and possessed rudimentary tusks. He did have a prehensile nose, though it was only thirty centimeters long. But she'd been way off on the massive part. Hastimukah stood only a meter high, if that. He put her in mind of a stuffed elephant she'd had as a child, one her parents had gotten for her after a visit to the holozoo on Europa. She'd named the toy Mr. Bo-Bo, and she'd lost it when her parents' transport had crashed.

The thought made her grin, and Hastimukah frowned. "Is something wrong, Commander?"

She shook her head. "No, not at all... Mr. Bo-Bo." And then she burst out laughing.

The others looked at one another and gave a group shrug.

"Careful, Kyoto," Adams said. "Keep it up, and you might cause Hastimukah to reconsider his assessment of the human race."

"You've reached a decision?" She'd been so busy helping the *Dardanus*'s techs with the Defender and Memory that she hadn't seen or spoken to anyone else for hours before she'd come to the bridge.

"I have," he said. "I'm going to recommend to the Ascendancy that humanity be given provisional membership in the Residuum. Provided your Council of Seven agrees, of course."

"That's wonderful news!" Kyoto said.

"Perhaps," Mudo allowed. "But it's difficult to say how the council, let alone the rest of the Colonists, will handle the revelation of the Residuum's existence. So far humanity's encounters with extraterrestrial life have been less than pleasant."

"We'll take it one step at a time, Doctor," Adams said. "And we'll just see how things play out."

"They'll be a lot more sympathetic when they hear how a Residuum ship helped up stop the Manti," Kyoto said.

"My only regret is we didn't have enough artillery left to attack the Manti after the Prime Mother's death," Kryllian said. "We had the opportunity to destroy them once and for all. We could've taken out the entire Weave." Kryllian's antennae waved about in frustration. "Instead all we could do was turn about and head home."

"The Residuum can always return with more ships," Adams said.

"If it's even necessary," Mudo added. "The Prana will likely try to do what they can, but without the Prime Mother to give them direction—or more importantly, to create new Manti—their species will eventually die out."

"Coming up on hyperspatial entry point," Suletu said.

"Prepare to make the transition to realspace everyone," Kryllian ordered.

As Suletu began to carry out his captain's command, Kyoto knew that they'd be returning to a very different Solar Colonies than she'd left—even if the Colonies themselves weren't aware of it yet. They were now provisional members of the Residuum, and the Manti threat had finally been eliminated once and for all.

But if that were true, why did she have the nagging feeling that it really wasn't over? That in some strange, unknown way, it was only just beginning?

Deep within the melted ruin that had once been the Prime Mother's pit, a single microscopic nanoparticle that had survived the destruction of the *Janus* began to stir. It cast about with its sensors and detected traces of biomaterial from what had once been the Prime Mother clinging to hundreds of inert nanoparticles. It sent a signal to awaken those sleeping particles, and then settled back to rest while it waited patiently for the others to come back online.

It would need all the strength it could muster, for there was a great deal of work to do. A great deal of work, indeed.